SPLENDID LITTLE SCHEMES

A NOVEL

ROBIN STRONG

PRAISE FOR SPLENDID LITTLE SCHEMES

"Strong crafts a hilarious story that borders on the absurd, and she knowingly winks at the reader page after page. Still, there are moments of genuine emotion... a smart critique that asks readers to consider what separates a victim from a villain. A clever and poignant suburban fever dream."

—Kirkus Reviews

"Strong is not afraid to ruffle some feathers. The novel is bold, engaging, funny, and uplifting... The well-developed plotline surprises us with many twists and turns. It touches on the destructive influence of predators on women's lives. I loved every page of this perfectly edited novel and highly recommend it."

—Nino Lobiladze, Readers' Favorite

"SPLENDID LITTLE SCHEMES proves to be a successful feminist contemporary novel about women seizing opportunities to lift themselves (and each other) up."

—Aimee Jodoin, IndieReader

ALSO BY ROBIN STRONG

Gods of The Garden (The Garden Series Book 1)

The Scrolls of Prophecy (The Garden Series Book 2)

SPLENDID LITTLE SCHEMES

A Novel

Robin Strong

Stay up to date on new books: www.robinstrongbooks.com

Cover design by R & T Creative
Author photo by Tom Konie

Library of Congress Control Number: 2024913867

ISBN 978-1-960597-03-8 (ebook)
ISBN 978-1-960597-04-5 (paperback)
ISBN 978-1-960597-05-2 (hardcover)
ISBN 978-1-960597-06-9 (audiobook)

For Tom, my favorite co-schemer

SPLENDID LITTLE SCHEMES

1

Victoria Sterling was on the hunt.

She pressed her rose-stained lips together and tousled her wavy blonde tresses at the roots. Her spine lengthened as she smoothed her skirt and adjusted the string of pearls around her neck. Shoulders back, legs crossed, chin high—she knew the key to a good kill was as much about beauty as it was skill. Lucky for Vicky, she had both.

From the stand where she sat, the congregation was in full display. Neighbors and friends filled the pews. Even the people whom Vicky couldn't identify by name had familiar faces. Little tic marks in her brain organized everyone into two lists: those who had joined her in the opportunity of a lifetime and those without the vision or grit to chase their dreams.

When the first counselor started the service, he began by welcoming a new family to the Splendor Springs Ward. Vicky's senses perked up.

Fresh meat.

A cute, freckled woman with bobbed brown hair sat with her

family of eight in the back row, taking up the entire middle bench. *What was her name again? Amelia something.* The husband was dozing off while four older children struggled to keep still. Amelia was wedged between twin toddler girls wearing the same face and matching polka dot dresses. She nudged her husband to keep the other children quiet. With folded arms against a bright yellow sweater, the woman's large smile couldn't fully mask the apprehension in her eyes as she focused on the speaker at the front of the meeting house.

Vicky zeroed in on her target. *Yes, she'll do just fine.*

All Vicky had to do was wait for her moment to attack, which was easier said than done. The last few minutes of church dragged like a parachute in mud. The puffy-faced High Councilor at the pulpit had already filled his allotted time. With his eyes glued to his notes, the man droned on about family history or family prayer or family home evening—Vicky wasn't sure which. Whatever the topic, the man turned it into a passive-aggressive guilt trip that could have easily doubled as a sleep aid.

Vicky's patent leather stilettos bounced impatiently. If the meeting ran too long, Amelia might run off before Vicky could catch her. She closed her eyes and silently hoped Jack would skip the closing hymn to speed things along, and even considered texting her husband to ensure he did. After all, the Bishop's wife should have some perks, right? If she were sitting in her usual front-row seat, it would be easy to send a quick message. But here on the stand? Vicky was too exposed to risk her reputation.

The rest of the congregation seemed just as eager for the meeting to end. Children bounced in their seats; teens had their faces glued to their phones. Tired mothers rocked screaming babies while toddlers crushed Cheerios into the crevices of the long, upholstered pews. Men in suits wrestled to stay awake, their heads tipping forward before snapping back to attention. Even Vicky's four children, the epitome of reverence, showed signs of sagging interest as they slumped forward. But Amelia and her yellow sweater sat bright and focused the way one does when trying to fit in—the perfect prey.

The speaker finally muttered a solemn *amen*. Sitting on the other side of the pulpit, Jack leaned over and whispered in one of his counselor's ears before standing up. His square jaw and slightly crooked smile made him authoritative but approachable. The little flecks of silver around his temples added a distinguished air. Tall, broad, and confident, Jack was aging like a fine wine—or at least that's what Vicky assumed, having never tried the stuff.

"Thank you, Brother Burton, for your thoughtful words," Jack said before nodding toward Vicky and the twelve-year-old youth speaker sitting beside her. "And thank you, Brother Perkins and Sister Sterling, for your talks. We certainly have been uplifted this beautiful Sabbath morning."

Vicky smiled at awkward teenager beside her as he shifted nervously in his seat. "You did great," she whispered. It was a lie, but what else was she supposed to say to the kid?

Jack shuffled through a small pile of papers, clearing his throat. "Before we close, I'd like to remind everyone that our ward has the opportunity to clean the building starting next month. We'll email each family's assignment this week." Dozens of eyes rolled at the reminder. "Due to the time, we'll skip the closing hymn and finish with the benediction."

Vicky slowly inhaled as she slipped her *Book of Mormon* into her bag. A petite, middle-aged woman with auburn hair approached the podium and waited for the congregation to bow their heads. Her small, apologetic voice could not compete with a babbling two-year-old in the third row. Vicky snuck a peek at the open aisle that led to Amelia's family, knowing it would quickly fill with people as soon as the meeting ended. Charting a course in her mind, Vicky tightened her core and wrapped her fingers around her purse, ready to pounce.

"Amen," the woman said—her final word echoed by the congregation.

Vicky popped to her feet just as the organist began bellowing a painfully slow version of *How Great Thou Art*. She threw an oversized purse over her shoulder and steadied herself for the chaos. Blaze waved from the front bench, urging his mom to relieve him of babysitting duties, but Vicky's eyes darted toward Amelia. She'd deal with her kids in a minute.

A lanky old man jumped in front of Vicky before she even reached the second row. "Beautiful talk today, Sister Sterling. I felt the Spirit so strongly."

"Thank you," Vicky said in her sweetest voice as her eyes narrowed on Amelia. "Excuse me. I'm trying to catch someone before they leave."

Without waiting for a reply, Vicky darted past a group of tweens giggling as they made faces at the boys on the other side of the chapel. A howling four-year-old nearly knocked Vicky over as he ran toward the front of the room. His mother rushed to catch him. "Sorry, Vicky! Great talk today. You're amazing!"

Vicky pushed her way through the crowds. With every passing row, another person tapped her shoulder or waved from a distance, trying to get her attention.

"Amazing job, Victoria. You're a natural speaker."

"Your story about overcoming your fear of imperfection was just what I needed!"

"The Sterling family is living up to their name. And your kids were so well-behaved! I don't know how you do it."

Vicky pressed forward, smiling and nodding politely as the compliments rained down, her mind still gripped on Amelia what's-her-name.

An old couple crept out of their seat, taking up more than half the aisle. Vicky sighed as the hunched-over man gingerly handed his wife her cane. A giant car seat with a sleeping baby took up the other side, making it impossible to get through. The wall of people separating Vicky from her goal grew thicker by the second. She strained her neck to peer over a Godzilla-sized man, catching a glimpse of Amelia's yellow sweater. *Almost there.*

The old couple finally shuffled to the side, and Vicky squeezed through the open space, apologizing when her purse whacked someone in the shoulder. She slipped around the monstrous man and nearly tripped on a diaper bag. As she steadied herself, her eyes met Amelia's.

Amelia smiled as she clung to her daughter's hand. The child tried to pull her mom toward the exit. Vicky tucked her hair behind her ear, sucked in her already flat stomach, and walked toward the woman. But just as her toes neared the finish line, Vicky was cut off by the worst kind of poacher: Tracy Monson.

Tracy was lean, rigid, and full of sharp angles. She sliced into Amelia's personal space with a predatorial intensity. "Oh, my gosh! What a beautiful family you have!" The words fell out of her mouth like sugar. "I just *had* to come over and introduce myself."

Vicky furrowed her brows and stood a little taller before inserting herself into the conversation. She reached out her hand, drawing the attention away from Tracy. "Hello! I'm—"

"Sister Sterling!" Amelia said. "Victoria, right? You did such an amazing job on your talk today."

"Please call me Vicky." A demure smile graced her face. "Your beautiful sweater caught my eye all the way from the stand. We're always excited to welcome new families. Bishop and I are here if you need anything." The bishop card always earned Vicky points. The Sterlings were like royalty in the Splendor Springs Ward.

Tracy pursed her lips and cleared her throat. "You have quite the crew here. I recognize some of these faces from primary today. I'm the Primary President, by the way." She crouched down and smiled at one of Amelia's boys, who responded by sticking a finger up his nose.

Amelia's cheeks turned bright red as she pulled the kid's hand from his face. "Hopefully, they were well-behaved."

The little girl pulled harder on Amelia's arm as she began to cry. "Moooommmmy. I wand wunch!"

Tracy smiled through gritted teeth. "Absolute angels."

Feeling the conversation slip away, Vicky knew small talk would get her nowhere. She needed to get Amelia alone. "You know," she said, trying to make it sound like the idea had just popped into her head, "I'd love to have you over some time. As the Relief Society President, I feel it's my job to show you around the neighborhood. What about Tuesday?"

"Oh, how sweet." Amelia picked up the toddler as she scoured her bag for some snacks. "Tracy just invited me to lunch on Tuesday, but I'm free Wednesday. Does that work?"

Tracy's smug smile was suffocating.

Vicky's mind raced, looking for a way to win this duel. She considered inviting the family over for dinner tonight, but the roast defrosting certainly wouldn't feed an extra eight mouths. What about an impromptu dessert bar? Scripture study? A joint family walk? A million ideas bounced in Vicky's brain, but they were all interrupted by a loud crash.

"Brynleigh!" Amelia put down the wiggly toddler who had just knocked the entire contents of the diaper bag onto the floor. She plopped the kid on the bench and hurried to pick everything up.

Tracy crossed her arms and waited while Vicky crouched to help.

Amelia swept up goldfish crackers into her hand. "Oh my gosh! I'm so embarrassed."

"Don't stress it, girl. I have four kids. I know the struggle."

Admittedly, Vicky couldn't remember her kids ever acting *this* bad, but Amelia didn't need to know that. She peeked under the bench, stretching her arm to grab a plastic bottle that had rolled away. Her fingers pulled it closer, revealing an all-too-familiar burgundy label with two cursive *J*s.

Vicky's heart plummeted. She stood, handing the bottle to Amelia. "Jolly Juice, huh?" She couldn't hide the disappointment in her voice. "Did someone give this to you, or—"

Amelia's entire face lit up. "I sell it! Have you tried it?" She pushed the bottle of juice back into Vicky's hand. "I swear this stuff saved me after my twins were born. I was so exhausted, my skin was a mess, and I had trouble producing enough milk for the girls. But after just one week of Jolly Juice, I was a new woman!"

Tracy scoffed, shaking her head. "My sister-in-law sells the stuff. It didn't work for me. You know what did? DreamWay's Pro-Eternity Vitamin Line." She continued blabbing about the benefits as she dug into her purse for a sample.

Game over.

Vicky politely handed the bottle to Amelia and excused herself as the two women rattled off their stale sales scripts. Vicky had been through it enough times to know the outcome. Amelia would never convince Tracy to enroll in Jolly Juice, just as Tracy wouldn't get Amelia to join DreamWay.

These women weren't hunters. They were scavengers satisfied with decaying, rotting corpses. Vicky was willing to work for something better—*someone* better. Anyone foolish enough to get caught up in Jolly Juice, DreamWay, or any other company that promised fast cash and subpar products wasn't the person for Vicky. After all, she didn't just need another customer. Vicky was looking for someone ready to build a business.

This self-awareness had propelled Vicky to the top—well, almost the top—of Puremetics in record time. She had been around the block enough to hear every pitch from every Network Marketer that dotted Utah County. Plenty of slimy companies were looking to take advantage of desperate stay-at-home moms wanting to earn some cash. None of them could hold a candle to Puremetics in terms of quality or opportunity.

It was a shame, too. Vicky really did like Amelia's sweater.

Blaze walked up the aisle with his younger siblings right behind. "Mom, everyone is hungry. Can we leave now?"

"Yes, sweetie." Vicky squeezed Blaze's shoulder. It was hard to believe her oldest had just turned seventeen. He looked like such a man and so much like Jack. "Thanks for holding down the fort today."

"Eh, it's not hard. You've trained these little goobers well." Blaze grinned at his seven-year-old brother.

The family moved toward the exit while Amelia and Tracy's voices continued to echo throughout the mostly empty chapel. Jack caught Vicky's eye as he waved from the front, still talking to his counselors. It would be the last interaction she'd get from her husband for hours. She sighed, trying to shake off her temporary defeat.

Blaze held the door open. "I'm guessing Dad has meetings?"

"Yeah, he won't be home until dinner."

The children piled into a shiny SUV—the one Vicky earned three months ago after hitting Presidential Emerald. She stood outside the car, letting the September sun soothe her soul. Never one to get bogged down by minor setbacks, Vicky closed her eyes and visualized the future she wanted.

An image of a woman took shape in Vicky's mind: confident, outgoing, faithful—practically a clone version of herself. That wasn't an accident. The rank of Royal Diamond was not easily achieved, so Vicky needed the best. She sent her request to the heavens with a silent prayer. Warmth filled her chest as she repeated her favorite affirmation. *It will all work out.*

It always did.

The short drive home refueled Vicky's enthusiasm. Scattered pioneer houses and expansive fields stretched along the road. Despite its rural reputation, Kinderhook, Utah was changing.

With the rush of well-to-do Mormons looking to preserve their idyllic life in a state experiencing a rush of California and Texas transplants, the little town was getting the ultimate glow-up. It reminded Vicky of her own transformation.

She turned into the nearly finished neighborhood of Splendor Springs, the epicenter of new beginnings. Rows of craftsman-style homes with steep rooflines and spacious floor plans passed by her window. Green lawns sprawled from driveway to driveway. Perfectly cut shrubberies and rose gardens lined walkways that led to enormous porches and thick, cedar doors. The towering Wasatch Mountains stood majestically in the background. Vicky smiled, taking it all in.

Her children laughed in the backseat. The diamond wedding band on her finger sparkled in the sun. Neighbors waved as the family drove by. Vicky pulled into house number 531 on New Hope Bluff, and she remembered how blessed her life was. Her hard work had gotten her this far—surely a sign her past mistakes had been forgiven. But there was still more to do. Vicky had bigger dreams to realize, things to prove, and doubts to shatter. She repeated her silent prayer and steadied her eyes, refusing to lose focus.

The hunt continued.

2

"At all times, you must *believe* you are in the right industry, with the right company, selling the right products. But mostly, you must believe in yourself."

Vicky paused the video and scribbled some notes in her journal. The glow from her laptop barely illuminated her words as she wrote. A sudden burst of light filled the kitchen, momentarily blinding her. Vicky looked over to see Jack opening the fridge. His mouth moved as he pulled out some orange juice and gestured to the lights overhead. Vicky removed her earbuds, but the early morning sounds of her kids getting ready upstairs flooded her senses. "Sorry? Did you say something?"

Jack leaned against the marble countertop as he sipped his juice. "I asked how you can work in the dark like that?"

"I enjoy the quiet."

Jack chuckled. "Lights don't make noise."

Vicky rolled her eyes. "I know. I can't explain it. It just *feels* quieter. Cozier." She put down her pen and straightened the papers on her desk. "Plus, I'm always afraid the kids will wake up if I turn the lights on. Suddenly, I'm back in mom mode. My early mornings are for me."

"Fair enough." Jack walked over to the built-in desk where Vicky sat. He leaned down to kiss her. "Mmmm... you smell good. Did you already shower?"

Vicky inhaled his cologne and smiled. "I already did a lot of things." She looked down at her planner, reviewing her morning to-dos.

1. ~~Spirituality: 20 minutes of scripture study and morning prayer~~
2. ~~Spirituality: 5 minutes of meditation and affirmations~~
3. ~~Creativity: Write a new blog post about fat burners~~
4. ~~Creativity: Edit photos for tomorrow's #OOTD post~~
5. ~~Creativity: Social media captions~~
6. Self-mastery: Review Convention talk, *"Power of Belief"*
7. Puremetics: Send out invitations for next week's recruiting party
8. Church: Relief Society agenda emailed to the presidency
9. Kids: Jaelyn's field trip form signed
10. Kids: New cleats for Blaze
11. House: Electrician appointment between 12 and 2

With a satisfied smile and a bright purple gel pen, Vicky crossed number six off her list. She closed her laptop and stretched her arms above her head. "Ready for breakfast? How about some eggs and toast?"

"I appreciate the offer, but I have an early meeting. I'm going to grab a bowl of cereal and call it good." Jack reached for a box of Cheerios in the cupboard.

Vicky scrunched her face. "That stuff will kill you."

"Then why did you buy it?"

Jack had a habit of questioning Vicky as if she couldn't possibly have a reason for her actions. Between cleaning the house, menu planning, grocery shopping, and ten million other invisible tasks that made Jack's life easier, hadn't she proved her competency after seventeen years of marriage?

She sighed. "Quinn never remembers snacks for Gigi." Vicky was careful to mask the annoyance in her voice. "At our last presidency meeting, Gigi screamed through the whole thing. I was hoping to bribe the child this week with some Cheerios."

Jack laughed. "So, it's okay for a toddler, but not me?"

"Excuse me for having higher standards than Quinn Baker. I read something about the glyphosate." Vicky contemplated pulling up the blog post to show him, but she knew he wouldn't read it. "I can make eggs. It will only take a minute."

Tiny Os fell into a porcelain bowl. "I think I'll be fine." Jack opened the large fridge behind him and groaned as he shuffled things around. "Where is the milk?"

"Dairy is full of hormones."

Jack closed the door and sighed. "Let me guess. You read that on a blog, too."

Vicky pushed back her chair and walked to the fridge. She smiled as she pulled out a shiny plastic bottle with a baby blue label. "Here. Almond milk. It's better for you."

"You know I can't stand this stuff." Jack slammed the bottle on the counter. He looked at his watch and sighed. "I'm going to be late. I'll grab something on the way to the office."

"Let me make you some eggs!" Vicky paused, afraid of her volume. She clenched her fists and exhaled slowly before forcing a smile. "Three minutes, Jack. That's all it will take."

He reached for his briefcase and gave Vicky a quick peck on the cheek. "I'm stopping by McDonald's."

Vicky opened her mouth to object; Jack quickly placed a finger on her lips.

"The occasional Egg McMuffin won't kill me." He reached for the almond milk and shoved it into her hands. "But this might." He threw on his sports jacket and grabbed his keys. "Please get some normal milk before I get home."

The garage door slammed. Tymberlee started singing *Let It Go* from the upstairs bathroom. Ryker was yelling that he was out of underwear. Vicky rubbed the side of her head, already missing her quiet time.

She contemplated her schedule, trying to factor in an impromptu trip to Green Goods Grocery. It was a long drive for just a gallon of milk, but Green Goods was her favorite place to shop—and not just for food. The store was brimming with Lululemon-clad women with too much time and a love for anything that promised to improve their health. It was the perfect place to find her last recruit. After all, one of Vicky's current leaders came from a conversation over acai berries in aisle seven.

As tempting as the trip was, there wasn't enough time.

An alarm rang, reminding Vicky to pack school lunches for the younger kids. She pulled three stainless steel bento boxes from the fridge. Each was carefully prepared the night before with homemade hummus, whole wheat pita chips, sliced strawberries, and organic yogurt. Vicky put a skillet on the burner and dropped a small pat of butter into the pan. She quickly hid the box of Cheerios before fetching eggs and the sourdough bread she made yesterday.

"Ryker! Tymber! Your bus leaves in twenty minutes."

As the pan heated up, Vicky grabbed her purple gel pen and quickly added *get milk* to her growing to-do list. She caught her reflection in the mirror hanging in the living room. She smiled and sighed. It was a shame to waste a perfect hair day on a trip to SuperMart.

Vicky's high heels clacked along the cold linoleum tiles as she trekked to the dairy section. In the five minutes since she had been in the store, she had already managed to avoid a pile of baby vomit near the bananas and someone's misplaced flip flop with a dirty Band-Aid stuck to the sole. Vicky was beginning to wish she had canceled the electrician appointment and made the trip to Green Goods instead.

Despite a less-than-ideal customer base, Vicky couldn't help sizing up every person she saw. She didn't expect to find her perfect recruit at SuperMart, but one woman looked promising. Dressed in activewear, she read labels on the back of two protein bars. *Health conscious. Cares about ingredients.* A sleeping infant in a car seat was nestled safely in her shopping cart. *New mom. Might want to earn money while staying home with the baby.*

Vicky smiled, flinging her hair behind her shoulder. With her purse tucked in the crook of her elbow, she took a confident step forward and tapped the woman on her shoulder. "Excuse me, I couldn't help but notice—"

"Oh my gosh, Vicky! It's been forever!" The woman turned with such energy it nearly knocked Vicky over.

Who was this woman?

Vicky would never admit to forgetting a name despite how often it happened. She smiled, regrouped, and popped her hand on her hip as she threw back her shoulder. "Right? How have you been, hun?" She cooed at the tiny baby. "Looks like you've been busy!"

The woman smiled, stroking the baby's head. "Meet little Adeline. Born at home three weeks ago. Jeff and I are absolutely smitten."

"She's precious. Congrats, and welcome to the Mom Club." Vicky tried to pull up the woman's name. *Carol? Christi?*

The woman beamed as she tossed a box of protein bars in the cart. "Thank you. She's what keeps me going. I'm hoping to hit Radiant Leader this year! I know it's nothing compared to your meteoric rise, but we can't all be like the great Victoria Sterling. I'm just lucky to have such an inspiring leader showing me the way. We're all excited to see you hit Royal Diamond!"

Cindy? Cynthia? Cici? Vicky gave up trying. Apparently, she had already recruited the woman. The fact that she was still slumming at the bottom rank proved she wasn't the leader Vicky needed. *Next.*

"Well, good luck and good work!" Vicky smiled politely and continued down the aisle.

The dairy section consumed the entire back wall of the store. Vicky perused the alternative milks first. Her fingers ran along the label of one made from coconut. Would Jack like this? She grabbed it along with his usual 2%.

"Oh my god! You're Victoria Sterling! Of *Sterling Style.*"

Vicky turned to see a woman in faded blue scrubs standing with her jaw dangling open. Her mousy brown hair was pulled back into a messy ponytail, revealing a makeup-free face and bags under her hazel eyes.

"Sorry, I didn't mean to yell." The woman blushed, shaking her head. "I've been reading your blog for years!"

"Ooh, a fan! How great." Vicky forced a smile, trying not to stare at the stain on the woman's top. "My readers are what keep me going. And please, call me Vicky."

The woman extended her hand. "I'm Anna."

Vicky stuffed the coconut milk under her arm so she could shake hands, hoping it would end the conversation. She turned toward the checkout line to leave.

"Can I ask you a question?" Anna followed her toward the front of the store.

"Oh, I'm sorry," Vicky said. "I don't do selfies."

"What? Oh, no. That's not—" Anna took a step closer, clearly not picking up on Vicky's leave-me-alone vibe. "I'm new in town and..."

I'm new in town was one of Vicky's favorite phrases. It was a giant green flag that screamed, *I need friends! I need direction! I need Puremetics!* She had been praying for someone to say those words for weeks, but this woman looked nothing like the star

Vicky had envisioned with her unpolished nails, clunky old sneakers, and invisible storm cloud hanging overhead. Vicky needed someone positive and inspiring—someone who believed they could build an empire, not this sad imposter.

But what if?

Vicky paused as a thought grabbed her by the throat. What if Heavenly Father was testing her? Maybe Anna was a diamond in the rough or a Cinderella story waiting to happen—one divinely handed to Vicky as the only person up to the task. She turned and decided to investigate this disturbing possibility.

"You're new, huh?" Vicky leaned in closer. "Where are you from?"

Anna's eyes shifted sideways. "Uh, Portland."

Promising. Vicky licked her lips. "How long have you been in Utah?"

"About a year." Anna looked less self-assured by the minute. "But I was in Provo for most of that time. I've only been in Kinderhook for a few days."

Very promising. "You have lots of friends back home?" Vicky took a step closer.

"I guess." Anna's eyes fell to the ground. "It's been a rough year, so I haven't really stayed in touch as I should."

Vicky placed her hand on her chest. Her voice grew so sweet it dripped with honey. "A rough year? Oh no, what happened?"

Anna's eyes drifted to a man walking toward them. He stopped at a display of batteries, and she quickly snapped her attention back to Vicky.

"I'd rather not get into it." Anna clasped her own hand, twisting the skin of her finger where a wedding band might have been. "I'm mostly focused on my daughter right now."

Struggling single mother? Jackpot.

Vicky reached out, squeezing Anna's elbow tenderly. "How old is your daughter? What's her name?"

Anna lit up a little. "Jane is sixteen," she said as a small smile crept along her face. "She's a junior at Splendor High. Just started last week."

"I have a son in the same grade! Maybe he knows her. Such a fun age, right?"

"Absolutely." Anna shifted from one foot to the other. "So, I just wanted to know if there were any good thrift stores around town. I remember all those amazing DIY upcycle projects you used to post on your blog. I figured you'd know the best spots."

A flood of memories filled Vicky's mind. It had been ages since her thrifting days, back when Jack was finishing law school, and they were barely scraping by. Vicky had remade their tiny townhouse into a Pottery Barn look alike. Dozens of projects, hundreds of blog posts, and a few million readers later, it was easy to forget how far Vicky had come.

"Provo has several options. Look up the nearest Deseret Industries."

"Awesome, thank you," Anna said, making a note of it in her phone. "I just moved into my new place and it's feeling a little barren. I was actually just looking at some of your old posts for inspiration. What are the odds I'd run into you at a random SuperMart?"

As Vicky walked to the checkout line, she asked herself the same question.

Part of her wanted to believe Anna was a distraction, a funny joke God had placed in the way before sending Vicky the leader she had been praying for. But the other part couldn't shake the feeling that Anna *was* the answer.

Vicky analyzed Anna, trying to make sense of a person so different from herself. The woman wasn't confident, poised, stylish, or outgoing, but there was a thoughtfulness to her. Anna looked like someone who had spent a lifetime quietly watching the world, seeing things everyone else missed, gathering secrets that could someday prove useful.

"So, what do you do, Anna?" Vicky gestured toward the faded blue scrubs. "Nurse?"

"Oh, no," Anna said, pulling nervously on her top. "I'm an Occupational Therapy Assistant and Certified Lymphedema Therapist. I'm part-time at Silver Lining Senior Living while I find a more permanent position. I used to work at St. Vincent's in Portland."

"You're looking for work?" Vicky placed the milk on the conveyor belt and smiled at the old man ringing her up.

"I'm trying to find where I can best use my skills in this new area," Anna said with a nervous smile.

Vicky was now confident the heavens had dropped Anna into her lap. "Do you believe in miracles?"

"Excuse me?"

"Miracles? Are you a woman of faith?"

"Well, I..."

Vicky shook her head, noticing the empty coffee cup in Anna's hand. "Forget I asked." God worked in mysterious ways. Maybe Puremetics wasn't just meant to change Anna's financial life. Perhaps Vicky was meant to lead Anna to the Gospel, too. Goosebumps ran down her arm just thinking about it.

"I'm hosting a little get-together at my house next week—a girl's night." Vicky took the bag from the cashier. "You should come."

"Oh?"

"I live just five minutes from here. You *have* to join us. It's super casual. There will be food, and we're going to do some spa treatments. You'll meet the greatest people in Kinderhook. Come. You look like someone who could use a little me time."

"Is it that obvious?" Anna asked, biting her lip. She pushed back a stray hair. "I'll think about it. Thanks."

"Do that. And then make sure the answer is *yes*." Vicky grabbed her phone, her eyes drilling into Anna's. "What's your number, hun? I'll text you the details and continue bothering you until you commit. I won't take no for an answer."

Anna rattled off her number, and Vicky sent the message. She smiled, suddenly energized by the potential she saw in Anna. Vicky had spent years turning beat-up dressers and crumbling nightstands into masterpieces. Why couldn't she do the same with this woman?

She pulled the keys from her purse and shook Anna's hand again. "I'm so happy you found me, Anna. I have a feeling we're going to be good friends. Welcome to Kinderhook."

3

"How was work?" Vicky asked, knife in hand.

The question drifted across the kitchen like a half-inflated balloon barely reaching Jack as he put his briefcase down. Vicky was too inside her head to realize she had even asked the question. The rhythm of the blade against the cutting board had lulled her into a meditative state, sharpening the one thing on her mind: transforming Anna Price.

With each slice, Vicky imagined cutting away Anna's flaws, starting with her clothes. *Slice.* Anna would need some new shoes, professional highlights, and the perfect shade of lipstick—*slice, slice, slice.*

Jack dropped the mail on the counter. "Busy," he said, loosening his tie, "but we made some headway on the Weston case." He nestled up behind Vicky as she reduced the carrot into tiny slivers. Jack wrapped his arms around her waist and pressed his lips against her neck.

His kiss broke the spell. Vicky put down the knife, realizing she had chopped a whole bag of carrots when she only needed two. She ran her fingers through her hair, accidentally bumping

Jack's chin with her elbow. She turned, reaching for his face. "Oh, sorry, sweetie!"

Jack chuckled, rubbing his jaw. "Someone's distracted."

On the contrary, Vicky was hyper-focused.

"I think I found a potential recruit," she said as she plopped some raw chicken on a second cutting board.

Jack walked over to the desk, picked up a letter opener, and ripped open an envelope. He pulled out its insides. "That's great, honey," he said, his eyes glued to the paper.

"This is a big deal, Jack. I just need one more qualifying leg to hit Royal Diamond. Only a dozen people have reached the company's top rank, and I'm on track to get there by Convention."

"I'm sure you'll reach all your goals." Jack picked up another bill. "But I thought you already found your last leader. Wasn't Jenny Taylor supposed to be *the one*? Just last week, you were raving about her potential."

"Don't get me started on Jenny Taylor." Vicky sliced the chicken breast in half, imagining it was Jenny Taylor's head. "Her nosy sister-in-law spooked her, and Jenny pulled out. Last I heard, she's working on some parenting coaching program, helping LDS families—and I quote—*Raise Celestial Children*."

Jack looked up. "Jenny Taylor is telling other people how to parent?"

Vicky nodded, a smile creeping along her face. "I thought you'd appreciate the irony." She gave a knowing look as Jack shook his head. On numerous occasions, she and Jack had over-heard screaming matchings from the Taylor household on their evening walks together.

"Just as well," Jack said, tossing a pile of catalogs into the recycling bin. "She was stirring up trouble a few months ago with that whole Kate Kelly business."

Vicky did not want to get into the Ordain Women argument

again. It had been a sore spot in their house ever since the group tried to gain access to the men-only session last year at General Conference. Even though Vicky insisted she had no desire to have the Priesthood, she could still sympathize with the women who did. But even her tepid understanding did not sit well with Jack, who considered their feminist agenda an attack on family values. He was quick to remind Vicky of women's sacred role in the home —their responsibilities were equal even if they weren't the same.

Blaze came bounding into the kitchen, a welcome interruption. "When will dinner be ready?" He pulled a bag from the cupboard, tore it open, and stuffed a handful of chips in his mouth.

"Soon," Vicky said as she seasoned the meat. "Put those away. You'll spoil your appetite."

"I'm hungry."

"He's a teenage boy," Jack said with a small laugh. "He could eat that whole bag and still want seconds tonight."

Vicky snapped at Blaze. "At the counter. No crumbs."

Blaze sauntered toward a stool and slumped down with his bag of chips.

"So, yeah," Vicky said to Jack, eager to get back on topic. "Jenny is out. But I have a good feeling about this new woman, Anna. She could be the one to get me to the top, and I think the business will be good for her, too."

Jack crossed his arms, leaning against the large kitchen island. "Why do you say that?"

"She's kind of sad and alone. She could be cute with some effort, but currently, she's a fixer upper." Vicky sighed, filling a pot with water. "I didn't see a wedding ring, so I'm guessing she's divorced, widowed, or just tragically single. She has a daughter who is a Junior at Splendor Springs High."

Jack pinched his brow. "And you think that will make her good at selling your supplements or body wraps or whatever it is you peddle these days?"

Vicky ignored the not-so-subtle dig and pressed on. "No, but it does make her eager for change. Having a big goal can transform a person's life. Besides, Puremetics is like a sisterhood. And trust me. This woman could use a little sisterly love."

After tossing the veggies into a pot, Vicky slid the chicken into the oven and closed the door with a loud thud. "But the real advantage is that Anna is not from around here. She's from Oregon."

"Meaning?" Jack removed his glasses and rubbed the bridge of his nose, clearly losing patience with the conversation.

"*Meaning*," Vicky said pointedly, "she's got friends and family out of state. She has access to a whole new market, one not as saturated as Utah County."

"Ah, right." Jack shook his head.

Vicky read between the lines of his expression. No matter how often Jack said he supported Vicky and Puremetics, it was the things he *didn't* say that made her defensive—like how Jack bit his lip whenever she mentioned a new promotion or the heavy sigh any time another box of products arrived. Dozens of clues forced Vicky to filter herself, ensuring she presented Puremetics in the best light possible. She was always afraid one wrong word would turn Jack decidedly against the whole endeavor.

Jack gathered his things and pecked her on the cheek. "Well, as long as it doesn't distract you from the kids and house, I'm happy you've found a hobby." He squeezed her arm and headed to his office.

And there it was, the familiar condescending tone. *Hobby.*

Vicky swallowed her pride—and her anger. She could have mentioned that her business had nearly matched Jack's income and that she managed it while serving as the Relief Society President, maintaining the house, and chauffeuring the younger kids everywhere. She was exhausted trying to prove she was more than a trophy wife who played pretend CEO while Jack did the actual work.

Did he forget what she gave up when she married him?

"Wait," Blaze said, interrupting the storm brewing inside Vicky. "This woman is from Oregon and has a daughter my age?"

Vicky unlocked her jaw and inhaled slowly. She turned to Blaze, trying to find her smile. "Yes. I think her name was Jane. Do you know her?"

"Yeah." Blaze leaned back, nodding. "She's my new biology partner. Just started last week."

"Oh! What a happy coincidence. Is she nice?"

Blaze shrugged. "Seems nice enough. She helped me a little with my homework yesterday. She's kinda weird, with neon blue hair and a bunch of piercings. But nice."

Blue hair? Multiple piercings? Vicky didn't love the sound of either.

"And she's smart. Mr. Broody kept trying to stump the class with some advanced questions, but Jane knew all the answers. It was pretty funny." Blaze stuffed another chip in his mouth. "You just met this lady, and you're already trying to recruit her? Is that a good idea?"

"Chew with your mouth closed, honey. And why wouldn't it be?" Vicky could feel her defenses accelerating again. "Anna could use some influential friends. I've seen Puremetics transform people's lives in ways you couldn't imagine. I think she'll do great, and I don't see why you should care either way."

Blaze fidgeted in his seat. "Remember your fallout with Diane West when she left Puremetics to join that Jiffy Juice thing, or whatever it's called?"

Vicky's fingernails dug into the sides of her pants just thinking about it. Diane had been on track to hit a new rank, too. *The traitor.*

"You blogged about the whole thing as if it were some *Real*

Housewives scandal, turning yourself into the hero. Seth stopped talking to me when everything went down, and he was my best friend. It sucked." Blaze pressed his hands into the marble countertop, looking down.

"You deserve better friends than Seth West."

Blaze shook his head as he crumpled the empty bag, refusing to meet Vicky's eyes. "Whatever. Just be nice, okay? I don't want you making it weird with Jane."

"Of course, I'll be nice. I'm always nice!"

Vicky didn't understand Blaze's concern. He barely knew the girl, and she certainly didn't sound like someone he'd be friends with. What happened with Diane was a fluke. Actually, it was a blessing in disguise. Vicky had heard Diane had stopped going to church and was mixed up with some anti-Mormon propaganda. *Good riddance.*

"So, this Jane girl," Vicky said, returning to the subject carefully. "Is she fitting in okay?"

"She's not some drug dealer if that's what you're worried about," Blaze said, his voice getting defensive.

"I never said she was a drug dealer." Although, admittedly, Vicky had wondered. After all, the girl *was* from Portland. "She sounds like she might have difficulty fitting in around here."

"Sure, she's a little different, but she seems fine. Keeps to herself mostly." Blaze stood and tossed the bag into the trash. "I honestly don't know much about her, but she is nice—and smart."

"Yeah, you said that." Vicky eyed Blaze, trying to read him. It wasn't like him to be so cryptic. Blaze had always been the most chatty and open of all her kids, but lately, he seemed more distant.

The soup began to bubble. "Just be careful," Vicky said, stirring the pot. "Kids these days like to express themselves in all sorts of ways, but that doesn't mean she's a good influence."

"Sheesh, Mom. We sit next to each other in biology. She helped me a little with my homework. I'm not marrying the girl."

"Good." Vicky rolled her shoulders back. "Speaking of girls, have you asked anyone to homecoming? It's only two weeks away, right? I heard Lexi Nader hasn't been asked to the dance yet. She's cute. Plus, she gave such a great talk in church a few weeks ago. Her family is one of the best in the ward."

"I didn't know you were ranking them now." Blaze furrowed his eyebrows as he crossed his arms. "Lexi is fine. I'm just really busy with classes and football. I was thinking of maybe skipping homecoming this year."

"Brigham Blaze Sterling, you will not disappoint some sweet girl dreaming about going to homecoming. I raised you better than that. It doesn't have to be Lexi. There are any number of amazing young women who would be thrilled to go with you. I'll pay for the ticket and a new suit. But you are going. End of discussion."

Blaze half-smiled, his eyes locking on Vicky's like a stubborn threat. "Maybe I'll ask Jane."

"Oh, well... I mean—" Vicky cleared her throat. She knew Blaze was testing her, but that didn't stop her from panicking. "What ward is she in?"

Blaze shook his head. "Oh, I don't think she's Mormon."

Vicky assumed as much, but having it confirmed spooked her. "Blaze, dear, we've talked about this. You marry who you date. Don't waste time with someone you can't take to the temple. I'm sure Jane is nice, and if you want to be her friend, I won't stop you. But I'm begging you to see the eternal picture here. There are plenty of other girls you can ask to the dance. Choose someone else."

"Is this even about me—or is it about you?" Blaze snapped back.

"Excuse me?" Vicky straightened her spine, locking eyes with her son. "I'm just looking out for you, sweetie. I don't want you to get caught up with the wrong crowd."

Blaze's lips clamped tight. Clearly, Vicky had struck a nerve.

"You have so much to offer the world," she said. "It's important you stay on the right path."

"The right path, or *your* path? I'm not you, Mom!" His voice cracked from exasperation. "One of these days, you need to let me live my own life instead of trying to force me to do things your way. You're worried about what the other moms will say if they see me hanging out with someone different. You can't stand the idea of anything ruining your picture-perfect family."

Blaze stood tall, towering over Vicky. "Don't you ever get tired of this bullshit? Sooner or later, you'll regret pushing away good people simply because they don't fit your stupid mold."

The sudden heat radiating from Blaze caught Vicky off guard. "Watch it," she said, her voice cold as ice.

They stood silent, both daring the other to look away first.

Finally, Blaze caved, cowering to Vicky's unrelenting glare. "I've got homework," he muttered. "Call me when dinner is ready."

The air around Vicky was thick from Blaze's outburst. Even in his absence, his words hung like menacing black clouds threatening to burst. Vicky's hand moved to her chest as she tried to ground her emotions before the electric charge building inside cracked her open.

Jack marched back into the kitchen with his phone pressed against his face. "Of course... Uh-huh... Yes, I understand. I'll be there in five minutes."

"What's going on?" Vicky asked, bracing herself for another storm.

"Sister Welch lost her temple recommend and has a family wedding tomorrow. She needs an interview tonight to get a new one, so she doesn't miss the ceremony."

"So, you're leaving now?" Vicky asked, glancing at the oven timer. "What about dinner? You do your interviews at seven. Why can't she wait until then?"

"She's not available later."

Vicky crossed her arms, her voice rising by the moment. "But you're not available now!"

Jack grabbed his keys and his jacket. "What am I supposed to do? She can't enter the temple without it. Would you have her miss her niece's wedding? Being the Bishop comes with some sacrifices. I'm sorry about dinner, but this is more important." The door slammed before she could respond.

Vicky slumped onto a kitchen stool and buried her head in her arms.

It took a lot to rattle Victoria Sterling. She was used to distant husbands and moody teenagers. She had built an empire while juggling the multifaceted demands of being a mother and wife. Vicky tried not to take these sudden outbursts or missed family dinners personally, but she couldn't help but feel like she was being punished somehow—that her past was finally catching up to her.

Vicky pushed down the lump in her throat just as the soup boiled over. She rushed to turn down the heat, wishing there was a similar knob for her emotions. She reached for a rag, swiping dangerously close to the gas flame, determined to clean up the mess even if she got burned.

When she finished, she turned to the pile of vegetable scraps and dirty cutting boards on the counter. The impulse to put everything back in place was intense. Vicky popped into action, filling the dishwasher and wiping the counters. She carefully set the table, trying not to break down when she accidentally set a place for Jack.

After the kitchen was sparkling and the dining room table stood ready for the three-course meal Vicky had meticulously prepared, the Sterling house was once again in pristine shape. Still, her stomach twisted into a knot—the truth unwilling to clean up as easily. No matter how hard Vicky worked to polish her life, she knew the foundation was rotting. One false step, and it could all come crashing down.

4

Anna Price's heart thumped so fast she half-expected to see wolves chasing her in the rearview mirror. So, that's what she imagined: three—no, four—fang-baring beasts nipping at the dented bumper of her Toyota Camry, waiting to overtake the car and gobble her up, skin and bones.

At least then Anna would have a reason for being so damned nervous.

She imagined a lot of things these days: the sun exploding, sinkholes swallowing her whole, seagulls pecking out her eyes. The more horrific and gruesome, the better. It was the only way Anna could overwrite the one memory that popped into her brain whenever her mind inevitably found its way back to Dale.

"In 500 feet, turn left onto Old Pioneer Way." Following the not-quite-human voice of her GPS, Anna drove along the winding road. Not a single wolf in sight.

The sun was low, casting a blue hue on everything. Kinderhook was a hodgepodge town that Anna was still trying to figure out. It was a strange mixture of old and new. One minute, you'd be cruising along vast hay fields and pioneer cabins; the next, you'd pass a luxurious subdivision.

Without roots or sheen, Anna couldn't figure out where she belonged in any of it. It didn't help that she had moved into the most uninspiring apartment on Gray Street. The small building, built in the seventies, had no historical appeal or shiny newness to make it stand out. Her apartment was cheap and available, so Anna made do, trying not to draw too many parallels between the building and her crumbling life.

Anna's phone rang, interrupting the GPS's navigation. Jane was calling. After fumbling with the buttons on her phone, Anna pulled to the side of the road to take the call.

Jane's voice filled the car. "Mom! I got your note. Where are you? I thought we were going to make cookies and watch *What's Up, Doc?*"

"I'm sorry, kid." Anna closed her eyes, bracing herself for the shock that would follow her next statement. "I'm actually on my way to a girl's night out."

Jane's silence was deafening.

Bumping her head against the steering wheel, Anna contemplated turning the car around and calling the whole thing off. A movie night with Jane would be infinitely more enjoyable—pajamas, homemade cookies, a cozy blanket. What could be better? Besides, Anna could use a little inspiration from her favorite character, Judy Maxwell, played flawlessly by the incomparable Barbara Streisand. Judy's willingness to go for what she wanted, without fear or filters, was inspiring.

Anna dreamed of cultivating the same kind of carefree confidence, being able to approach anyone with the self-assurance of a star, who could say everything they needed with just a glance or simple catchphrase. *What's up, doc?* She liked to think she shared Judy's wit and surprising intelligence, but no matter how hard Anna tried, she lacked Judy's boldness. Anna was unwilling to take up space, terrified to show her true self.

It was even more reason to skip Vicky's party.

"Are you mad? I can cancel." Anna held her breath, hoping Jane would beg her to come home.

"Good for you," Jane finally said. "I think it's great you're meeting new people. We'll ogle Ryan O'Neal another time."

"Deal." Anna tried to hide her disappointment. "I'm hoping to be home by nine. Make sure you eat something, okay? Feel free to order a pizza." She cringed, knowing funds were tight. "Or there's still plenty of last night's chicken and rice in the fridge. Why don't you finish that up?"

"Sure thing," Jane said, her voice heavy with understanding. "And good luck!"

"Thanks, kid." Anna ended the call and checked for traffic before merging back onto the road.

"In 200 feet, turn right onto Glitter Lane."

A large stone sign with *Splendor Springs* etched on its face welcomed Anna to the neighborhood. The street widened, and an island of trees split the road into two one-way lanes. Large houses passed her window, most with garages bigger than her entire apartment.

"Fancy," Anna whispered, feeling even more nervous.

Anna thumped her fingers against the steering wheel, trying to center herself. She was already late, which only added to her nerves. Following her phone's orders, she moved further into the neighborhood, where the houses grew even more grand.

A final turn onto New Hope Drive brought Anna onto a narrow, rocky road. The pomp and circumstance of the neighborhood were suddenly gone. She followed the tiny lane until it came to a dead end. Her car sputtered to a stop in front of a small cottage from the nineteenth century. Well-maintained but plain and unassuming, it looked nothing like the mansions she had passed to get there.

"This can't be right."

Anna reread Vicky's text: *Come for a girls' night of pampering!!! Wed, Sep. 24. @ 7 PM. My house. 531 New Hope Drive.*

A hand-painted *531* over a tiny carport marked the address. Cars were parked outside the house, suggesting a party-sized crowd. Anna wrinkled her nose and peeked out her window at the green street sign, confirming what her app had already told her.

This was the place.

New Hope Drive. It sounded pleasant enough, but then again, so had Dale's suggestion to move to Utah last year. "Hope for a better tomorrow!" her ex-husband had said. "That's what this new job offers!"

Anna had doubts, but Dale convinced her it was the best option for the family. So, she packed up, pulled Jane away from her friends, quit a job she loved, and followed him over the Rocky Mountains to this strange new world, leaving behind the only life she had known.

It took less than six months for all hope to crumble.

Anna's fingers gripped the steering wheel as she squeezed her eyeballs shut, trying to keep the unthinkable image out of her brain. But Dale's bare ass, hovering over a twenty-something graduate student in *their* bed, came fully into view.

She popped her eyes open, renewed with rage.

"If you want things to change, you must be willing to change," Anna said, pumping herself up. She took a huge breath and puffed her chest like she was preparing for war. Throwing her purse over her shoulder, Anna marched up the driveway. Her shaky hand formed a loose fist and tapped three times.

The door swung open. A dozen eyeballs from the small but crowded living room turned in Anna's direction. She tried to find Vicky's face among the women, but it didn't take long to realize she wouldn't find it.

This was the wrong house.

"Can I help you?" The sturdy but petite woman at the door smiled. Silver curls bounced like confetti from her scalp. Ruby red lips matched the brightly colored glasses that framed hazel eyes accented by deeply set crow's feet.

"I'm sorry," Anna said, pressing her sweaty palms into her jeans. "I'm looking for Vicky Sterling. She invited me to a party, and this is the address she sent, but I'm guessing there was a mix up."

"This is New Hope *Drive*," one woman in the living room yelled. "That fancy schmancy neighborhood down the street has all kinds of variations: New Hope Circle, New Hope Boulevard, New Hope Lane, New Hope Court—"

"—I think she gets it, Emily." The woman at the door cut her off as she leaned in closer as if trying to read the fine lines etched on Anna's face. "I'm sorry, did you say Vicky Sterling? As in Victoria Sterling?"

Feeling like a kid snitching at recess, Anna swallowed hard. "I'm sorry to bother you. I'll leave."

"No!" The woman's voice stopped Anna in her tracks. She opened the door wider, gesturing for Anna to come inside. "What I mean is, you're not bothering anyone. Come in. We'll help you find where you need to be."

Anna's stomach dropped at the invitation. The voice in her head begged her to return home, put on some pajamas, and call it a day. But the scene bursting from inside the plain old house beckoned her to come inside for a closer look. Loud, colorful furniture and unique knickknacks popped out from the cozy space. A massive mural with a kaleidoscope of colors made the room feel alive. Anna's imagination grabbed onto every detail, holding her interest hostage.

"You okay, honey?"

Anna woke from her transfixed state to find every eye still stuck on her. Half a dozen women in their sixties and seventies sat like a gathering of modern-day Mother Goose characters. Their bold patterns and unique accessories gave each lady a distinct style, while the same owl brooch pinned near the collarbone united the women with its golden shine.

Even with her impressive imagination, Anna never expected to stumble on these mysterious crones. Her feet rooted to the porch, unsure what the next step should be. By the looks of the women's faces, they were talking business, not pleasure. But what kind of business could these silver-haired women have? Were they widows who murdered their husbands? Crazy cat ladies starting a cult? Witches summoning the spirits of their ancestors? Anna was delighted and terrified by every possibility. Before she knew what was happening, her curiosity had pulled her closer until she stood in the entryway.

"I'm Gloria," the first woman said. "Welcome to my home."

"Thanks." Anna took another timid step toward the group. Tucking her chestnut hair behind her ears, she inhaled slowly, waiting for someone to say something. Instead, Gloria whispered to another woman. They smiled, nodding as they turned their attention back to Anna.

Gloria gestured for one of the women on the emerald couch to make room. "Before we help you find your party, we have a few questions."

"Oh, okay." Anna sat carefully on the sofa, her hands running along the velvet cushions.

Gloria smiled; her eyes twinkled. "What do you know about Puremetics?"

5

Anna's head spun, matching the swirling paint of the large mural in front of her. Thick brushstrokes of grays and yellows dripped downward, slowly morphing into a circular spiral that enveloped a woman in the middle. Eyes closed and chin up—the subject's profile lifted heavenward, facing a tidal wave of reds and whites that morphed into a phoenix above her. It was hard to tell where the woman ended and the bird began. Connected by the tornado of colors, both subjects struggled to break free from the storm surrounding them.

Gloria tapped Anna's shoulder. "Anna?"

Pressing her eyes tight, Anna tried to shake off the artwork's pull. The vibrant painting had captivated her attention the moment she entered Gloria's house, feeding her imagination.

"I'm sorry. What did you say?" Anna looked at the silver-haired woman whose friendly gaze had morphed into an urgent request.

"Will you do it? Will you help us?"

On the surface, it was such a benign question. The woman's plea tugged at Anna's heart, begging her to give in, but the last twenty minutes had put every other part of her body on high alert. What started with one simple question—*what do you know about Puremetics*—turned into a whirlwind of corporate conspiracies, shocking accusations, and an interrogation into Anna's life and personal moral compass. Anna wasn't even entirely sure what these women wanted from her, only that this unlikely group of senior citizens had taken on a mission so ambitious it seemed almost laughable.

Gloria leaned in and locked eyes with Anna. The rest of the group sat quietly at the edge of their seats, equally eager for a reply.

Anna could barely think. The deluge of information had drenched her senses, leaving her numb. "Can we back up a bit?" She rubbed the sides of her head. "What exactly is this little group of yours?"

Gloria tapped the gold brooch on her lapel. "We're The OWLS: The Old Wise Ladies' Society."

The other women in the room chuckled.

"It started as a joke," Claire explained. Short and peppy, her asymmetrical purple pixie and oversized earrings made her seem younger than the rest of the group. The gray roots and lines across her forehead suggested otherwise. "We've considered changing it multiple times—at least the *Old* part."

Emily leaned back in a rocking chair, crossing her arms firmly in front of her chest. With her stick-straight hair, pale skin, and icy blue eyes, Emily was Gloria's opposite: Calculating, cold, and rigid.

"There are so many better options: Outstanding, Open-minded, Optimistic, Observant. But *somebody*," Emily said, pointing to Gloria, "insists on keeping the word *Old*."

"Because *old* isn't a bad word." Gloria met Emily's gaze with a satisfied smirk. "Twenty-year-old me has nothing on this wiser, kinder, and tougher version of myself. Do you know how many fucks I give at this age?"

"None!" the group yelled in unison, raising their porcelain teacups in a salute.

Gloria nodded her head. "Exactly."

Emily huffed. "It makes us sound like cranky spinsters with too much time on our hands."

"Well, if the shoe fits." Gloria shrugged.

The room erupted in laughter. Anna couldn't help but notice the way everyone gravitated toward Gloria. Even grumpy Emily in the corner seemed to orbit around the de facto leader's magnetic pole.

"Okay," Anna said, trying to get back on topic. "You're—what? A group of spies who work in secret to bring about justice? Like Batman?"

Claire giggled. "I wish!"

"We're not spies, nor do we go around fighting crime in costumes." Emily had already established herself as the lawyer-type who was hellbent on ensuring Anna's language was accurate. "We're just women, Anna. Activists. We want to see the world change for the better." She scoffed, setting her teacup down on the table. "Gloria, we're wasting our time with this. We don't need her."

"I disagree," Gloria said, her eyes still firmly planted on Anna. "After what happened last month, we need to cover all our bases. Having someone on the inside would be invaluable."

"Oh, I see." Anna nodded slowly. "So, you just want *me* to spy." As intrigued as she had been about the group, their mysterious appeal was wearing thin now that they wanted her help. Anna stood, trying to remember where she had put her purse. "Ladies, I applaud your efforts, but I am not the right person for the job."

Gloria quickly interceded, gently pushing Anna back down in her seat. "You're wrong. Based on what you've told us, you are *the* person for the job. You are bright and caring, and you already know Victoria Sterling."

"Well, I mean..." Anna stumbled on her words, wishing she had never mentioned Vicky's name. Over the last few days, she had imagined being Vicky's new best friend. In her mind, they had an unstoppable bond that would pull Anna from the brink of despair and lift her to where Vicky stood in her glorious perfection. It was this fantasy that had convinced Anna to go to Vicky's party in the first place. Now that Gloria was looking to capitalize on this potential relationship, the illusion quickly vanished.

Anna was *not* Vicky's friend, but that didn't mean she couldn't be.

"I met her a week ago, and we've texted a couple of times." Anna tugged on the hem of her shirt. "She invited me to a party that I have now rudely missed. She probably wouldn't trust me enough for your plan to work."

"You haven't missed the party," Emily said with some bite. "You're just late."

Gloria clapped her hands. "Exactly! We'll help you get to Vicky's. You'll earn her trust. And it will all work out!"

"Can we please stop calling it a party?" Emily pointed to a giant sketchpad on an easel in the corner of the room. Large letters in red marker revealed the key points they had discussed earlier with Anna. "We went over this, remember? It's a recruiting scheme for Puremetics."

Of course, it was. Anna wasn't stupid. She had read enough of Vicky's blog to know about Puremetics. Why else would Vicky invite a perfect stranger to her home ten minutes after meeting her?

But what Emily, Gloria, and the others didn't seem to understand was that Anna *wanted* to enroll. She was eager to buy whatever Vicky was selling—willing to do anything to get a taste of her rarefied life.

Or at least she had been until Gloria came along and smothered the dream.

Anna plopped back on the sofa. "Is Puremetics really so awful? Whatever Vicky is doing, it seems to be working well for her. According to her blog, she's helped countless people find financial freedom. It's all about women supporting women. Shouldn't we cheer that on?"

Claire shook her head. "Don't believe the hype. Ninety-nine percent of people lose money in MLMs. But Puremetics is even worse. Don't forget who is running the show. I'll give you a hint: It's not Vicky."

Anna ran her fingers through her hair, trying to untangle her thoughts. "Right. The evil CEO. What was his name? Chris, something?"

"Christian White," Emily said, pointing to his name on the sketchpad.

Anna nodded. "Who—according to you—has lied, cheated, and done all kinds of bad stuff."

Gloria flinched. "To put it mildly."

It was clear Gloria wasn't telling Anna everything. The OWLS had presented a brief but cryptic list of the man's supposed misdeeds. Sure, he sounded awful, but not any worse than your typical shady rich guy. What made Christian White worthy of being the target of this crusade?

"I'm sorry," Anna finally said with a slight scoff. "Do I look like someone who can defeat a powerful CEO?" She already knew the answer to that question was a resounding *no*.

Gloria leaned forward. "You'll be working as part of a team. You won't be alone. This isn't some thrown-together plan."

"Right." Anna jutted her chin. "You knew I'd show up tonight. I forgot about your magical foresight."

"No," Gloria said. "You are a happy accident. But this is not our first time trying to take this man down. We need someone who can work up the ranks and earn the trust of those on top."

Anna lowered her voice, trying to find a crack in Gloria's conviction. "Why don't one of you enroll with Vicky? Why risk putting such an important task on someone you don't even know."

Gloria smiled. "We would, but as I said, our attempt at this most recent convention didn't go well. Puremetics knows who we are. But you," she said, squeezing Anna's arm tenderly, "you've already been invited to the inner circle. You're young, new, and without ties to our group."

Anna felt sick, unable to enjoy that someone called her young for the first time in a decade. She pressed her fingers against the temples of her head. "You said you want me to sabotage their big convention next summer. Is that even legal?"

The exchanged glances between the women made Anna's stomach churn. But Gloria's earnest expression was even worse. It was a look that said *I trust you. You can do this. You're special.* Anna worried she'd follow the crazy old woman to hell. She needed to leave before she did just that.

Anna found her purse on a side table and flung it over her shoulder. "I wish you luck and will cheer you on silently from afar, but as I said before, I am not the right person for this job." A handful of women raised their voices at once, sending Anna to the edge of a panic attack as she maneuvered through the group, making her way to the door.

Gloria followed and gently pushed the door shut, inserting herself between it and Anna. "Listen, I know this is crazy. I know we're asking a lot, but we have no chance of making this work if we don't have someone on the inside. We're not asking you to confront Christian or take him down on your own, and I promise to do everything in my power to ensure you are safe from any legal implications. You will be our eyes and ears among those we can't get close to."

Anna felt her muscles tense as a dozen eyeballs drilled into her. Despite Gloria's persistence, Anna knew not everyone in the room was eager to welcome her into their little band of misfits—Emily had made that clear. But Gloria's belief that

Anna could do something meaningful gave her the briefest feeling of hope.

What if she *could* pull this off?

What if she *was* brave enough?

What if this was the thing that would change her life?

Gloria locked eyes with Anna. "The fact that you stuck around as long as you did tells me you're open to change."

The words hit Anna like bullets. For months, she had been begging for a change. Anna felt stuck long before the divorce, even before Dale cheated. At forty, she felt past her prime, but it wasn't just her growing waistline or the gradual descent of her once perky breasts that made her feel undesirable. Anna had a lifetime of saying less than she thought, shrinking herself to be acceptable until she was suddenly invisible. More than anything, she wanted to matter. Anna wanted to know the world hadn't ignored her—that life hadn't dumped her in the middle of nowhere, forgotten and unwanted.

As Gloria stared into her eyes, Anna felt seen, which was terrifying because it made staying put impossible.

"Okay," Anna finally said. She rubbed her temples, already afraid she made the wrong choice. "Where do we start?"

A victorious smile spread across Gloria's face. She wrapped her arms around Anna's shoulder, leading her back into the middle of the room.

"We start by getting you to Vicky's house!"

6

Vicky's fingers drummed against the marbled countertop as she rechecked the time. It was almost a quarter to eight, and Anna still hadn't shown. She slammed her phone down and snapped a carrot stick in half.

"Vicky! Get over here," Becki yelled from the living room. "You've got to hear this. You'll never believe what Jenny posted today."

A ripple of laughter moved through the group as they shared the latest gossip.

Vicky wasn't in the mood. She reached for another carrot, held it close to her lips, and grimaced. After spending the past week building a rapport, offering thrifting tips and insider info about the area, Vicky couldn't believe Anna would bail on the party. *The nerve.* Considering the colossal risk of inviting someone like Anna into her home, the least she could do was offer a reasonable excuse for not coming.

She tossed the vegetable in the trash and grabbed a potato chip, running it deeply through Wendy's signature dip, nicknamed the Fat Bomb. Vicky shoved the dip-smothered chip into her mouth, ignoring the promise she had made earlier to avoid the sinful treat.

It was time to get the party started. Even if Vicky's own hopeful recruit was a no-show, the other leaders of her organization had come with starry-eyed newbies, ready to enroll. Sure, none of these women would help Vicky rank up, but they would still add to her overall bottom line. The night wouldn't be a total waste.

Vicky stuffed another chip in her mouth just as the doorbell rang. A spark of hope flickered as she sprinted to the door. Anna stood on the front porch looking as timid as ever. She clung to her purse like a life jacket. Her smile faltered when her eyes met Vicky.

"I'm sorry I'm late," Anna said, holding her phone for Vicky to see. "I went to New Hope *Drive* instead of New Hope *Bluff*."

"Oh, dear. Sorry about the mix-up." Vicky read the typo on Anna's phone. She knew she should be embarrassed about the mistyped address, but she was more annoyed Anna was shoving her mistake in her face. After all, it was nearly eight o'clock. Anna could have texted her sooner.

Vicky forced a smile, telling herself to keep the big picture in mind. "Well, I'm glad you found your way to us. Come in. I'll introduce you to the girls."

Anna's eyes bulged as she entered the house. "Wow. Your home is beautiful."

"Aw, thank you! Kick your shoes off. We're just about to start the spa treatments."

Anna carefully removed her dingy sneakers, and Vicky tried not to judge Anna's faded sweater or baggy jeans, but she did make a mental note of it. If this was going to work, Anna's makeover would need to happen sooner rather than later. The thought made her giddy. She always loved a good project.

But first, Vicky needed to close the deal.

The large, circular entryway featured a grand spiral staircase that loomed nearly ten feet over Vicky's head. Walking past an adjoining music room with a grand piano, Vicky led Anna into the kitchen. The counter was full of appetizers, desserts, and sparkling flavored water. Bouquets and a colorful pom-pom banner across the large window added a festive flare to the space. Baskets full of Puremetics products and brochures covered the kitchen table.

They walked into the living room, where nearly a dozen women waited. Like pearls strung across a necklace, they sat evenly spaced out, mirroring Vicky's flawless style with their colored skinny jeans, shiny hair, and well-manicured nails. One by one, the women looked up, each lifting a suspecting eyebrow at Anna.

"Everyone, this is Anna. Anna, this is Becki, Jenna, Liz, Dana, Sarah, Molly, Grace, Cali, Jennifer, and Wendy." Vicky rattled through the names like an auctioneer. She knew Anna would never remember them all, nor did she care. Half the women were already enrolled in Puremetics—each a part of Vicky's downline in one way or another—and the other half were the first half's hopeful recruits.

But Anna was Vicky's.

"Nice to meet you all," Anna said, carefully sitting at the edge of the couch. "Thanks for having me."

Becki and Cali exchanged looks, making Vicky's stomach turn. She could practically hear their snide telepathic remarks. Sure, Anna was a little rough around the edges. Her hair needed some volume, her skin was dull, and her wardrobe was depressing, but all those things just made Anna more moldable. Vicky had built her online empire by transforming old, outdated junk into masterpieces. It would be no different with Anna. The others would see.

"Where are you from, Anna? I don't think I've seen you around Splendor Springs," Dana said, crossing her legs.

Anna squeezed a throw pillow, practically choking it. "I'm

originally from Portland. I moved to Utah last year and to Kinderhook a few weeks ago. I don't live in Splendor Springs."

"That makes sense," Dana said, eyeing Molly. The two women smirked.

Anna shifted in her seat. "Do you all live in the neighborhood?"

"Most do, but not everyone." Vicky snapped down on a carrot stick, wishing it dripped with dip. She pointed to a long-legged blonde with a chunky necklace. "Grace is my sister-in-law. She lives in Rockford Hallows."

"Gorgeous neighborhood," Becki said, swooning at the very mention of it. The other women nodded in agreement while Grace curtsied her head as if receiving a lifetime achievement award.

Vicky pointed to a brunette with glowing white teeth. "And Wendy lives in an old historic house on Main Street."

Liz laughed. "Historic *mansion* is more like it."

"Completely renovated, too." Wendy tossed her silky brown hair over her shoulder. "New roof, new porch, updated kitchen and bathrooms. Heaven knows we don't need another decaying old house in this valley. Seriously, when is the city going to tear those blemishes down?"

"They should start with Ghostly Manor," Dana said, rolling her eyes. She pursed her ruby lips. "I hate driving past the thing every time I take Braxton to soccer."

"Ghostly Manor?" Anna asked.

"It's the most decrepit shack you'll ever see. Legend says it's haunted, but really, it's just hideous. The windows are all boarded up. It has graffiti all over the rotting siding. I wouldn't be surprised if there were bodies buried in the backyard."

Anna bit her lip. Her voice was barely audible. "Are you talking about the abandoned house on Gray Street?"

"Yes!" Dana threw her arms up. "Oh. My. Gosh. It's the *worst*. And it's right next to those crappy apartments that also need to go. I swear only druggies or prostitutes live there. Those ratty old buildings are ruining our property values."

The other women sighed collectively, adding their impassioned agreements. Anna's cheeks went flush as she sunk deeper into the chair.

Sensing Anna's growing discomfort, Vicky clapped her hands. "Okay, ladies. It's time! What's it going to be tonight? Facials or body wraps?"

Becki pinched her stomach, unable to grab anything but skin. "Ugh, body wraps please. I'm still trying to lose this baby weight from little Omni."

"Yes!" Dana said, matching Becki's energy. "It's been two months since the twins came, and I still can't shake these last three pounds."

Vicky turned her back, gathering the requested supplies while quietly rolling her eyes. Leave it to the two thinnest women of the group to make everyone else feel like hippos. Plus, she couldn't help but think their comments were directed at Anna. After all, she was the only one who needed the body wrap. But she pushed these thoughts aside, determined to stay focused on her goal. She plastered a smile on her face, grabbed a couple of boxes, and held them up like a model on *The Price is Right*.

"Okay, ladies. Let's melt some belly fat!"

"Oh my god! It burns!"

Anna gripped the edge of her seat, holding back tears. Her shirt was tucked in her bra, making space for the plastic wrap that clung to her belly like a leech. The cream Vicky had applied to Anna's stomach was frigid initially, but now, her skin was on fire after being wrapped like a burrito for forty-five minutes.

Vicky perked up and smiled. "That means it's working!"

Nobody else seemed bothered. Anna couldn't decide if they

were better at hiding their pain or if she was just being a wuss. She tried to ignore the most obvious possibility that she was suffering from an allergic reaction. The last thing Anna wanted was to draw unnecessary attention to herself by requiring medical attention.

"These wraps helped me fit into my pre-pregnancy jeans," Wendy said. "You ladies are getting spoiled tonight!"

Molly took a sip of her sparkling water. "I also sleep better after each wrap session. The detox is ah-mazing."

"Tell me about it." Vicky passed around another set of hand-outs. "I wish I had these when I was pregnant. I got huge with Ryker."

"Hardly," Grace, the sister-in-law, said. "You were a glowing goddess."

"Well, since you were the only one who knew me back then, I'm going to let everyone assume you're telling the truth." Vicky cocked her head and laughed.

As the women let their bellies ferment, Vicky continued her little spiel about Puremetics. She had briefly covered the compensation plan (*uncapped earning potential!*) and the community (*women empowering women!*)—now, she was pitching the products.

"As you can see on page two," Vicky said, pointing to the purple brochure, "these wraps use powerful, active botanicals to help pull away toxins, tone your midsection, and enhance the overall skin texture. It's perfect for targeting all your problem areas."

Even without Gloria's warnings of too-good-to-be-true promises, Anna could see the red flags a mile away. A simple cream wasn't going to do shit to her belly fat and calling out someone's "problem areas" didn't feel very empowering. Besides, Anna had more important things to worry about than the size of her pants.

A timer buzzed. Anna began unwrapping herself in a frantic

attempt to break free. She tugged away the gooey plastic, revealing tomato-red skin. Hints of blood stained the washcloth as she rubbed her body clean.

"Is this normal?" she whispered to a woman whose name she could not remember.

The woman shrugged and turned to chat with someone else.

Anna tapped Vicky on the shoulder. "Where is the bathroom?"

Vicky pointed down the hall. As soon as Anna locked the door, she let out a small whimper. Her fingers gently pressed against the skin, and the pain nearly knocked her over. She rolled up a wad of toilet paper, ran it under the cool water, and pressed it against her stomach, achieving the slightest hint of relief.

Anna leaned over the sink, staring at her reflection. Tears welled in the corner of her eyes. "I can't do this."

It wasn't just the broken skin—Anna's spirit busted wide open. The whole night had been one emotionally draining disappointment after the other. She would never fit in with Vicky and her friends. And while that no longer seemed like a massive loss after spending the past hour with these women, not fitting in meant letting Gloria down. How could Anna possibly be the eyes and ears for the OWLS if she couldn't even get through one product pitch?

Anna pulled out her phone, ready to text Gloria and tell her she was out. She unlocked the device but stopped as her eyes landed on the phone's background image.

It was a photo of Ghostly Manor.

Anna had snapped the pic on her first day at the new apartment, the one Vicky's minions were eager to tear down. Her bedroom window perfectly framed the decrepit old house. Anna hated that Ghostly Manor's sagging roof and graffitied walls would be the first thing she'd see each morning when she opened the blinds. It felt like a cruel reminder of how far she had fallen. But then Jane had pointed out the faded curtain half-hanging from inside a broken window.

"It's crazy to think someone used to live there," Jane said, a smile stretching from cheek to cheek. "Think about how many happy memories must have happened inside that home. How many stories are locked inside those walls?"

It was an innocuous observation, but it ignited Anna's imagination. Suddenly, she saw the house as it must have looked more than a century ago. Someone had carefully built it, hoping for a stable, safe harbor from the world. She pictured a little family sitting around a fire, singing Christmas carols, a mother hugging a child, and countless dinners served. How many celebrations took place under that roof? How many babies had been born? How many hard lessons won?

When Anna snapped the photo and set it as her phone's wallpaper, she had no idea the decaying shack had a nickname. She wanted a visual reminder, not for what Ghostly Manor was but for what it *used* to be—and what it *could* be again if given the chance.

There was a knock on the door. "Anna, everything okay in there?" Vicky asked from the other side.

"Yep! Be out in a sec!"

Anna put away her phone and stared at her reflection. Some would say *she* was past her prime. Her chestnut-colored hair was flat and dull, and her face was rounder than she remembered. The changes over the past decade or two had been so slow and subtle that it was hard to recognize the middle-aged woman staring back at her. There were days when Anna felt haunted and worthy of being torn down, days when what she saw on the outside proved she was too far gone ever to be loved again.

But all she had to do was look past the face staring back at her to see the fire burning behind her hazel eyes. Anna was still standing, too stubborn to fall, which had to mean something. Maybe she wasn't up to the task, but she would not give up on this mission as long as Gloria believed in her. Just like that not-so-haunted house everyone was desperate to demolish, Anna knew she had more to give.

Puremetics was going down.

Anna swung the door open, surprised to see Vicky standing just outside.

"Oh good! I was getting worried." Vicky folded her arms. "So, what do you think? Don't you just love the products? I'm telling you, there's nothing like Puremetics."

"You're right," Anna said, no longer worried about the rash burning across her stomach. The fire raging within consumed her. "You've convinced me, Vicky. Sign me up."

7

"You have *got* to be kidding me."

Vicky's cheeks burned as she pulled into the tiny parking lot of the run-down apartment building. She rubbed her temples, feeling a rush of delayed embarrassment as her mind replayed last night's conversation—the one where her friends had described, in painful detail, their wishes to see this exact building torn down. No wonder Anna had looked so uncomfortable.

Vicky grabbed her laptop and brochures and marched up the stairs to Anna's apartment.

I can fix this.

Of course, by *fixing it*, she meant helping Anna earn enough money to escape this hellhole. Puremetics was the answer to everything.

A girl with vibrant blue hair opened the door. *Ah, the infamous Jane.* She was cuter than Vicky had expected. Still, her dark, doe-like eyes and bright complexion gave her a childlike innocence that Vicky didn't trust.

"Hi!" Vicky said, shooting out her hand. "You must be Anna's daughter. I'm—"

"Vicky Sterling. Yeah, I know who you are. You look older in person."

The words hit Vicky like a fist in the throat. She gasped for air, unsure how to recover. "I'm sorry, what?"

"I just mean, you look older compared to your blog photos," Jane said, not missing a beat. "My mom used to show me all your projects, but that was eight or nine years ago."

"Of course," Vicky muttered as she made a mental note to schedule another Botox session.

"Mom! Vicky is here," Jane yelled as she moved out of the way to let her inside.

Vicky couldn't believe how cramped the space was as she subconsciously counted square footage, betting that the whole kitchen/dining/living area could fit inside her foyer. She bent down to remove her shoes, but some faded stains on the carpet changed her mind. The apartment was tidy enough, but there was too much evidence of past inhabitants' lives—rust along the stovetop, scuff marks on the wall, and a faint, musty smell that Vicky couldn't quite place that made her wish she had offered to do the onboarding at her house instead.

"So, what exactly is going on with you two?" Jane asked as she moved toward the kitchen and filled a glass of water from the tap. "Mom was a little cryptic after she came home last night."

It wasn't Vicky's place to fill Jane in, but she did wonder why Anna might have chosen to hide any information. Maybe she still had doubts. Without wanting to jump to conclusions, Vicky couldn't help but remember how Jenny Taylor had bailed at the last second. "Your mom didn't say anything?"

Jane tapped the outside of her glass, eyes firmly set on Vicky. "Just that she may have found a way to earn some extra money, but I assumed it was with a rehab center, not from the local Avon lady."

"I would never sell Avon," Vicky said, unnerved by Jane's brazen confidence.

"Hey, Vicky!" Anna said, cutting the awkward conversation short. Anna wore a faded Oregon State hoodie, jeans, and a flat smile. "You really didn't need to come over. I'm sure I could have enrolled myself."

Vicky couldn't tell if Anna was being polite or just embarrassed to have someone in her home. The second option seemed more likely. Ultimately, it didn't matter. Vicky insisted on personally onboarding each person. Sure, it was easy enough for anyone to hop online and enroll, but it was also easy for a recruit to get spooked by a minor detail and change their mind before closing the deal. There was a reason Vicky was the fastest-growing leader in Puremetics. She never let her prey get away.

"Nonsense. I'm happy to help walk you through the process. While it's pretty straightforward, you may have questions I can answer. I want you to know that I am one hundred percent here to support you on this journey, starting with this first step."

Jane rolled her eyes as she sipped her water. She slithered from the kitchen to the living room and slumped into the sofa. Vicky couldn't help but feel that the girl was watching her every move, even with Jane glued to her phone.

Vicky cleared her throat, reminding herself to keep her eye on the prize. "So, Anna, what convinced you to join? The products? The compensation plan? The people?"

Anna fidgeted with the string of her sweatshirt as she shifted in her chair. "Well, uh, it just seemed like a good opportunity." Her nail scraped at a small ketchup stain on the table. She glanced at Jane. "I guess I'm just ready for a change."

"It was the body wrap, right?" Vicky leaned in, searching for a glimmer of passion in Anna's eyes. "All my girls swear by them."

Jane scoffed.

"Actually," Anna said, shifting uncomfortably in her seat, "the cream gave me a pretty nasty chemical burn."

Vicky pursed her lips. "Those active ingredients are potent, but I doubt it's a burn. As I said last night, the intense sensation means the product works. Beauty comes with a price! No pain, no gain, am I right?" She laughed, trying to compensate for the annoyance creeping up her throat.

Anna grabbed one of Vicky's brochures and thumbed through it. "Wow, this looks complicated. What are all these terms: PV, OVG, Downlines, Uplines?"

Vicky swiped the booklet from Anna. "Don't stress about those things yet. I'll be here to teach you everything. Puremetics is simple when you get down to it. Basically, you get paid for sharing any of their hundreds of amazing products. But first, we need to get you enrolled!" She clapped her hands as if the matter was settled because, in her mind, it was.

"Step one: I need your social security number and billing information." Vicky opened her laptop and clicked the Puremetics bookmark at the top.

"You need my social security number? Why?" Anna's eyes grew large. "And why am I getting billed? I thought I was the one selling the product."

Vicky sighed. She had answered all these questions last night. Why didn't people listen?

"The social security number is so that Puremetics can send tax information at the end of the year. Nothing shady, I promise. You'll work as a 1099 independent contractor, which is great because Puremetics doesn't take taxes out of your commission checks!" Vicky made a mental note to explain later that Anna would need to put money aside for taxes, but that detail wasn't important now.

"As for the billing information, you must purchase a starter kit. This is a business, after all. The kits provide you with samples and information packets you can share. Plus, you'll get a nice assortment of products to try so you can get familiar with what you're selling."

Anna leaned closer to the screen. "I guess that makes sense. How much are we talking?"

"They have basic kits and more premium ones. Like any venture, you need to spend money to make money. But really, it's such a tiny investment compared to literally any other kind of business. Do you know how much it would cost to open your own retail store?"

Anna sighed. "I guess I'll take the basic kit. How much is that?"

Vicky felt her stomach twist. This was what she was afraid of. The people who went for the cheapest kits were the same people who quit by the third month. She needed to entice Anna to see beyond the price tag and recognize the value of leveling up from the start.

Why was it so hard for people to see the vision?

"Here's the thing," Vicky said carefully, not wanting to scare Anna off. "The basic starter kit is really just for customers who want membership prices on the products."

Technically, that was a lie. There were no rules about the kind of kit you needed to get started as a distributor, but it *was* true that nobody who went with the basic kit ever got past the third rank.

"You're going to want a business builder kit. It will help you hit the ground running. Plus, you'll earn so much more going this route. It's the smartest financial decision you can make."

Jane cleared her throat and shifted in her seat.

Vicky pressed on as her manicured nails clacked on the keyboard. "There are three options: Brilliant Bronze, Shiny Silver, and Glitter is Gold."

"Okay, I'll take the bronze package. How much is that?"

"The Bronze Kit is $249, but it just makes sense to go for Gold as it will give you everything you need to excel, and it's only a little more. It's basically a business in a box *and* the best value as you'll end up using all the products for yourself or as samples for your customers. My most successful girls have all gone Gold."

Anna leaned forward to view the $999 price tag. Her eyes grew so wide Vicky thought they would pop out of her head. Thankfully, Anna pressed her lids shut before they could fall onto the matted carpet.

"Fine," Anna said, shaking her head. "Add it to the cart."

"Mom!" Jane's hand slapped the arm of the couch. "Can I talk to you?" Her eyes drilled into Vicky's as if she was threatening her life. "Alone?"

"Give us a sec," Anna said with a pained smile. She gestured toward the bedrooms, and Jane followed.

Vicky strained her ears, trying to hear their private conversation, when the apartment next door suddenly started blaring Metallica. Vicky's muscles tensed, trying to create a protective armor from the sudden sensory onslaught. The paper-thin walls rattled, making her wonder if the whole complex would crash. A voice from the first floor yelled as they banged on the ceiling. "Turn your fucking music down!"

Even when the music stopped, Vicky's head continued to spin. Anna was slipping away from her grasp; she could feel it. Other recruits had been pulled away by family members who refused to think big. Vicky threw her face into her hands, breathing deeply before her emotions spiraled out of control. Her dream was slipping from her fingers all because some know-it-all teenager couldn't mind her own business.

When Anna returned, Vicky prepared herself for the bad news. "Everything okay?"

Anna smiled. "Everything is fine. The Gold package sounds great."

"Oh!" Vicky said, unable to hide the utter surprise in her voice. She sat with her mouth open while her brain processed this unexpected twist. "That's great! For a second, I thought—"

She smiled and shook her head. "You know what? It doesn't matter. I'm proud of you!"

The surge of relief washed over Vicky as the finish line came into view. Anna was on board. She was proving her commitment. Vicky tapped furiously on the keyboard as if racing the clock. Like a runner reaching that last mile, a sudden burst of adrenaline gave her the energy to push forward. *Let's finish this thing.*

"All we need to do is set up your auto-ship."

"My what?"

"Your monthly subscription." Vicky pulled up the information online. "But don't worry, you can always change what products you order before they ship each month."

Anna leaned back in her chair with her arms crossed. "I thought the cool thing about this business was that I didn't need to keep inventory."

Vicky laughed, her diminishing patience evident in the forced nature of it. She hated how Anna had twisted her words from last night into an almost mocking tone.

"Your auto-ship isn't inventory. It's products you use so you can sell them authentically. Plus, to qualify for commissions, you need to keep your PV—that's personal volume or the products you purchase personally—at 100 points each month. Now, most people—"

Anna cut her off. "Wait, I have to buy products *each* month just to get paid for whatever I sell?"

With a flick of her wrist, Vicky brushed Anna's concerns aside. "Trust me, between the vitamins, home products, and skincare line, you'll probably reach your PV just getting the things you'd normally buy elsewhere. And remember, Target won't pay you commissions the way Puremetics does!"

Vicky's heart was in her throat as she pushed the laptop toward Anna. The finish line was so close. "You just need to accept the terms and conditions and then—"

"Hey, Mom." Jane suddenly materialized like a ghost in a horror film. "Can you check the message I just sent you?" She pursed her lips as she stared Vicky down. "It's, uh, school related."

Vicky tried to peek over Anna's shoulder as she unlocked her phone. Her eyes caught the words *Pyramid Scheme* before Anna stuffed her device in her pocket. Vicky dug her nails into the rickety wood table. She wasn't in the mood to deal with this blue-haired nuisance.

"Jane," Anna said with a firm but calm voice, "I know what I'm doing. Okay?"

"But!"

"Leave us alone. *Please.*"

Vicky's nostrils flared as she puffed her chest triumphantly. Her syrup-sweet voice pushed forward. "Okay, hun, just one electronic signature, and it will be official!"

Anna took the mouse from Vicky, ticked a box, typed her name, and clicked *Enroll Now*. Vicky's eyes lit up as the total price of more than $1200 disappeared into the void. Pixels of confetti dotted the screen as the message unfurled itself: *Welcome to the Puremetics Family, Anna!*

Vicky exhaled a breath she didn't know she was holding. She released her grip on the table and looked up to see Jane's eyes in the shadow of the hallway. Vicky snapped her laptop shut and smiled in the girl's direction, feeling victorious in this unspoken duel.

Anna was in the game. Now, the real work could begin.

8

"I don't know what was worse, the shocking price tag or the look of betrayal on Jane's face." Anna slammed her head against the back of Gloria's velvet couch, her mind replaying every horrible moment of Vicky's visit.

Gloria pushed a silver curl out of her face as she reached for her purse. "I told you not to worry about the price. We'll cover it. You just do whatever Vicky says, okay? She needs to believe you're fully onboard."

"I just didn't expect it to feel so icky, you know?"

Gloria nodded. "What was the total cost?"

Anna lifted her eyebrows as she locked eyes with Gloria. "One thousand two hundred and twelve dollars."

"Damn!" Gloria's mouth hit the ground. "What's in those supplements? Cocaine?"

Anna laughed, her loose ponytail bobbing. It was the first hint of relief she had felt since agreeing to this insane plan. Her nerves were working overtime, trying to extinguish whatever fire she had felt before.

"I can't decide if Vicky is delusional or just another out-of-touch rich person who doesn't understand that some people live paycheck to paycheck."

"Both, probably." Gloria tilted her head back and grinned as she ripped out a check and handed it to Anna.

"Does she really think Puremetics will turn me into a millionaire?" Anna popped to her feet, stuffing the money into her back pocket. She began pacing along the floor, feeling her entire body tighten. "Vicky sat in my god-awful apartment and didn't think twice about pressuring me to spend three times my rent on some fucking supplements!" She pressed her palms into her hair, shaking her head. "And I can't stop thinking about Jane, who flat-out told me it was a pyramid scheme. She must think I'm an idiot!"

Gloria rested her hands on Anna's shoulders, gently guiding her back to the sofa. "Breathe, Anna. It's going to be okay."

"Is it? Because it kinda feels like it won't."

"I promise it will be fine." Gloria smiled, her steady presence an anchor.

Anna exhaled slowly. A lump formed in her throat just thinking about Jane, who had single-handedly kept her from drowning this past year. Anna hated the idea of keeping this secret from the one person she trusted most. "Are you sure I can't tell Jane what I'm doing?"

"As I said last night, you can't tell anyone. We've got a lot riding on this plan, and we can't risk it getting leaked before we're ready to strike."

Anna nodded, unable to hide her disappointment.

The front door burst open, and a tornado in the shape of a person ripped through the small living room. Anna remembered Gloria's friend Emily from last night's OWLS meeting. Her stern, authoritative manner kept Anna on edge. A large stack of files in her arms hid half of Emily's face. She dropped the pile on the coffee table. Its heavy thud rattled the teacups at the other end.

Gloria leaned over, inspecting the folders. "What you got there, Em?"

"You told me to come over and brief Anna on White. This is everything I have on him."

"Oh, your thoroughness delights me," Gloria said, reaching for her tea. "Buckle up, Anna. You're about to get a crash course in Puremetics."

Emily inhaled deeply and took a seat next to Anna. "You didn't look too convinced last night when we told you Christian White was worthy of our rage, so I wanted to put your mind at ease with all the facts."

Anna smiled politely as a new batch of nerves twisted her stomach into knots.

"Over the past two years, I've combed through all of Puremetics's social media posts, press releases, and extensive marketing materials." Emily picked up a third of the folders. "This pile contains all the information readily available to the public."

"If it's public, it can't be too bad, right?"

Gloria laughed. "You'd think. But Emily's research has shown the company's tendency to backtrack, gaslight, and erase anything that doesn't comply with their current policies, which are always changing thanks to the FTC cracking down on them."

Emily pulled out a brochure. A smiling woman on a beach with a laptop graced the glossy trifold. The headline across the top read: *Puremetics Means Financial Freedom! Earn Six-Figures Anywhere Your Life Takes You.*

"Two years ago, the company published this advertisement. The FTC pushed back, threatening to shut Puremetics down because of unsubstantiated income claims." Emily placed a copy of the FTC's letter on the brochure.

"Rather than own up to the mistake, Puremetics tweaked the message." Emily plopped another brochure on top of the growing pile. The same woman and laptop spanned the cover, but the headline had changed: *Puremetics Lets Her Work from The Beach. Where Will It Take You?*[*]

"Notice the tiny asterisk?" Emily said, pointing to a barely visible star beside the question mark. "If you look closely at the bottom, you'll find a new, FTC-approved income disclaimer."

Anna picked up the document, squinting to read the fine print:

[*]Puremetics makes no promises or guarantees regarding income. The success or failure of each Puremetics Independent Contractor, like any other business, depends on your skills and personal effort. You should not rely on the results of other Puremetics distributors as an indicator of what you will earn. Please read our income disclosure statement for more details.

"Okay, that's a little slimy," Anna said, putting the pamphlet down. "But I'm not sure it's any worse than other MLMs or work-from-home scams."

Gloria laughed. "Oh, she's just getting started."

Over the next two hours, Emily poured through her research. She had copies of financial records, whistleblower testimonies, distributor complaints, lawsuits, product testing results, and regulatory violations.

Anna leaned back, running her fingers through her hair. "I don't get it. Half of their products don't contain the ingredients listed on the bottles. There's a string of sexual assault accusations and an undeniable track record of exploiting distributors in a way that will haunt me forever."

"What don't you get?" Emily asked. "He's a garbage person. Now you see why we have to take this man down."

"How is he still standing?" Anna threw her arms up. "Shouldn't he be in jail already?"

Gloria tapped the side of her cup. "Money, Anna. Money, power, and connections to people willing to sweep anything under the rug."

Emily leaned back in her chair and huffed. "When you make billions of dollars, a hefty FTC fine or a multimillion-dollar settlement is considered the cost of doing business."

"Exactly," Gloria chimed in. "It's like buying toilet paper—they'll keep paying to flush it down."

Anna sighed as she slumped back into her seat. "Then how the hell do you expect us to do anything when all these other agencies, lawyers, and regulations can't?"

"Simple," Gloria said with a mischievous smile. "By publicly blasting everything all at once before it can be flushed away. We're going to clog the toilet with all of White's shit until the truth comes flooding out."

Emily shook her head as she organized the documents on the coffee table. "So ladylike, Glo."

Gloria shrugged. "I just call it like I see it, and everything Christian White does is gross."

It wasn't just gross. It was overwhelming. Anna closed her eyes, trying to keep the room from spinning. She opened them only to find herself staring at the large mural with its whirlpool of color. Getting lost in the paint swirls was too easy, especially with a real-life storm brewing.

"And what's my part in all this?" Anna asked quietly. "You don't need me as a spy. You're swimming in evidence."

"You're right," Gloria said, eyeing Emily. "We need something else from you."

Emily interlaced her fingers, sitting tall. "Are you familiar with the Puremetics distributor ranks?"

"Vaguely," Anna said, recalling Vicky's presentation last night.

Emily opened her laptop and navigated to the Puremetics compensation plan. "Now that you've joined, you're at the bottom of the pyramid: a Pure Apprentice. Once you enroll your first person, you'll move up to the level of Spark Coordinator."

Gloria scoffed. "They make the first rank super easy to achieve, giving a false sense of success."

Anna grabbed a pen from her purse and started jotting notes. "How many ranks are there?"

"Not counting Pure Apprentice, there are seven." Emily pointed to the screen. "Vicky is currently sitting at the second highest rank: Presidential Emerald. From what we know, she's just one qualifying leg away from hitting Royal Diamond."

Gloria leaned forward, locking eyes with Anna. "Enter you."

Anna shook her head. "I don't understand."

"Vicky can only hit her target if *you* reach the level of Ruby Director."

"Okay?" Anna pressed the top of her pen to her lips.

"Vicky is invested in your success," Emily said, "giving you a better chance of ranking up. That is what we're asking you to do. We want you to go all in, pose as a starry-eyed distributor, and reach the rank of Sapphire Executive."

"I thought you said I needed to be a Ruby Director," Anna said, skimming her notes.

"No," Gloria smirked. "That's what Vicky needs. We need you to go one higher."

Anna was so confused she wanted to scream. "But *why*? What's the endgame?"

Gloria rubbed her hands together. "You're going to help us get a confession from Christian White."

The sound that erupted from Anna's mouth startled her more than Gloria or Emily. She didn't mean to laugh. It was the natural release of the mounting absurdities of the past twenty-four hours. "How am I supposed to do that?"

Gloria took Emily's laptop and pulled up a video. A dozen women in sparkling ball gowns stood in the spotlight of a darkened arena, waving like they were beauty queens. In the middle of the glossy-haired bunch was a tall man with salt and pepper hair and a dimpled smile.

"This," Gloria said, tapping the screen, "is the Leadership Gala that happens every year at the company's big convention. Anyone who achieves a new rank of Sapphire Executive or higher gets fifteen minutes of fame on the big stage with the leading man."

Anna could feel a headache forming. "Okay, and?"

Gloria's eyes narrowed as the video zoomed in on the CEO. "A tradition of the Leadership Gala is that each woman offers White a small gift."

"Of course it is," Anna said, rolling her eyes.

"Your gift will be a small lapel brooch with a hidden microphone. All you need to do is pin it on him. We'll take care of the rest."

"That doesn't seem too bad." The knot in Anna's stomach relaxed ever so slightly. "So how do I hit rank?"

Emily took over, moving back to the compensation plan. "There are three factors that determine your eligibility to level up: Your PV—"

"Personal Volume!" Anna yelled, excited there was at least one familiar term. "Vicky talked about that. Apparently, I have to buy stuff each month just to get a commission check. Is that really a thing?"

Emily nodded. "Generally, one dollar of product translates into one PV. You'll spend at least one hundred dollars each month to earn a check and qualify for rank advancements."

Gloria shook her head. "Can you imagine if all jobs forced their employees to buy their product each month to get their paycheck? Newsflash: The distributors *are* the customers."

"We'll cover the cost of your monthly orders," Emily said, "so don't stress about that. But along with your PV, there's also your OGV: Overall Group Volume. That number is based on how much product the people you've enrolled buy each month."

Anna scribbled another acronym in her notebook. "Oh my god. How does anyone keep this straight?" And more importantly, how was Anna supposed to follow Vicky's lead? Just thinking about pressuring someone to buy these products made her queasy.

"Ah, but there's more!" Gloria smiled. "Each time you sign someone up, that person has the potential to enroll their own people. When that downline gets big enough, it's considered a qualifying leg. So, to rank up, you need a certain amount of PV, a certain number of OGV, and enough qualifying legs that meet their own PV and OGV requirements. Does that make sense?"

Anna rubbed her temples. "Cut to the chase, please."

Emily clicked the mouse and switched tabs. The banner across the top read: *PureExpo 2015.* "This is our firm deadline. The Puremetics convention is happening next August."

"Oh, so we have lots of time!" A rush of relief washed over Anna but was quickly replaced with one glaring concern: How would she keep this secret from Jane that long?

"Uh..." Gloria shot Emily a look. "That's not a lot of time. For starters, you'll need to hit rank by the end of July to qualify for the Leadership Gala in August. Second, Sapphire Executive is the third rank from the top. Less than 0.1% of distributors even make it that high, and those that do typically take a couple of years. Vicky was the fastest person in Puremetics history to hit the rank, and it took her just over a year."

"And I'm supposed to do it in like ten months?" The blood rushed from Anna's face. She steadied herself against the couch. "What if all the OWLS sign up under me? Wouldn't that be a good start?"

Gloria sighed. "As I mentioned last night, we're all blocked from the company after a failed mission."

Anna closed her eyes and shook her head. "How am I supposed to do this?"

"It won't be easy," Gloria said, squeezing Anna's shoulder. "But we will help you however we can."

A pained groan escaped Anna's lips as she fell back into the couch cushions. Once again, she stared at the woman trapped on Gloria's wall. Even with the phoenix flying above the woman's face—born from the ashes and promising a new beginning—the woman seemed unable to break free from the chaos that pulled her in.

And here Anna was, wishing she could trade places with her.

Gloria moved closer, her eyes following Anna's gaze. "I painted that mural."

"Really? I didn't know you were an artist. It's stunning."

Emily walked over and stared at the painting. She tilted her head as if she was still uncovering the artwork's mystery. "Gloria is an amazing artist."

Anna was thrilled to be talking about anything other than Puremetics, even if it was just for a moment. "The woman in the painting, is she someone you know?"

A hint of moisture glistened in the corner of Gloria's eyes. "You could say that."

Emily cleared her throat. "The least you can do is tell her the truth, Glo."

"Yes, Anna," Gloria said with a sigh. "She is someone I know —or at least, someone I used to know. She was a dear friend, my roommate. But that was years ago. Decades." She inhaled slowly, puffing up her chest. "She's the reason I'm doing all this."

"I don't understand." Anna turned. "I thought you're doing this because Christian White is evil."

Emily scowled. "Two things can be true."

Gloria walked toward the painting, her hand gently tracing the outline of the woman's profile. "She was Christian's first victim."

Anna could feel the tension in the room press against her chest. "Who is she?"

"Her name is Fiona. She's Christian White's wife."

9

"What a day!" Gloria dropped her purse near the front door. She walked past Fiona on the couch and into the kitchen, looking for something to eat.

"Mrs. Garrett came home just as the kids found her lingerie drawer. Tiffany used one of the bras as a slingshot while little Nate wore leopard print panties on his head." Gloria laughed, pulling out a cutting board.

"The look on their mom's face—oh, boy! I thought she was going to fire me on the spot." Gloria opened a jar of peanut butter after cutting some apple slices. "It will go down as one of the most terrifying and hilarious moments of my life. When I signed up for this nanny gig, I never thought I'd be spending so much time pretending not to notice all the weird shit these kids find in their parents' bedroom."

Dipping an apple slice into the jar, Gloria scooped a huge pile of peanut butter. She stuffed it in her mouth, relieved to eat something after a six-hour shift. Nannying was supposed to be a temporary way to pay the bills as she focused on her art at night.

But it turned out watching four small children was exhausting. It had been months since she pulled out her paints.

Gloria made her way to the living room with the jar in hand. "How was your day?"

Fiona sat with her hands tucked in her lap. Her pale skin looked almost translucent against the emerald sofa. With her brown curls pulled back into a ponytail, Fiona's cheekbones jutted out like a warning sign. "We need to talk."

Gloria swallowed the chunk of apple lodged in her throat. "Everything okay?"

"No," Fiona said, looking up with red and puffy eyes. "It's not."

The sudden wave of tension sucked the air from Gloria's lungs.

Fiona had been the one bright spot in an otherwise disappointing life. Even though they had only met last year, the roommates had been inseparable since New Year's Eve at Jen's house. Connecting over a shared obsession with Madonna, the two women danced all night. Even after the party ended, they stayed up until nearly four in the morning, talking about everything from family traditions to their favorite flavor of Lip Smackers.

That night, they forged an unbreakable friendship. Fiona would revel in Gloria's stories from her nanny job, listening to the terrorizing shenanigans of the Garrett children. In return, Gloria would listen to Fiona as she talked about her boyfriend and whatever cruel thing he had recently done to make Fiona upset. No matter what drama or frustrations came their way, the women found solace in each other's company.

Now Gloria sensed a bombshell coming as Fiona sat motionless on the couch. She leaned against the wall, strangling the jar of peanut butter in her hands as her heart raced on. "Is this about last night? I told you this morning; I'm sorry. I didn't mean to rush into anything. I promise I'll let you take the lead. You don't have to worry about me."

Fiona smiled for a split-second, her eyes catching the light. "You're not the one I'm worried about." She wiped her nose with her hand and cleared her throat. "I'm moving out."

The detonation was worse than Gloria had imagined. Her eyes widened as sweat pooled in every crease of her body. "What? Moving out? No, you can't! Why would you?"

"I think you know why."

A week ago, Fiona had finally dumped her loser boyfriend, Chris. The two women had stayed up all night, shoveling ice cream in their mouths while watching *Footloose*. Gloria pointed out Chris's many flaws and why Fiona was so much better off without him. By midnight, the energy in the apartment had shifted. The two women had shared countless secrets, unlocking Gloria's heart—something she had boarded up years ago.

She fell hard and fast, but Gloria knew her feelings were one-sided. After all, Fiona was still getting over her boyfriend. Plus, there was that nagging issue of Fiona's Mormon beliefs—a hurdle Gloria now realized was bigger than she imagined.

Still, there had been little signs that gave Gloria hope. The way Fiona's hand would accidentally graze hers as they got ready in the morning—the flirty laughs and lingering looks. After years of believing she would live alone, Gloria started wondering if there could be a future with Fiona.

Gloria panicked, trying to find any excuse to keep Fiona from leaving. "You can't go. You still got three months left on your lease."

Fiona shook her head. "I can't stay here. You'll find someone else." Her eyes locked on Gloria, tears welling up inside. "I can't see you anymore."

The room spun as all the blood rushed from Gloria's head. She couldn't understand what was happening, only that whatever it was, it felt like a death. "Fi, no," she pleaded. "Don't do this."

"We both know what's been going on. Last night, when—"

Fiona choked on her words, shaking her head. She pushed a tear away, struggling to regain her composure. "I don't trust myself to stay here. It can't happen again. Ever. It was wrong."

No, it was a miracle.

Chris came by the apartment last night angry, looking for a fight. He was desperate to get Fiona back, but Gloria was in no mood for his rantings. She called the cops, who thankfully took the complaint seriously. Fiona was understandably upset. Emotionally exhausted, she snuggled against Gloria and nuzzled her head into her shoulder. Nothing had ever felt more right. Gloria's heart pounded against her chest as she sat, frozen and unwilling to do anything that could disrupt the bliss that had unexpectedly enveloped her.

When Fiona looked up and locked eyes, Gloria took her shot.

Like a magnet, the women found each other. The sweet taste of Fiona's lips lingered on Gloria's like fine wine. Soft and gentle caresses grew into powerful urges that Gloria no longer wanted to deny. One hand wrapped around Fiona's waist as the other moved to the hem of her shirt, lifting it.

Fiona pulled back, breathless. "Stop," she said quietly. "This can't, I can't…" Pulling down her blouse, she stood. "I'm sorry." Flushed and shaking, Fiona vacated the living room, slamming the bedroom door behind her.

Gloria berated herself for moving too far, too fast. Still, she couldn't help but smile, knowing that Fiona felt *something*. It was the hope she had been waiting for, the sign that gave her breath. Unable to sleep, Gloria spent most of the night staring at the ceiling, lost in memory of Fiona's taste.

Eighteen hours later, Gloria was clinging to a dream that was fading fast.

"It wasn't wrong, Fi." Gloria sat down, taking her hand. "What I feel for you, what I hope you feel for me—it's good. It's grown from love, admiration, and connection. How could any of that be bad?"

Fiona pulled her hand back, shaking her head. "It's not of God. It's not part of His plan."

"Says who? Some old book? A group of men? How do you know they speak for God? How do we even know who or what God is? Or that there even is one?" Gloria's voice continued to rise. These were the same questions she had wrestled with for years, only to be kept in the dark.

Decades of loneliness, abandonment, and loss rushed to the surface, igniting Gloria's senses. All her life, she knew she was different, attracted to people and ideas others told her were wrong. Growing up in Salt Lake City made it even harder to understand the discrepancies between what she heard in church, from her parents, and everyone around her compared to what she felt in her heart.

Gloria began to guard her thoughts and deny her feelings. She tried to pretend she was someone else but couldn't endure that kind of hell. Breaking free from the religion was simple; erasing the layers of shame that had become encrusted over the years took much, much longer. Finding someone she could trust seemed impossible. Gloria always assumed she'd live alone. At thirty-six, she had finally come to terms with it.

Then Fiona came along.

"I knew you wouldn't understand," Fiona said, pushing back. "I know you think my beliefs are weird, that I'm in a cult. But you haven't experienced the Spirit the way I have. I know because if you did, you would understand just how dangerous of a line we crossed last night." She leaned into Gloria, her hand shaking as she placed it on her shoulder. "I have feelings for you. Okay?"

Gloria felt a brief relief, a rise of hope that was quickly crushed.

"But those feelings are evil," Fiona said flatly. She sat tall, smoothing the wrinkles in her skirt. "I cannot risk my eternal salvation on a few butterflies in the stomach. I won't. I have made up my mind, so please accept it and let me go."

A dam broke loose in Gloria's heart. Tears flooded the surface as she choked on her words. "Please... don't do this."

"You'll be okay," Fiona whispered, her breath catching her words. "You're the strongest person I know."

Fiona stood, taking a key out of her pocket and placing it in Gloria's hand. Her fingers lingered as they brushed against Gloria's wrist. Fiona moved toward the front door, grabbing a moving box as she left. It was only then that Gloria realized Fiona had already packed her things. She was gone before Gloria could even say goodbye.

10

"This might work." Vicky dropped another blouse on the growing pile. She dragged her fingers along a rack of maxi skirts, trying to decide on a color.

Anna juggled the awkward jumble of clothes in her arms. "Do I really need all this?"

Vicky pretended not to hear as she grabbed a yellow skirt and beelined to the sweaters. Nondescript indie pop played softly overhead as a fresh, citrusy perfume wafted through the air. This small boutique was a favorite, with its high-end showstoppers and quality basics. It was a shame Vicky wasn't shopping for herself; these fall trends were on point.

If pressed, Vicky could create twelve flawless outfits using only the items within reach—all without breaking a sweat. That would translate into a dozen blog articles and even more Instagram posts. It made Vicky wonder: If Anna was such a fan of her website, how was it possible she didn't own a single acceptable piece of clothing?

Wiggling her hand out from the pile, Anna flipped the price

tag of the most recently added garment. Her eyes bulged. "Oh shit."

Vicky whipped around. "Language."

Transforming Anna was a monumental task, but Vicky hadn't expected it to be *this* difficult. It was hard to envision a beautiful rose garden among Anna's weeds—a new flaw sprouted every minute.

Anna adjusted her arms to keep the clothes from tipping over. "I spend most of my time in scrubs. It's not like I can wear any of this to work."

Vicky reached for a navy cashmere sweater. The dark blue would look lovely against Anna's eyes, so she tossed it onto the pile. "We've been over this. If you want to be successful, you've got to dress the part. Puremetics is more than its products. It's an opportunity—a lifestyle." She turned, gesturing in Anna's general direction. "Who is going to believe the dream if you look like *that*?"

Anna's cheeks flushed red. Her nostrils flared as she inhaled slowly. "I can't afford this."

"You don't have to buy all of it. Just try them on and see what you love the most. You need a power outfit, Anna—something that lights you up and makes you feel confident. You'd be amazed how clothes can change a person. Trust me. This is just as much an investment in you as it is in your business."

Anna followed Vicky towards the fitting room and plopped everything on a bench. She picked up a large chevron infinity scarf that fell to the ground. "But these clothes aren't me."

"Exactly. You could use an upgrade, sweetie." Vicky offered a small chuckle to soften the blow. She corralled Anna into the fitting room and closed the door as she waited outside. "Don't you *want* to look nice? Or do you enjoy looking like you just pulled a double shift at the local ER? What do you usually wear when you go out?"

"I've got other clothes." A loud zip punctuated Anna's words.

"You saw them in my closet. There was that gray pantsuit for work conferences and a cocktail dress or two—although I'm not sure they fit me anymore. I got them before Jane was born."

Vicky leaned against the door as she examined her cuticles, shaking her head. She had seen Anna's closet. It's what spurred this emergency shopping spree in the first place. "You're just proving my point, hun."

A layer of fabric muffled Anna's voice. "Okay, but shouldn't I wait until I'm actually making money in the business?"

Vicky didn't know how many times she had to tell Anna that success required investment. She sighed. "Just let me see what you put on."

Anna stepped out, biting her lip. It wasn't half bad. The navy sweater needed to be tucked in, and the adorable yellow maxi begged for some shape. The long, leather boots were incredible. Vicky dug through the pile and found the belt she had picked out. "Put this on and wait here. You need one more thing."

Vicky turned the corner and marched toward the back wall of accessories. A wide-brimmed, khaki-colored boater hat caught her eye—just like the one that trendy life coach she followed online wore. It might be too daring for Anna, but it would pull the outfit together nicely.

"OMG, I love that hat," a woman said as she peeked through a pair of sunglasses she was trying out. "I keep thinking about getting one, but I don't know if hats are my thing."

Vicky smiled politely. "It's adorable, right? But you do need the right face to pull it off." She tipped her head, examining the young woman. "I think it would look cute on you."

The woman blushed. "Oh, thanks."

Vicky rushed back to the fitting room and handed Anna the hat. "Try this."

Anna put it on. Vicky grimaced, whipped it off, and tossed it in the *no* pile.

"You know," Anna said as she turned in the mirror, "I work

with a bunch of old people. My neighbor is a twenty-something metalhead. You've already recruited anyone I might meet in the area. That means my best shot for enrolling others is probably by hitting up my friends back in Oregon."

"Oh, I hadn't thought about that," Vicky said as if Anna's out-of-state network weren't her most alluring quality.

"Since I'll be doing most of my recruiting online, it really doesn't matter what I wear, right?"

Vicky could feel her blood pressure rising. "You're missing the point! You don't know where your next recruit might be. The beauty of this business is that you can work it anywhere—assuming you look the part." As she punctuated the last few words, an idea flashed in Vicky's mind, tugging the corners of her mouth into a wide smile. She grabbed Anna by the arm. "Come here."

"My purse and stuff are still—"

"They'll be fine. Follow me." Vicky led Anna around the corner, hoping the hat lady was still nearby. Her eyes lit up when she saw her looking at earrings. "There—see her?"

"Yeah."

"Go talk to her about Puremetics."

"What! Are you kidding?" Anna snuck back to the fitting rooms.

Vicky followed, spinning Anna around and pushing her out toward the woman. "It will be fine."

"I wouldn't even know where to start." Anna's entire body tensed as she dug her heels into the hardwood floor.

Vicky took a quick inventory of the target, looking for any flaw she could capitalize on. Despite being well dressed, the woman had a small muffin top from pants that were a little too small, her foundation didn't quite match her skin, and her hair desperately needed a trim.

"Compliment her outfit," Vicky said, whispering in Anna's

ears as she pushed her forward. "Tell her how much you love her jacket. Once you've got her attention, make a connection."

A familiar hint of guilt pricked the pit of Vicky's stomach. She felt it whenever she taught a recruit how to push the business. It wasn't that Vicky was ashamed of the tactics she taught. She just knew the smarter ones might look back at their own interactions with Vicky and see the same patterns. It was hard to come off as genuine when you had your people skills down to a science.

"Find something you have in common. Tell her how you used to struggle to find a good foundation or how your pants fit better now after trying this cool new product. And then *BAM*! You've made the perfect inroad to discuss our skin-match makeup line or our amazing body wraps!"

"No." Anna's voice grew desperate as they got closer.

"Offer her a free sample," Vicky whispered. "Once she's hooked, just reel her in."

Anna flipped around, pushing Vicky backward. "I can't do that! I rarely wear makeup, and I'm not a huge fan of the body wraps, remember?"

"Enough with the rash! You might be in a smaller pant size if you gave the wraps an honest chance!" Vicky rubbed her temples while doing the deep belly breaths her yoga instructor had taught her. "Fine, I'll show you how it's done. Stay close and pay attention."

Anna looked like a deer in headlights but nodded nonetheless.

Vicky rolled her shoulders back, wiggling away the tension that had steadily risen over the last few minutes. She marched toward the woman and tapped her on the shoulder.

"Hey, hun! Remember me? Hat lady." Vicky forced a laugh.

"Oh, hey." The woman picked up another set of earrings. "Did you decide to get it?"

"On the fence still."

Vicky picked up a necklace, running the delicate chain through her fingers. It was time to show Anna how to do this thing. *Step one: offer a compliment.* "By the way, I absolutely love your jacket. It's so cute!"

The woman looked down, pulling at the hem of the garment. "Oh, thanks. I've had it for years."

Step two: make a connection. "I could never wear white denim like that with my little guy." Vicky laughed. "Do you have kids?"

It was the easiest way to build rapport with women in Utah, not to mention the fastest inroad to talking about the body wraps. There was a reason it was Puremetics's number one product. What young mother didn't miss her pre-baby body?

"Kids? Oh, no. Too busy for any of that." The woman shifted her eyes toward the exit.

Swing and a miss. Vicky was not deterred, but she would need to find a better connection. She started over with a new compliment. "You have the nicest skin."

"Thank you?" The woman shifted, taking a step away.

Vicky panicked. She never panicked. The woman was giving every signal for Vicky to back off, but she couldn't give up. Anna was watching. Even more important than closing a sale, Vicky had to model leaving your comfort zone. She swallowed her pride and carried on.

"You know, I just switched to this new makeup line that really transformed my skin. They have so many shades, which makes finding the perfect color easy," Vicky said, gesturing to the woman's jawline. "You'll never have to worry about your face not matching your neck."

"Excuse me?" The woman pulled back as her face twisted with disgust.

"Oh, no! You look great, honestly." Vicky laughed a little too loudly. "I just love this new makeup so much that I feel like a missionary spreading the good word. I could get you a free sample if you like?"

"I'm good, thanks." The woman put the earrings back and headed straight for the exit.

Vicky cringed. She spun around, taking note of Anna's slightly terrorized expression.

"Honestly, that was perfect." Vicky was determined to spin straw into gold. "It's not always going to be a *yes*. You must be okay with hearing *no* in this business—a lot. Most people are too small-minded to think big. But, when you consistently put yourself out there, you'll eventually attract those willing to take a chance on their dreams."

"Sure," Anna said carefully. She sighed, looking down at her outfit. "But I still don't think I can afford the clothes."

"Oh, hell!" Vicky's patience snapped in half. "I'll buy the damn outfit for you!"

Anna smirked. "Language."

Vicky blushed and chuckled, relaxing slightly at Anna's attempt to break the tension. "Fair enough," she said with a heavy sigh. "I'm just passionate about this stuff. I know how much this business can change your life. I don't want you playing small."

"I appreciate it." Anna rubbed the back of her neck. "And even if I'm hesitant about the clothes, I am determined to succeed in the business. Tell me what I need to do."

Vicky was surprised by Anna's words, mainly because they directly contradicted everything her body was saying. Still, it was a good sign. Maybe Anna was just shy. Vicky could work with shy.

"You need to jump in with both feet. Commit."

Anna nodded. "I am committed."

Something about Anna was intriguing. She was like a puzzle that couldn't be solved—a book Vicky couldn't quite understand.

After building an empire on her unmatched ability to read others, Anna offered Vicky a frustrating yet refreshing challenge.

It was a pity Vicky would have to change everything about her.

"I don't just want you to say it," Vicky said, crossing her arms. "I want you to *prove* it. Enroll one person by next week—someone in person. We'll tackle your network in Oregon later. First, you need to demonstrate you're willing to get uncomfortable. Can you do it?"

Anna straightened up, her face as serious and unreadable as a medical journal. "If you can make a fool of yourself in front of a complete stranger, I can find one person to sign up."

"Good," Vicky said, trying to move past the whole *fool* part. "This time next week, you'll be a Spark Coordinator. And that's only the beginning. You need to keep showing up. There will be plenty of rejection as you build your team. Don't let me down."

"I promise," Anna said before she disappeared into the fitting room.

A dozen thoughts unraveled as Vicky waited for Anna to change. She wanted to believe Anna would pull through—that this was a turning point. After all, a promise was a promise. And even if Anna wasn't the most stylish or confident, she did seem like someone who kept her word.

Still, Vicky pulled out her credit card. Some new clothes couldn't hurt.

11

Anna held her breath as she swung open the heavy door to Silver Lining Senior Living, bracing herself for Peter's inevitable whiny demands. As Director of Rehabilitation, he always dumped a million tasks on Anna, yet anytime she mentioned moving into a full-time position, he was suddenly concerned that they didn't have enough work for her. In other words, Peter was an ass.

There was no way Anna could muster the patience she needed to deal with her annoying DOR—not today. Anna had a mission to accomplish, a promise to keep. Vicky had challenged her to enroll a new person within a week, and time was running out. Anna was desperate to untangle herself from this new scheme, and the only way out was through. There was just one problem: She had no clue who to enroll.

The obvious answer was to start messaging her network back in Oregon, but Vicky insisted Anna recruit someone in person. So, Anna considered her options. Her landlord, Mr. Talbot, wasn't exactly the body wrap kind of guy, nor was her metalhead neighbor. *Next.* Strangers at SuperMart? There was no way Anna was willing to pounce people in the grocery store. *Hard pass.* That left work as the only possible setting to catch her prize.

But even that seemed like fishing in a swimming pool.

Silver Lining Senior Living wasn't hopping with starry-eyed entrepreneurs. Anna's patients were often on their last leg, worried more about not falling off the toilet than about the quality of their mascara. The very idea of trying to recruit such a vulnerable population wasn't just unprofessional. It was downright unethical—a line Anna refused to cross.

If not her patients, that left enrolling a coworker. So, that's what Anna set out to do. She arrived thirty minutes early, hoping to catch Ruth or Jackie in the staff room before they rushed off to make their morning rounds. Anna had spent all night rehearsing fake conversations in the bathroom mirror, trying to find a natural way to bring up Puremetics. She went to bed with little hope she could pull it off. Most interactions at work revolved around treatment plans and patient updates. As the only Certified Lymphedema Therapist on staff, Anna barely had a chance to eat lunch. Finding time to chat about body wash or makeup seemed unlikely—and mortifying.

All these thoughts competed for attention as Anna walked down the hall. She felt woozy from the pressure, and the beige walls and vomit-colored carpet did little to help.

"Hey Anna!" Jackie said, walking out of the bathroom.

This was her chance. Anna opened her mouth to respond but stumbled on her words. She cleared her throat and barely squeaked a simple "Hey."

Jackie leaned in, whispering with a satisfied smile. "Did you hear the news?"

"What news?" Anna halted to attention, surprised by Jackie's sinister tone. The nurses only stopped to chat if they needed something from Anna or to inform her of a resident's passing. This sounded like Jackie had gossip to share, which was noteworthy in and of itself.

"Peter is out," Jackie said, cocking her head back.

Anna's eyes narrowed. "What do you mean?"

Jackie crossed her arms and smirked. "Canned. Friday. Turns out he was being a little handsy with one of the patient's daughters."

"Oh, gross." The image of it instantly nauseated Anna. "Are you serious?"

"Yep. There's a new DOR—a woman, and from my thirty-second interaction with her in the breakroom, she will be a welcome change to Peter the Tyrant."

"Wow." Anna stood, shaking her head. She let the news roll in her mind, wondering what it meant for her future at the nursing facility.

"Anyway, gotta run! There's a bedpan emergency in B6."

Frozen, Anna processed this information as Jackie disappeared into one of the rooms down the long hallway. Only after Jackie was out of sight did Anna realize she hadn't even said *goodbye,* let alone mention Puremetics. It wasn't a promising start to the day.

Her shoulders drooped as she scolded herself internally. Still, Anna felt a hint of relief. The idea of preying on her coworkers—expecting them to pay money for a company Anna knew was awful—left a bad taste in her mouth. She kept telling herself it was for a good cause, but that didn't change the fact that she would have to lie to see this mission through.

Anna hated lying.

As she moved to the staff room, Anna dumped her stuff in her locker. She grabbed her tablet and checked her schedule for the day, making sure nothing urgent had popped on her plate over the weekend.

"Oh, hello!"

Anna looked up. A tall, statuesque woman stood in the doorway.

"I don't think we've met," the woman said, extending her hand. "I'm Lisa, the new Director of Rehab."

"Oh, hey!" Anna fumbled, trying to straighten up. She nearly dropped her tablet as she pushed her hand to shake Lisa's. "I heard we had a new DOR. Welcome to Silver Lining. I'm Anna."

"Thank you, Anna. It's certainly been a run-before-you-walk kind of situation, but I'm happy to be here."

"Where are you from?" Anna cringed the moment she heard the words. Lisa's rich brown skin, dark eyes, and bouncy black curls certainly stood out in this corner of Utah County, where spelling names creatively counted as diversity. Anna's tone made the question feel loaded in a way she couldn't quite place, but she blushed all the same.

"Houston," Lisa said, unfazed. Her assured posture and warm gaze put Anna at ease. "A love for the mountains brought me out here. The job sealed the deal."

"I've only been in Utah for a year and haven't trekked any mountains yet."

"We need to change that!" Lisa said, jutting her hip out. "Once I'm settled, I'm taking you for a hike. There's nothing like it. You'll see."

Anna smiled even though she was sure she might die trying to keep up with someone as fit as Lisa. Still, she was thrilled to be invited.

Lisa glanced at the clock. "Shoot, I've got to run. It was lovely meeting you, Anna. I look forward to getting to know you better and am serious about hiking. Plan on it." With a quick smile, the woman bolted out of the room.

Anna stood, spellbound by the brief interaction. She spent the rest of the day reliving that one-minute conversation. It was the first genuine connection she had felt with anyone at work. As the hope of making an actual friend pricked Anna's brain, her mind hijacked it, positioning Lisa as the answer to Vicky's challenge.

Lisa could be her recruit. The woman's tasteful makeup and dewy complexion suggested a certain level of self-care—like she was willing to spend a little money on quality products. Lisa was new to the area and needed friends and community. She probably had a bunch of people back in Texas she could enroll. It all added up.

Was it possible the universe was finally giving Anna a break?

Anna decided not to overthink it. She knew the guilt of roping someone into this company would take over if she didn't move fast. So, Anna focused on Gloria and the OWLS. She thought of all the women she would be helping by taking down this company. Besides, Vicky's one-week deadline was approaching, and Anna knew it was now or never. So, she set her target on Lisa and started formulating a plan.

The idea was to catch Lisa as she left for the day. Anna stayed an extra hour after her shift and tried remembering some of Vicky's tips and tactics from the weekly mastermind calls.

Why is leveling up important?

What would extra income mean to you?

Where do you want to go?

Who are you ready to become?

These were the questions Vicky insisted every Puremetics distributor must know to be successful. Now that Anna had a potential recruit in sight, she realized none of Vicky's platitudes provided any valuable skills to promote the product—products Anna hadn't even tried yet, with the unfortunate exception of those damn body wraps. But apparently, that didn't matter. According to Vicky, you could fake it before you made it. You could *act* being successful. You could *pretend* to look the part. And apparently, you could even talk up a product you've never tried.

As Lisa walked out of the building, Anna hoped it was true.

"Lisa!" she yelled, waving. Anna had purposely moved her car to be next to Lisa's during lunch. It seemed like a tactic Vicky would approve of.

Lisa looked up from her phone and waved back.

Anna's heart skipped a beat. There was no turning back now.

She bit her lip, trying to remember Vicky's advice from the boutique. The first step was to make a connection.

"So, now that it's been a whole day, how are you liking Silver Lining?" Anna turned the key, unlocking her car as if she were just getting ready to leave. Lisa didn't need to know she'd been standing there for seven minutes.

"It's been a crazy eight hours, but it seems promising." Lisa tossed her phone in her purse. "We have a great rehab team. I was worried, knowing it can be difficult to staff small facilities like this. You did a great job with Edna in C9 today. The swelling really went down after your drainage massage. Impressive."

Anna paused, taken back by the compliment. She couldn't remember the last time someone genuinely praised her work. "Oh, thanks," she said quietly.

An alarm blared inside Anna's head, telling her to call off the plan. Lisa was a breath of fresh air in an otherwise sterile world. Did she want to risk losing that by introducing Puremetics? Did she really want to ask this woman to spend good money on an evil corporation?

The doubts were piling up, and Anna forced herself to remember what was at stake. Gloria was counting on her. Anna might only be a pawn in a bigger game, but she had to believe her part mattered. It had been months since she felt needed—like her life had a purpose. Anna couldn't just give that up.

This Jekyll and Hyde debate continued in Anna's head as Lisa pulled out some hand lotion from her bag.

"I'm not used to how dry it is here," Lisa said as she popped the lid open.

Damn. There it was—a connection.

Anna forced a small laugh. "Tell me about. I'm from Oregon originally."

She wanted that to be her final word on the matter. In any other normal situation, it would be. Anna had always been a better listener than a talker, and she sincerely wanted to know more about Lisa. But her mouth rattled on without her permission.

"I really struggled with the dry air, too." Anna couldn't stand the sudden, sugary, sweet tone in her voice. "I found this awesome skincare line that helped my patchy elbows."

Sweat pooled in Anna's armpits as she twisted in place, trying to escape the gnawing shame that climbed up her spine. Nothing about this script was true. For all she knew, the Puremetics line didn't even address dry skin. What if it was as awful as the body wrap? What if it cost a hundred dollars? But no matter how icky Anna felt about shoving this baby-new relationship into the Puremetics marketing machine, she couldn't stop.

"I could get you some free samples if you like."

Lisa finished rubbing the lotion into her hands and snapped the lid shut. She gently put the container back in her purse, crossed her arms, and lifted an eyebrow. "What are you trying to sell me, Anna? Is this how you want to start our friendship?"

"Oh my god." Anna closed her eyes and wished the ground beneath her would crack open and swallow her whole. She pushed down the lump in her throat and wiped her sweaty palms against her scrubs. "No, this is not how I want to start things."

"So don't," Lisa said, pulling out her keys.

It felt like someone had grabbed Anna by the throat, squeezing until she couldn't speak. She gasped for air, trying to pry herself free from the stranglehold on her brain. She didn't know what to say or how to act. All she could do was stand there, burning in her well-deserved shame. But the silence didn't last. A tremor from deep within began to rattle Anna Price until words spewed from her mouth as if somebody was shaking them loose, forcing out the secret she had promised to keep.

"I'm working undercover as an MLM rep to take down a shitty CEO!"

Anna's hands flew to her mouth to keep anything else from leaking.

Lisa stood, frozen.

A car flew by the parking lot, throwing a pile of leaves into the air in its wake. Neither woman batted an eye.

Finally, Lisa opened her mouth but said nothing. Her lips pinched to one side as she furrowed her brows, trying to understand the scene she had landed in. "Are you serious?"

Anna blinked twice, her face blank. "Dead."

Lisa bit her lip as if stifling a laugh. She shook her head and closed her eyes, letting out a small chuckle.

That's all Anna needed to fall apart. It started as a simple release, a small noise bubbling to the surface. But before she knew what was happening, a hearty, unstoppable laughter had taken over.

Tears bubbled to Lisa's eyes as she followed Anna's lead. She braced herself against the side of her car, clutching her sides. "Girl, this is a story I need to hear. Wanna grab a coffee?"

Anna nodded and offered to drive. What else could she do? She couldn't believe she had broken Gloria's promise not to tell anyone, but she also couldn't deny the relief of releasing this heavy secret. For the next hour, Anna shared the entire saga—meeting Vicky at SuperMart, the typo that sent her crashing the OWLS meeting, Christian White, the plan for the convention, all of it. As Lisa absorbed every detail, her face jumped back and forth between disbelief and amusement.

"This is wild," Lisa said, shaking her head.

Anna took a sip of her now cold mocha decaf. "I know."

Lisa leaned back in the seat, tapping her mug. "Okay, I'm in."

It took a moment for the words to register. "What?"

"I'll enroll. Let me be your first step toward this crazy goal."

Anna tried to pick her jaw up from the ground. There was no way Lisa could be serious. "The products aren't cheap," she said. "You really don't need to do this."

Lisa brushed her off as she unlocked her phone. "I'm a single lady with no kids living in the cheapest apartment I could find because it's close to the mountains. Don't you worry about me. If I can help take down some evil CEO, I'm totally on board."

Anna smiled, triumphant at this unbelievable stroke of luck. Not only could she tell Vicky and Gloria that she had enrolled her first person, but finding Lisa seemed like a genuine miracle from the universe. When was the last time someone had offered to do something for *her*?

"Just tell me what to do." Lisa pulled up the Puremetics website.

"You're like my new favorite person," Anna said, trying to keep her emotions in check.

As she walked Lisa through the enrollment steps, she made one more promise—this time to herself. No matter what, Anna vowed to make this gift from the universe worth it. She would not take Lisa for granted or waste her trust. Anna was done playing small.

"And finished!" Lisa said, clicking the *Enroll Now* button.

"Oh my god. Thank you!" Anna leaned back, her smile unbreakable. She shook her head and chuckled. "Just remember, whatever you do, do *not* buy the body wraps."

Lisa smiled. "I like your honesty, friend."

Anna beamed. *Friend.*

12

Vicky pinched her nose as she walked up the stairs to Anna's place. She couldn't believe she was back at the dumpy apartment building, but it had been more than a month since Anna had enrolled her first—and *only*—person. Desperate measures were required.

It was time to light a fire.

Holding her breath and hoping that smell was not coming from Anna's apartment, Vicky knocked. Muffled chatter from the other side stopped, and the door creaked open. Anna stood with an expression that was more surprised than pleased.

"Oh. Hi, Vicky."

Vicky didn't wait for an invitation to come in. She shuffled past the doorway with her bag clenched to her side. As soon as the door closed, she exhaled, welcoming the hint of vanilla, butter, and sugar that wafted through Anna's home.

"Come on in, I guess," Anna said flatly. "Cookies will be out soon if you want to stay a minute."

Vicky sat her bag down on the kitchen table. "I'm sorry to

show up unannounced, but you haven't responded to my last few texts. I wanted to make sure everything was okay." She spun around. Her eyes grew wide as they landed on an unfamiliar woman sitting on the couch. "Oh! I didn't know you had company."

The woman stood, extending her hand. "Hey, I'm Lisa."

"Oh! Our newest Pure Apprentice!" Vicky flung her hair over her shoulder and moved in to shake Lisa's hand. "Well, this is fortuitous. I was just dropping by to give Anna a little gift—one for her and her new recruit!"

Vicky dug through her bag, pulling out two copies of the same bright pink book as a handful of Puremetics samples spilled out onto the table. Jack always made fun of her for stuffing her purse full of them, but Vicky knew how essential it was to be prepared.

"Don't let the cover fool you." Vicky passed the book to Anna and stuffed the samples back in her purse. "The information inside is gold."

A photograph of a woman sitting in an oversized leather chair was on the back cover. She could have been Vicky's twin with her perfectly tailored white pantsuit, bubble-gum stilettos, and cascading blonde hair.

Anna flipped the book over, reading the title. "*Get It, Girl— How to Take Your Network Marketing Business to the Next Level.*" Anna held the book up for Lisa to see. "Wow, I don't know what to say."

"That book helped me reach Presidential Emerald in a year," Vicky said as she handed Lisa her own copy. "I especially think you'll enjoy principle seven."

Anna flipped the pages until she found the chapter. "Become An Expert in Rejection." She bit her lip, shaking her head. "This is great, Vicky. Just... wow. Thank you."

"I read that chapter every night for a month to help me over-come the anxiety of approaching strangers at the store." Vicky snapped her purse shut, beaming like she had just cured cancer. "It's like I told you before. If you want people to say *yes* to your business, you must get used to hearing *no* first."

Anna and Lisa exchanged glances.

The microwave timer beeped. Anna swooped into the kitchen and pulled cookies out of the oven. Vicky's mouth watered as their sweet aroma tempted her like a siren's song.

"Who wants one?" Anna asked as she slid the gooey morsels onto a cooling rack.

Lisa jumped to her feet and headed to the kitchen table. "You don't have to ask me twice."

"No, thank you," Vicky said, determined to stick to her *No-Sugar November* pledge. "But I'll take some water."

The three women sat at the table with a pile of cookies in front of them. Vicky tapped her glass as she tried to find the right inroad to the conversation she'd rehearsed for a week.

"Anna, you did such a great job recruiting this rockstar here," Vicky said, squeezing Lisa's arm. Lisa did not smile back, and Vicky quickly recoiled, placing her hands in her lap. "And I know you invested a lot to get started with Puremetics. As your upline, I want to ensure you succeed. By now, you should be making enough to cover your monthly costs and working toward earning back the full price of the starter kit."

"Well, I'm not there yet, but I am trying," Anna said.

Vicky doubted it. She'd been doing this long enough to know most people cold-messaged a few former friends and called it quits when those people didn't immediately jump on board. MLM haters loved to talk about how nobody makes good money in this business, which was a blatant lie. Vicky was on track to earn over a million dollars this year alone. The only reason people failed at this business was because they didn't put in the effort.

"Who have you talked to?" Vicky asked.

Anna brushed a cookie crumb off the table. "I sent messages to more than two dozen former friends and neighbors."

Vicky perked up at this. "Really? That's great!" She had assumed that Anna had dropped the ball entirely based on her lack of sales, but maybe she was planting seeds. With time, the harvest would come. Vicky felt her shoulders relax at the thought of this possibility. "What did you tell them?"

"I followed the script you gave me."

Another good sign. "Can I see?"

Anna hesitated for a moment, biting her lip. Finally, she opened her message app. Vicky snatched the phone and read the text:

Hey, hun! I hope this message finds you well! *Smile Emoji.* Your kiddos are so adorable and getting so big! [Switch this part out to make it personal.] I know it's been a long time since we've been in touch, but I am reaching out because I just started a business with Puremetics. Not only do they have the most amazing products, but this company also offers an incredible opportunity for women like us. You have been on my mind lately. I know you could rock this business, and the world needs more boss babes like you! *Lips Emoji.* Besides, who couldn't use some extra cash these days? *Money Bag Emoji.* Anyway, I just had to reach out to see if you're interested. *Heart Emoji. Heart Emoji. Heart Emoji.*

It was the exact sample script Vicky gave all her recruits—the same one passed down from her own upline. Duplication equaled success. That rule was drilled into distributors' brains the day they enrolled. *Don't reinvent the wheel*, those on top would say. *Just duplicate what's already working.* But seeing this copy-and-paste monstrosity had Vicky rethinking everything.

"You typed out the word for each emoji?" Vicky's eyes bulged from their sockets. "You were supposed to insert the actual icons, not spell them out!"

Anna dropped her head into her hands. "I'm sorry! I've never talked in cartoon hieroglyphics before. I'm not the most technically savvy person."

Vicky pursed her lips, unable to look away from the train wreck inside the message bubble. "And you didn't delete the instructions. Did you even read what you sent? The part about kids was an example of how you could personalize the script. You're supposed to change it for each person. Please tell me this woman has children."

"*She* does." Anna's emphasis made it clear not everyone who got her message did. "I changed that part after someone pointed it out to me. They weren't all bad, I swear."

Vicky's body grew hot from secondhand embarrassment. Even without the stupid mistakes, this script sounded nothing like Anna—and for that, Vicky could only blame herself. Well, actually, she blamed Clara, her upline. After all, Vicky was only doing what she had been taught. That was how this business worked.

Although, only sometimes, apparently.

Lisa, who had been annoyingly quiet, chuckled softly. She took another cookie from the pile. "Did anyone respond?"

Anna shook her head as her eyes drilled into the table. "Well, Joyce did, but only to point out my mistakes and tell me I was in a cult." She hunched over, burying her face in her hands. "And Maggie, who yelled at me for asking about her kids when I knew she was struggling with infertility."

Lisa grimaced. "Oh, shit."

Vicky bit her lip. She didn't know Lisa well enough to call out her foul language.

"It's okay," Vicky said with a sharp inhale. "We can fix this. Give it a few weeks, let the awkwardness fade, and you can reach out again—this time with a different, more Anna-like message. I'll write it myself if I have to."

"But leave poor Maggie alone, for the love of God." Lisa shook her head.

Vicky was ready to move on from this dumpster fire. She turned her attention to Lisa as her voice moved almost an octave higher. "In the meantime, let's focus on building your downline!"

Lisa choked on her cookie. Her hand flew to her lips to keep the crumbs from spilling out. "I'm sorry, what?"

Didn't Anna pitch the business opportunity to Lisa? Why was it so hard for people to follow the process? Vicky inhaled slowly, trying to keep her annoyance from bubbling into rage.

"Oh, I just assumed you'd want to earn some easy money." Vicky pulled a small laminate card from her purse: a mini version of the Puremetics compensation plan. She pointed to the second rank from the bottom. "I mean, even if you only joined for the incredible products, the beauty of Puremetics is that you can cover the cost of your monthly auto-ship simply by signing up one or two people. It doesn't have to be a full-time thing. Most people start by enrolling their sisters or mom."

"My mom is dead," Lisa said, her face stone cold.

The words struck Vicky like daggers. Her hands popped to her mouth. "Oh, my gosh. I'm so sorry." Without thinking, she grabbed a cookie and stuffed the whole thing in her mouth, hoping it would push down the shame.

Anna leaned forward, inserting herself like a referee. "Lisa isn't interested in the business aspect of Puremetics just yet, but she's very excited about the products, right?" She turned to Lisa, nodding her head.

Lisa mirrored the action, moving her chin up and down as if she had been trained to comply.

Vicky swallowed the hunk of cookie in her throat. "I see. No problem." She made a mental note to ignore Lisa. It seemed safer that way. "Anna," she said, hoping to get things back on track, "you mentioned not having a lot of potential recruits where you work, but after your success with Lisa, is it possible there are others who might want to join? You're a massage therapist of some kind, right?"

"I'm a COTA and a CLT."

Vicky huffed. "In English, please."

"I'm a Certified Occupational Therapy Assistant and a Certified Lymphedema Therapist," Anna said.

"Right, a therapist of sorts, like I said. Anyway, I'm sure your clients would love our products. We have a great massage oil."

Anna cleared her throat and sat tall with a surprising self-assurance. "My patients are almost exclusively senior citizens who are dying, disabled, or learning to deal with a life-changing diagnosis. I am not about to pitch beauty products to them."

The strength of Anna's voice surprised Vicky, but she admired the display of integrity, even if she didn't fully agree with it. "You know, we have a senior line of supplements with the highest qual—"

"No," Anna said firmly.

Vicky leaned back, her arms up in surrender. "So, you're just giving up then?"

"I didn't say that." Anna's eyes shifted toward Lisa, almost like she was asking for help.

Lisa seemed to decipher the silent plea. "Of course not! You just need some ideas on where to find the right people. Maybe you should quit your job and hang out around day spas or yoga studios."

Anna ribbed Lisa in the side. "Ha ha."

Vicky sighed. "But it really is too bad you don't work with a younger, more health-conscious crowd like that."

Lisa chuckled. "You know, back at the medical center where

I worked in Houston, one of our CLTs ran her own mobile side business doing lymphatic therapy for plastic surgery patients. She spent her afternoons and weekends helping women who were recovering from boob jobs and tummy tucks."

"What's your point?" Vicky asked.

Lisa shrugged. "You wished Anna worked with a younger, more beauty-obsessed crowd."

"Health-conscious, not beauty-obsessed," Vicky snapped back.

"Whatever." Lisa flicked her wrist. "I was just putting two and two together: Anna's training and the kind of women who would *love* Puremetics."

Vicky hated the tone in Lisa's voice. *The kind of women*—what did that even mean? Still, she wasn't about to dismiss any potential idea. She was desperate. "And Anna could do that kind of work? Is she qualified?"

Lisa rolled her eyes.

"It's what I'm trained to do," Anna said. She turned back to Lisa and smiled. "I'll just call up my list of plastic surgeon friends and get this new business up by Monday. Piece of cake."

The two of them laughed.

"Oh my gosh! This is brilliant!" Vicky sat up tall, her excitement practically oozing from her body. "I have a friend who is a plastic surgeon. I could make an introduction."

Lisa tossed the last bite of the cookie in her mouth. "You know we were kidding, right?"

Anna shook her head and laughed. "I'm not starting another side hustle to make this first side hustle viable. I already work thirty hours a week at my *real* job."

"Why not?" Vicky said, suddenly very serious. She wasn't used to seeing Anna like this—the laughter and sarcasm. Even without knowing Anna well, it seemed evident Lisa was a bad influence. Vicky was not a fan. "For starters," she continued, "Puremetics is a *real* job. And it's this kind of out-of-the-box thinking that can change someone's life. Isn't that what you want, Anna? I thought you were ready to commit."

Anna sat, frozen in her seat.

Vicky's heart jackhammered against her chest, ready to bust out if Anna didn't agree to this plan. She was already mentally composing the email she'd send Dr. Davis. In front of her was a beautiful solution to an increasingly desperate problem. What was Anna waiting for?

The sound of laughter from another room snapped Vicky back to attention.

Jane emerged from the hallway and stopped when she saw Vicky. "Oh! Mrs. Sterling. I didn't know you were here." She turned her back, shrugging at a shadow walking up behind her.

Blaze walked into the room. "Mom?"

Vicky's mouth dropped. What was Blaze doing at Anna's house? No, better question: What was he doing in *Jane's bedroom*? Her stomach knotted around itself, thinking about the two teenagers alone, unsupervised. Were they friends? Did they hang out often? Did they like each other? And why were they here at Anna's horrible little apartment instead of Vicky's home, where it was safe and flea-free?

"I thought you were doing homework," Vicky said, her mouth dry.

Blaze shrugged. "Yeah. Jane and I have been prepping for our bio test. I told you I was heading out to study."

"You didn't say *where*."

Any thought of Anna or Puremetics had vanished. Vicky was eager to rush Blaze home, lock him up forever, and discuss an emergency plan with Jack. She needed answers about her precious boy. Fast.

Jane walked past the group into the kitchen. She grabbed two glasses from the cupboard and milk from the fridge. "He's seventeen years old," she said with a laugh. "I don't think you need to know his every move."

Vicky snapped her attention toward the blue-headed freak trying to seduce her son. "It's not him I'm worried about."

"Hey!" Anna said, standing up. "Let's calm down." She turned to Vicky. "The kids were just studying. I've been here the whole time. Nothing bad was going on."

"You're right, you're right." Vicky forced a tiny laugh, realizing how unhinged she must sound. "I'm sorry. Must be the sugar talking."

Overreacting or not, for seventeen years, Vicky had paved a path for Blaze, ensuring he always did the right thing by keeping him away from anything that could lead him astray. She expected him to live up to the Sterling name, mostly because she promised herself that her kids would not have to live with regret like she did.

Vicky exhaled slowly, trying to regain a semblance of composure. "I didn't realize you two were hanging out. It caught me off guard, that's all."

Blaze took the glass of milk Jane handed him. He shrugged. "Didn't mean to spook you."

"You didn't, sweetie." *Jane, on the other hand.* Vicky reached for her glass of water, chugging it down in a frantic attempt to calm her nerves.

Jane sat beside her mother, reached for a cookie, and passed the plate to Blaze. Vicky tried not to cringe when her son grabbed three for himself. Anna probably didn't use organic ingredients.

"How goes the studying?" Anna asked. "Almost done?"

"Great!" Jane said.

"Yeah." Blaze took a huge bite of a cookie. "Just finishing up the section on genes and sexual reproduction."

Vicky choked on her water, spewing droplets all over the table. She reached for a napkin, wiping away the evidence. "Oh my gosh, I'm so sorry."

It was all too much. Up until now, all of Blaze's close friends were guys. Now, this Jane was suddenly in the picture. Why *her*? There were a dozen girls who would kill to have Blaze Sterling in their house—girls with parents who were equally diligent in ensuring their kids remained pure. Why was he lowering his standards?

It was getting harder to breathe.

"I think I've crashed your little party long enough. I should go." Vicky stood and grabbed her bag. "Blaze, why don't you come with me."

"Uh, I drove myself."

"Well, it's time to drive yourself home then."

Blaze rolled his eyes at Jane, and the two chuckled softly. "I guess I'll talk to you tomorrow." He turned to Anna. "Thanks for the cookies."

The exchange felt like an arrow to Vicky's heart.

"You're welcome." Anna pushed back her chair and walked mother and son to the door. "Thank you for the book, Vicky."

"Read it." It was more a command than an invitation, but Vicky had no choice. Anna would only stop playing small if Vicky forced her to think big. "I'm going to email my surgeon friend. The least you can do is talk to him. I know you think it's crazy, but big dreams sometimes require a little crazy."

Vicky left before Anna could respond, giving Anna no chance to say *no*; sometimes, you had to force a *yes*. Working with plastic surgery patients was a solid plan, and right now, Vicky needed to know Anna had her feet planted in a firm direction. And with the decision made, she could focus on the more pressing matter: Blaze's eternal soul.

As Vicky made her way to her car, she tried to convince herself she was overreacting about the whole Jane thing. She wanted to see it like Anna did: an innocent study session with no ulterior motives. It didn't work. Vicky knew you could have the best intentions in the world and still mess up.

13

"I'm supposed to meet with the guy on Tuesday." Anna stood at the front of Gloria's living room, giving an update at the OWLS monthly meeting. The crackling fire behind her matched the women across from her—each a little spark of energy bundled into cozy knit sweaters. Meanwhile, Anna's own mood mirrored the blistering weather outside. It had only been a few days since Vicky demanded Anna meet with her plastic surgeon friend, and Anna still wasn't sure which way the wind would blow.

"Vicky didn't even wait for my response," Anna said, hoping to garner sympathy for her frustration. "She just went ahead and made the appointment for me."

Gloria rocked back in her chair, clutching her cup of tea. "The woman has moxie, that's for sure."

"She sounds like a nightmare," Claire said, one of the group's more vocal members. She ran her finger through her purple pixie, tossing her head back. Her voice turned syrupy sweet as she did her best Vicky impersonation. "Look at me. I'm Victoria

Sterling. I live in a mansion and think shilling vitamins to my neighbors makes me a CEO."

Another woman—Anna couldn't remember her name—jumped in with her own impression. "I'm a Boss Babe who doesn't think twice about pressuring people into joining my pyramid scheme." She flung her wispy white hair over her shoulder. "I've earned everything that comes my way because I'm hashtag-so-blessed."

The group laughed as they clucked, gobbling up the latest gossip like they were starving for a meal. Anna didn't mean to turn her monthly report into a venting session, but Vicky's nonstop pressure was taking its toll.

"So, are you going to do it?" Emily asked Anna, her arms crossed in their familiar shield-like fashion, clearly annoyed the group had veered off the agenda. "It's not the worst idea, and it could work."

It could work—that's what Anna hated most. Vicky had taken Lisa's off-hand remark and ran with it, turning the joke into a legitimate plan. There was no way around it. Teaming up with a plastic surgeon *would* put ideal clients in her path.

Anna sighed. "I'm going to talk to the guy and see if he is even willing to refer his patients. I would need to buy a massage table and a few other essentials. Between that and setting up an LLC, getting insurance, and creating a website, I'd only commit if the doctor thinks there is enough interest to justify the costs."

At this point, Anna wasn't thinking about nabbing extra Puremetics recruits. She had her own reasons for talking to this plastic surgeon. Working at Silver Lining Senior Living was taking its toll. The work was exhausting. The pay wasn't close to what she earned in Oregon. And except for Lisa, Anna's coworkers made her feel lonely and out of place. Even with her part-time schedule, she felt like she was burning out. The more she imagined walking down this path Lisa had paved, even if it was in jest, the more it made sense. Heaven knows she could use the money after having to dip into Jane's college fund to help cover moving and attorney expenses. Besides, Anna was kind of excited about the prospect of starting her own business as long as she didn't think about recruiting people into Puremetics.

"I could also contact some midwives and birthing centers," she said. "Expecting and postpartum moms are another group who benefit from lymphatic massage."

"Oh! More potential recruits!" Gloria clapped her hands. "This is all very promising, Anna!" She popped to her feet and patted her on the back. "We don't want to put any more pressure on you, but time is of the essence. How long will it be until you're taking on new clients?"

Anna did the math in her head, thinking about all the steps required. It wasn't the best time to jump into a new endeavor like this. Thanksgiving was next week, and then December was always rough. "Hopefully by mid-January? February at the latest," she said, wishing she sounded more confident.

"Fantastic! Thank you for a very thorough report. Hopefully, there will be some exciting updates at our next meeting."

Gloria was giving Anna the cue to wrap things up, but there was more to discuss. She hadn't told the group about Lisa yet. For weeks, Anna debated just how much to share about her recruit. Did the OWLS need to know she had accidentally revealed the plot to her new friend, or was it better to keep that information to herself? Anna preferred honesty but was terrified that these women would think less of her if they knew how quickly she had caved. Since everyone looked ready to move on, Anna decided to shelve the issue for now.

"Sounds good," Anna said, taking her place on the sofa.

Silence filled the room. The occasional spoon tinkling against a teacup magnified the sudden lack of conversation, leaving Anna wondering if she was supposed to say something else. The other women exchanged glances, shifting uncomfortably in their seats.

Emily cleared her throat. "That's all we need from you today, Anna. Thank you. You can see yourself out."

"Oh." Anna looked around the room. "You want me to go?"

"Claire, you're up next," Gloria said, gesturing to her friend. "Why don't you take the floor, and I'll see Anna to her car." She smiled warmly, grabbed her coat off the rack, and hurried Anna out of the house.

Anna waited until they were outside. "What was that about? Why can't I stay for the rest of the meeting? Shouldn't I know what's going on?"

"I'm sorry, sweetie. I should have been clearer when I invited you. We only needed a quick update from you. The rest of the meeting is for other projects."

"Other projects?"

Gloria raised her eyebrows. "Of course! This Puremetics stuff is just one of several ongoing missions we're working on."

Anna's eyes grew wide. "Seriously?"

"What? You don't think a bunch of old ladies can handle more than one covert mission at a time?"

"No!" Anna felt her cheeks get hot. "That's not it. I just figured this was a one-time thing." She lowered her voice. "You know, avenging your friend Fiona by taking down her shitty husband."

At the mention of Fiona, Gloria's smile faltered. "Right. I forgot I told you about that." She stiffened her spine. "Yes, this specific mission is very personal for me. I've been trying to expose White for years, but it's far from our only gig. The OWLS were hesitant to take on Puremetics at first."

Gloria sat on the porch swing, blowing warm air on her red fingers. She zipped up her coat and stuffed her hands in her pocket. "They all thought I was too attached to the cause. They were worried it would be easier to trace things back to me if things went badly—you know, because of my history with Christian."

Her history. Anna was curious to know just how entangled their lives were. She sat beside Gloria, eager to hear more.

"After I showed the mounting evidence of his corruption—thanks to Emily's impeccable detective skills—the rest of the group realized his business was harming thousands of people. They jumped on board with their full support. And even after things didn't work out this past summer, they were willing to try again at next year's convention."

"What exactly happened before?"

"We don't talk about it," Gloria said with a smile.

Anna chuckled as she watched the clouds drift by, fantasizing about having a group of friends who had each other's back. She had envied the women ever since stumbling into that first meeting. A spark of hope told her that if she did a good enough job this time, they would invite her to stay on as an official OWL despite being twenty or so years younger than them all.

"So, what about these other projects? How long have you guys been doing this work?"

Gloria laughed. "A while. It started eight or so years ago. We met at a school board meeting. There was this horrible board member who was hellbent on banning a beloved book. Those of us fighting the ban kept crossing paths, and eventually, we realized we had more in common than our age. We all wanted a better world and have been working to that goal ever since."

"Did you succeed?" Anna asked. "Did you stop the book ban?"

Gloria shook her head. "No, unfortunately. There was a large group of parents who outvoted us. But that only fueled our desire to do more."

"Like what?"

"Oh, I can't tell you," Gloria said with a wink. "The first rule of OWLS is you don't talk about OWLS."

Anna chuckled.

"But seriously," Gloria said, lowering her voice. "Over the years, our work has gone more underground. And while we haven't done anything technically illegal, we have worked close to the line."

Anna shook her head, smiling as her imagination drafted a hundred potential secret missions. "It's hard to believe. You guys look like you could be a sweet little knitting group or a book club."

"Exactly!" Gloria laughed. "Women of a certain age are generally invisible to society. We decided to use that to our advantage. Nobody expects us to get our hands dirty." She leaned in and whispered, "But sometimes that's the only way to make a change."

A mixture of awe and envy swirled inside Anna's mind. She felt lucky to have stumbled into this unsuspecting world of silver-haired vigilantes, but now she couldn't help but feel a twinge of resentment as Gloria escorted her away from the group. Hadn't Anna proved she was worthy of joining the OWLS? She was reluctant to leave but not brave enough to ask for an invitation.

"One more thing," Gloria said, following Anna to her car. "Victoria Sterling can be demanding and difficult."

"You think?" Anna said with a laugh.

"Just remember, she's not the villain here. I know Claire and some of the others love to point out her irritating flaws and highlight every hypocrisy that escapes her lips, but I think it's important to remember she's also a victim of Christian White."

"Yeah, I'm not so sure." Anna's mind replayed the moment in her kitchen when Vicky didn't bat an eye as she asked Anna to spend twelve hundred dollars on supplements. "She's making a fortune off the people she enrolls without any concern about their ability to afford it. I wouldn't exactly call her innocent."

"That may be true," Gloria said. She paused, pulling her coat tightly around her body as the wind picked up. "But I'd be careful not to paint her with such a broad stroke. I've been watching Vicky for many months. The woman has flaws. She's made mistakes. But don't let those things keep you from seeing who's pulling her strings. Don't let the puppet distract you from the puppet master."

"Fair enough," Anna said, still not convinced.

"Enjoy the rest of your day, dear. Let me know how the meeting with the surgeon goes." Gloria squeezed Anna's shoulder and hurried back into the house.

Anna tucked her arms in her coat, hoping to glimpse the action happening inside. Emily's stern profile stood framed in the window like a guard dog. Once again, Anna was on the outside staring in, but there was a spark of hope this time. If she could pull off this plan and prove to the OWLS that she was one of them, maybe they'd invite Anna inside for good.

14

OCTOBER 1986

The pile of mail hit the table with a whack. Gloria's hands shook as she held the envelope addressed in Fiona's unmistakable handwriting.

It had been seven months since Fiona walked away from Gloria's life. Thirty weeks with no word or update. Two hundred and twelve days with no way of finding her.

The emergency contact information from Fiona's lease agreement only listed a former roommate from college who had no clue where Fiona was this many years later. Gloria spent hours looking up addresses in the White Pages, but there were thousands of Andersons to sift through in Salt Lake County, and the only Fiona Anderson on the list was a retired Swedish immigrant.

Gloria didn't know if Fiona had moved in with her parents or moved out of Salt Lake City altogether. Brothers? Sisters? Fiona never mentioned them. Even the restaurant where she had worked when they were roommates couldn't help. Fiona quit her job the day after she left.

Grabbing a knife, she sliced the envelope open. Inside was a cream-colored card—an invitation of some kind. Gloria's mouth went dry; her hands turned clammy as she realized what she was holding. She pulled out the heavy cardstock, confirming her worst fear.

Fiona was getting married.

The room started spinning. Gloria braced herself against the kitchen table and finally slumped into the chair, reading and rereading every line of the message she was sure would destroy her.

Kyle and Cheryl Anderson
together with
Harold and Martha Blackwell
are pleased to announce the sealing of their children
Fiona Leslie Anderson
and
Christian Gordon Blackwell
in the Salt Lake City Temple of
The Church of Jesus Christ of Latter-Day Saints

She pulled out a photo of the couple. Fiona's thick brown curls draped over her shoulder. A conservative, navy blue and white floral dress matched her eyes. The smiling faces on the glossy paper mocked Gloria until she looked closer at Fiona's expression. Her lips were curved upward, but her eyes were missing their usual spark.

Chris stood behind his fiancée, dressed in a suit and tie. His sandy brown hair was parted to one side, and an irritating smirk highlighted his face. Chris wrapped his arms around Fiona's petite frame. His entire expression was one of triumph, not love. It was as if he was declaring to the world: *Fiona is mine.*

The truth smacked Gloria in the face. Fiona didn't just leave. She left to marry her emotionally abusive ex-boyfriend. This invitation was a sucker punch, leaving Gloria gasping for air and doubled over in pain.

How could Fiona marry *that* man?

Gloria crumbled the invitation in her hand and banged her fist. With a guttural roar, she swept all the mail off the kitchen table. But the rage died quickly, leaving her alone with the heartbreak that she was sure would kill her.

The tears burst like a dam breaking. Gloria's breaths became more erratic as her chest convulsed. She had already let go of the idea of ever being with Fiona, but knowing the love of her life was committing herself to such a man was too much. The sobs grew so intense that Gloria could only hope they would eventually drown her. Minutes passed—maybe longer. After the last tears drenched her cheeks, Gloria wiped the snot from her face and stood.

She picked up the scattered mail from the floor. When her fingers reached for the envelope that had delivered the bad news, Gloria found a small scrap of notebook paper tucked inside. She unfolded it and read the hastily scribbled note:

Glo, I know this news must come as a shock. I didn't make this decision lightly. Chris is a righteous man who has promised me a good life. My whole family has prayed about it. We know this is Heavenly Father's plan for me. I'm not asking you to come to the wedding. It's probably best that you don't. But I wanted you to know that there is happiness in the Gospel. If God has a plan for me, I know He has one for you, too.

- Fi

Outside the window, far enough in the distance to have never bothered Gloria before, she could see the sun reflecting off the golden Angel Moroni that stood on top of the Salt Lake City temple. She knew little about what happened inside those white, granite walls—having extracted herself from that world long ago. But suddenly, the building took on new meaning in Gloria's life. It wasn't just a city landmark or a remnant reminder of her past. Knowing Fiona would marry Chris inside the temple made it impossible for Gloria to stay put. The spires jutting upward from the skyline were no longer just a reminder that she was an outsider. They were a symbol of what she had lost.

Gloria tossed the invitation and note in the trash. She grabbed her keys and started to drive, not knowing exactly where she was going—just that she needed to get away. The city was bustling with five o'clock traffic, and Gloria's heart gripped tighter against her ribs with every delay. She strangled the steering wheel, trying to wring out her frustration, wishing she could plow through the rows of cars keeping her from the freedom she craved.

After slogging along the city roads, Gloria finally reached I-15. She merged onto the freeway and headed south, past the Murray smokestacks toward Utah County. She zoomed forward, beyond the Point of the Mountain, the Lehi Roller Mills, and even Brigham Young University. After more than an hour of driving, she finally exited the highway and found a hint of peace as she moved toward the rural farmlands of southern Utah County. Meandering Salem and Santaquin's scattered neighborhoods and tiny city centers, Gloria felt a shift. The oppressive weight lifted ever so slightly, helping her breathe easier. When she reached the unfamiliar city of Kinderhook, a place barely big enough to be called a town, Gloria finally stopped.

Nestled against the majestic Wasatch Mountains, a small cottage poked its head from among the fields. A *For Rent* sign punctuated the lawn. Alone in what must have once been the home for a local farmer, a small, plain house stood quiet and solemn, promising safety from a world collapsing before Gloria's eyes.

One week later, Gloria made the little cottage her home.

15

6 MONTHS UNTIL CONVENTION

"Okay, let's do this." Vicky inhaled sharply, steadying herself for what was sure to be a stamina-testing night. After rushing through dinner and cleaning up, she changed her clothes and touched up her makeup. After all, there were bound to be selfies. Poised and ready, Vicky sat at the kitchen desk, rolled her shoulders back, and logged into her Puremetics group forum.

"Let the month-end madness begin!"

More than a dozen notifications filled the screen, an alarming foreshadowing. Vicky had been messaging her downline all day, ensuring everyone in her organization was working to meet their monthly quotas. She plastered the forum's feed with motivational quotes and tips for recruiting last-minute hopefuls. If someone was falling behind, there was a not-so-subtle push to stock up on products to meet sales minimums.

When someone did hit rank, Vicky snapped a photo of herself holding a purple sign with a fancy *Congratulations* written across it. She would tag the new leader, sing their praises, and testify that anything was possible for those willing to do the work. There was nothing like singling out the winners to light a fire under everyone else. Vicky had mastered her role as a caring leader who wouldn't accept anyone falling short of their goals.

Because if any of them fell short, so would Vicky.

It was a familiar dance that happened every thirty or so days since all ranks reset at the start of each month. When January began, Vicky's numbers plummeted to zero—just like the other twenty thousand Puremetics distributors. But unlike the majority struggling to earn enough to cover the cost of their products, it was a quick climb back to the top for Vicky. As long as her people kept their autoships active and pushed their customers to buy products, she'd hit rank and earn her six-figure check.

Still, Vicky knew nothing was guaranteed. Inevitably, someone would decide to leave the business or buy fewer products than they did the month before, so this frantic push was necessary. There was no going down for Victoria Sterling, only up.

Jack wandered into the living room and plopped into his favorite chair. A moment later, the television was on. Two snarky sportscasters blabbered about some athlete's sprained ankle while the constant squeak of sneakers against the waxed floor filled the room.

"Can you turn it down, please?" Vicky was careful to keep her tone light. "I'm trying to work."

"I've put in nearly sixty hours this week," Jack said, not policing his tone even a little. "You already canceled date night. I'm not giving up my game."

Date night was sacred in the Sterling household. On their wedding day, the temple sealer who officiated the ceremony encouraged the couple to make it a priority. *Once you are married, your spouse is the most important person in your life, except for God Himself.* So, of course, Vicky had considered this advice another commandment she couldn't break. But just like so many other non-negotiables, Puremetics had pushed Vicky to make tweaks and exceptions more often than she cared to admit.

Vicky moaned quietly. "I told you; we'll do date night tomorrow. And I'm not asking you to give up your game. I'm asking you to turn it down." She spun her chair around, meeting her husband's gaze. "Please, Jack. My work is important, too."

Jack let out an exaggerated sigh and stood. "Fine. I'll watch it in my office." He dragged his feet across the floor, stopping by Vicky to give her a quick peck on the cheek.

"Thank you, sweetie!"

The doorbell rang. Jack let Becki in before retreating to his office.

"In here, Becks!" Vicky yelled to her neighbor.

Becki Young was Vicky's closest friend and highest-ranking distributor—just one title below Vicky. Becki stumbled into the kitchen with her arms full. Her usually bright complexion had turned ashen gray. "We've got a problem."

There was always a problem with Becki. The woman lived for drama and wasn't afraid to stir the pot if it meant dredging up someone's misfortune.

"Tell me," Vicky said, scrolling through messages from her downline. She carefully clicked *like* on each post and added a quick comment with encouragement.

Becki moved a dining room chair next to Vicky and sat. "Remember Rachel, my cousin who lives in Alpine? She was one of my first recruits and a top leader in my organization."

Vicky nodded, typing Rachel's name in the search bar to pull up her distributor report.

"Well," Becki said, "she's still struggling to lose weight after having baby number six almost a year ago."

Vicky could not imagine what this had to do with Puremetics. "And?"

"A few months ago, she decided to do a Puremetics challenge

and made a big deal about it on her blog and social media." Becki leaned back in her chair. "As you know, she has a massive following."

"Yeah," Vicky said. "So, what's the problem?" The screen finished loading and populated Rachel's numbers from the past year.

Becki pointed to the laptop. "See this spike in her OGV back in September? This is when she first posted about the challenge. She invited her followers to join her as she worked to lose thirty pounds in three months using only Puremetics products. She got a *ton* of people to enroll. They bought all the extras like body wraps, fat burners, and slimline supplements."

"I remember," Vicky said. "She hit Ruby Director right after that, which helped you reach Sapphire Executive."

"—which boosted you to Presidential Emerald," Becki said with a smile.

Vicky still wasn't sure where Becki was going with all this. "What's the problem?"

Becki scrolled down to January's numbers. "This. Do you see this cliff? After she posted about the challenge, Rachel steadily climbed in sales. But this month, she may not even reach Opal, let alone Ruby."

That was concerning. Vicky leaned in to study the numbers. If Rachel couldn't hit Ruby, Becki might not reach Sapphire. And if Becki's OGV dropped too low, Vicky would drop a rank, too. Unacceptable.

Vicky sighed. "What happened?"

Becki rolled her eyes, shaking her head. "The challenge was a flop. She lost maybe three pounds. After weeks of posting updates with little or no change, Rachel tried to move on, hoping nobody would notice. When some followers asked how things were going with the experiment, Rachel deleted any posts and comments that mentioned the challenge."

"Don't tell me—"

"Yep," Becki said with a scoff. "One of those anti-MLM bloggers caught wind of the situation. She published an article shaming Rachel and insisting it was proof that Puremetics did nothing to help people lose weight."

"Dang it." Vicky stood and began pacing around the kitchen, trying to work the problem out in her mind. There were more and more of these anti-MLM trolls these days, little monsters looking for any tiny issue that they would turn into some exaggerated click-bait article. Vicky nearly lost one of her rising leaders to an online rant about some ridiculous rumor that Puremetics products didn't contain the ingredients listed on the bottles.

"The first thing we need to do is keep Rachel from losing rank," Vicky said. "How far off is her OGV?"

"She needs at least two or three thousand dollars in sales."

Vicky whistled. "Okay, let's start messaging her people individually and ask them to make an extra purchase in the next hour or two. If anyone pushes back, remind them they may need this sort of group assistance in the future. No excuses. They can always buy gift cards if they don't need more products right now."

"On it." Becki pulled her laptop from her bag and set it on Vicky's counter.

"That should solve the immediate problem, but we still need a long-term solution." Vicky pulled two sparkling waters from her fridge and handed one to Becki. "It would be great if we could get her to lose that extra weight. If she could show a killer before/after photo, it would prove the trolls wrong and spike her sales again."

"Yeah, I'm not sure her body is cooperating. Rachel was diligent with all the products. At least, that's what she told me." Becki took a long sip before resting her elbows on the counter. She tapped the aluminum can with her finger. "It's too bad there isn't a Puremetics Tummy Tuck," she said with a chuckle.

The thought came instantly. Of course, it did. Dr. Davis had been on Vicky's mind for weeks. She had just followed up with him two days ago to see if Anna had ever taken on his referrals.

"Do you think Rachel would be interested in... a surgical alternative?" Vicky's voice was barely a whisper. As soon as the words left her lips, a surge of shame swelled in her gut. She wished she could take them back, but they had already landed on Becki's ears.

"Oh! That could work!" Becki clapped her hands as her voice picked up speed. "A little nip and tuck would make for some incredible after-shots. Rachel could have a new blog post up in a matter of weeks, showing off her killer body and putting all those anti-MLM trolls to shame. I love it, girl!"

Vicky took a large gulp of water to wash down the guilt. "You don't think it's a little... deceitful?"

"No more than wearing makeup or getting Botox," Becki said, her smile spreading by the moment. "Besides, this past year has been hard for Rachel. Bouncing back after six kids is no joke, and I'm sure she'd love to speed the process along."

Even if that were true, it didn't change the lie Rachel would have to tell to pass surgery off as a Puremetics miracle. Vicky was all for women doing whatever they needed to feel as confident and beautiful as they wanted. And sure, she had exaggerated some of the benefits of certain products. It was easy with Vicky's genes. But passing off a tummy tuck as if it were the result of some fat burners was a line Vicky hesitated to cross.

"I'll talk to her," Becki said, seemingly unbothered by the ethics of it all and ready to move on.

"Don't push it," Vicky said, hoping it was enough to wash her hands of the whole thing.

Becki took another sip. "How is your last leg coming along? Anna, right? Are you still working with her?"

"Ugh, don't even get me started with Anna Price." Vicky was happy to change subjects, but not if it meant talking about Anna.

"She still only has one recruit. I practically handed her a golden opportunity, and she wasted it. If things don't change quickly, there's no way she'll meet the requirements I need for my final leg."

"I may know someone you could enroll," Becki said with a shrug.

"Who?" Vicky felt like a lifeline was being thrown her way until she realized who was tossing it. "And why wouldn't you enroll this person yourself?"

Becki blew a raspberry. "Dave won't let me. It's his therapist, and he says it would be out of line for me to approach her. Never mind the fact that he's seeing a female therapist after I told him it made me uncomfortable." She pressed her lips together, shaking off layers of frustration. "Whatever. That's not the point. Her name is Stephanie, and I think she'd be great."

"Am I supposed to just call her up? That wouldn't be awkward or anything." Vicky laughed but immediately pulled out a pen and notepad. At this point, she was desperate enough to pick up the phone and try.

"I've run into Steph several times at the Yoga Studio in Spanish Fork. You could come to a class with me one of these weeks, and I'll introduce you."

Vicky's eyes lit up. "Oh my gosh! That would be amazing. Do you think she'd do a good job with the business?"

"Better than that Anna chick," Becki said with a shrug. "It couldn't hurt to hedge your bets a little."

Vicky bit down on her purple pen, loving the idea of having a backup plan. Anna vs. Stephanie—it was like a Puremetics game show where Vicky was the winner either way.

"I'm in," she said with a grin. "Thank you!"

"My pleasure." Becki turned back to her laptop and started messaging Rachel's downline. "But if I do this for you, you'll owe me."

The women buried their heads in their work for the next

hour, messaging distributors and posting motivational selfies. Vicky was grateful for Becki's dedication, which helped fuel her own desire to do more. After all, Vicky did not want Becki to reach Royal Diamond before she did. Just the thought of it made her type faster.

The garage door rumbled, knocking Vicky out of her meditative dance at the keyboard. She turned to see Blaze enter the kitchen and felt her breath catch when Jane followed behind.

"Jane! What a lovely surprise," Vicky said as her jaw clenched.

It had been weeks without any mention of the girl, and Vicky had assumed her little chat with Blaze had worked. "I'm not sure Jane's a great influence for you," she had said. "With your mission right around the corner, it's probably best to focus on school and seminary." Blaze had promised they were only friends —that Vicky was blowing things out of proportion, but she held her ground. When he stopped mentioning Jane's name, Vicky assumed things were back on track.

Now, the girl was in her kitchen, taking a drink from Blaze's hand. Her blue hair was pulled into a high ponytail, showing off her brunette roots growing in. A small stud in her nose and a dozen rings around the edge of one ear all mocked the image Vicky had created over the years of Blaze's future wife. This girl would never see the inside of the temple. That fact alone made her unworthy to be linked to her son.

The two teens laughed as they shared an inside joke. Vicky couldn't help but notice how relaxed and happy her son seemed around Jane. Blaze never mentioned crushes or talked much about girls. Vicky always assumed he kept that part of his life private. She watched, obsessively looking for clues that this friendship was heading in another direction, disappointed that her earlier warnings had made no noticeable impact.

"I know you're working, Mom." Blaze grabbed some chips from the cupboard. "We'll be out of your hair in just a sec."

"What are you guys doing?" Vicky asked, realizing her tone sounded more policing than she intended.

"We're going up to my room to watch a movie."

To the bedroom? Over Vicky's dead body. "Why don't you watch it down here?"

"Because during dinner, you threatened to skewer us kids if we bothered you tonight."

Becki chuckled, seemingly amused by the image.

Jane stood behind Blaze with one hand tucked in her back pocket while the other held her drink. Vicky tried to read her expression. It was no use. Jane's neutral gaze and relaxed smile made it impossible to decipher any clandestine plans.

Vicky turned on her primary voice—the sickening sweet one Blaze said she only used when talking to the kids at church. "I insist you guys watch your movie here on the big TV. You won't bother us at all, right?" She looked at Becki for confirmation.

"I'm used to working with a baby and a toddler screaming in my face," Becki said. "A little background movie is a walk in the park."

"See? We're fine." Vicky turned to Jane. "What's the movie?"

"*What's up, Doc?*" Jane rocked back on her heels, looking uncomfortable. "It's a favorite in our house."

Vicky leaned back in her chair. "Never heard of it."

"It's great!" Jane said, perking up. "It's an older show—from the seventies, I think. Ryan O'Neal plays Dr. Howard Bannister, a musicologist engaged to this tightly wound, overbearing woman."

Vicky flinched at the subtle smirk that lifted the corners of Jane's mouth when she said it, as if it was a personal dig at Vicky.

"He meets Judy Maxwell, played by Barbara Streisand—a witty magnet for trouble. Judy pursues Howard. Hijinks ensue. It's hilarious."

"It's about a woman trying to break up a happily engaged couple?" Vicky eyed Blaze with a *you should know better* glance.

"Well, I wouldn't use the word happily," Jane said, pushing back firmly. "It's super innocent, I promise. It's a screwball comedy, not some home-wrecker drama."

Vicky leaned in, her eyebrows furrowed. "What's it rated?"

"What's with the third degree?" Blaze snapped. "It's not like we're watching porn!"

Jane laughed, pulling the movie out from her bag. "Relax. It's rated G."

Vicky still had her mouth gaping wide at Blaze's porn remark. She was sure her cheeks were tomato red. "Sounds fun," Vicky said with a nervous laugh. Her fingers still gripped her desk as she pretended to get back to work. "Enjoy the movie."

The teens moved into the living room and slipped in the DVD. Vicky took a few deep breaths, trying to understand why she was acting so crazy. She wished Blaze had never met the girl, wished the family had never moved to Kinderhook. Had she inadvertently attracted Jane to Blaze by working with her mother? That thought made her even more eager to find someone to replace Anna. It wasn't like the woman was succeeding with Puremetics anyway.

Vicky nudged Becki. "When's the next yoga class?"

Becki looked up from her laptop. "Tuesday. Why?"

"I want to meet this Stephanie person. The sooner, the better."

16

Anna precariously balanced the portable massage table under her arm as she grabbed her bag from the trunk. With ten new inches of snow on the ground, fears of broken ankles loomed as she thought of trekking up Mrs. Nelson's steep driveway. She steadied herself, careful not to slip on the ice as she made the climb.

The neighborhood reminded Anna of Splendor Springs, although it was ten or twenty years older. A long string of brick and stone mansions stood on steep inclines, pulled back from the road that winded further up the foothills. As Anna reached the front door, she gasped for air and wondered how long it had been since her last visit to the gym.

Despite the sub-zero temperature, Anna could feel sweat beading under her arms at the thought of screwing up this appointment. Mrs. Nelson was the first plastic surgery patient referred from Dr. Davis's office—and Anna's last chance to make this Puremetics thing work.

Anna had done thousands of lymphatic massages during her career. She was good at her job, able to relieve swelling and improve circulation with an almost magical touch—or so her patients had said. But her clenched muscles and throbbing heart told a different story—one tangled with secret missions and sales scripts. Between the fear of letting Gloria down and the stress of being found out, disaster seemed like the only possible outcome. Anna wanted this first meeting with Mrs. Nelson to be a new beginning, not a complicated subplot.

Nevertheless, the pressure to recruit persisted.

The door swung open before Anna knocked. A young woman in jeans and a ponytail smiled. "You must be the lymphedema therapist! Come on in. Mrs. Nelson is waiting for you."

"Sorry I'm late," Anna said, wiping her soaking feet on the mat outside. "The roads were crazy."

"No worries. I'm Mandy, the nanny. Can I help you with anything?" She gestured to the armful of stuff in Anna's hands.

"Thanks." Anna passed her bag and adjusted her grip on the table.

She followed Mandy through a long hallway lined with family photos. A half dozen portraits showcased a blond-haired, blue-eyed girl—all different ages. Anna wondered if the pictures were of one person throughout the years or six separate children. As she walked into the living room, she found her answer. A massive, framed photo hung above the mantel, showcasing six golden-haired children, from baby to budding teenager, standing on either side of their gorgeous parents.

"Wow, big family!"

Mandy shot a knowing look and smiled. "You could say that." She led Anna into a beautifully furnished library off the kitchen with oversized leather armchairs and the most envy-inducing bookshelf Anna had ever seen. A woman sat in one of the chairs with her feet on an upholstered ottoman.

"You must be Anna," the woman said, barely opening an eye as Anna entered the room. "I'm so thankful you make house calls. The doctor said recovery wouldn't be too painful." She scoffed, wincing as she did. "He's the type who probably says giving birth isn't a big deal."

Anna laughed, pleasantly surprised by the woman's candor. She had half-expected to find a stuffy snob inside a house this grand. "It's nice to meet you, Mrs. Nelson."

"Please, call me Rachel."

"Right, Rachel." Anna pushed the coffee table aside and began setting up her equipment. "How's the swelling?"

"I feel like an overinflated balloon," Rachel said with a groan. The woman's frown didn't match the smiling wife in the living room photograph, but she had *just* had surgery.

Anna smiled. "Let's see if we can deflate you a little."

Even with the bruising and puffiness, it was clear the woman's genes had been kissed by God, making Anna wonder what had prompted her to go for Dr. Davis's Mommy Makeover package in the first place. Between the breast surgery, tummy tuck, and liposuction, it seemed like a lot of risk, time, and money for someone who probably had a stack of business cards from modeling agencies tucked away somewhere in this chateau.

For the next forty-five minutes, Anna worked her magic as Rachel talked about her children and the latest drama within the PTA. Anna smiled politely, offering a sympathetic ear but saying little beyond what was needed to do her job. Still, as Rachel blabbered on, Anna saw the appeal of working for herself. Rachel's beautiful home was far more pleasant than the stuffy, sterile nursing facility. And leading the rehab process without a supervisor calling the shots was rewarding in unexpected ways. It reminded Anna that, in the right setting, she was downright capable—confident, even.

"Make sure you stay hydrated," Anna said after they finished. "And don't be surprised if you have an increased need to urinate. That's totally normal."

Rachel was back in the leather armchair with a relaxed smile. "That was lovely. I already feel better."

"As we discussed on the phone, the healing process varies from person to person. Based on what I saw today, six to eight sessions will get you back to feeling like your old self."

"Do you have any product recommendations for the incision scars?" Rachel asked as she reached for a glass of water from the side table.

Anna paused, suddenly aware of the opportunity in front of her. It was like the universe had dropped a beautifully wrapped present in her lap, but she wasn't sure she should open it yet. The plan was to hold off on saying anything about Puremetics for the first few sessions. After blowing her pitch with Lisa, Anna knew coming on too fast or soon was a bad idea. Besides, she had loved not thinking about Puremetics, focusing only on the client's needs. Yet here was Rachel, opening a door that could shut any moment.

"Actually," Anna said, taking a deep breath, "there's this really great product line with the best natural ingredients that might do the trick." She remembered how Vicky had coached her to say the next bit. "It's like a spa day for your—"

"—face," Rachel said, finishing Anna's sentence. She smiled, shaking her head. "Let me guess, Puremetics?"

Anna felt caught like a cat with feathers in its mouth, too shocked to hide her guilt. "Oh, you've heard of it?" Her stomach tensed, prepared to be called out again.

"Girl," Rachel said, sitting up. "I'm a Ruby Director!"

That was three ranks above Anna's pathetic Spark Coordinator. Somehow, this was even more disappointing than losing out on a potential enrollee. Desperate to remain composed, Anna forced a smile. "Oh, so you know how great they are." Her flat voice barely carried her words across the room.

Rachel rolled her eyes and chuckled. "If I thought the products were good, I wouldn't have asked for a recommendation. I mean, don't get me wrong. Some of their stuff is fine. My thirteen-year-old thinks their makeup is phenomenal, but that's because she hasn't tried anything else and hears me singing its praises to everyone I meet. The skincare line is mediocre at best. I swear the moisturizer gave me my first pimple. And the body wraps are an absolute scam."

"Oh, sure." Anna didn't know what else to say. How did this woman rank so high if she hated the products this much?

"I signed up last year under Becki Young. Do you know her? She's my cousin and one of Vicky Sterling's top leaders. I'm assuming you know Vicky—*everyone* knows Vicky. She's something of a Puremetics legend around here."

Anna nodded slowly.

"See what I mean? Legend." Rachel chuckled. "Anyway, that's why I got the Mommy Makeover package from Dr. Davis."

"Wait, what?" Anna's brain paused, looking for a rewind button.

"Yeah, Becki insisted it would help my business. My confidence took a hit after having baby number six." Rachel lifted her shirt an inch and tenderly inspected the incision on her abdomen. "Network Marketing is all about selling a lifestyle. You must know that."

"Sure." Anna looked around at the luxurious house. It was clear the Nelsons had a very different lifestyle than she did.

"I'm hoping to reach Sapphire Executive by Convention." Rachel grabbed a couple of pills and popped them in her mouth. "Going under the knife was worse than I thought, though. So, it better be worth it."

Was this woman going to use her post-surgery body to help her sell Puremetics? There was no way anyone could be so blasé about something so objectively unethical. Anna had to be missing something. She backed up, trying to withhold judgment until she had all the details.

"So, Becki made you get a tummy tuck and boob job—to sell Puremetics?"

Rachel's eyes grew wide. "Oh! Of course not."

A sharp exhale escaped Anna's lips. "Oh, good. For a second, I thought—"

"—It's not like Becki held a gun to my head," Rachel said, interrupting. "I could have said *no*. But honestly, I had tried *everything* to lose the baby weight. Desperate measures, you know? Besides, lots of people get cosmetic surgery." Rachel leaned back, plopping her legs on the ottoman. "The fact that it can help my sales is an extra perk. Impressive before and after pictures can be very compelling."

"But it's a lie," Anna said, pressing the subject.

Rachel's expression turned sour. "I'm not telling people my results came from Puremetics."

"Oh. Then what *are* you doing?"

"My blog took a hit a while back after some trolls made a big fuss that I hadn't lost the baby weight, insisting it was proof Puremetics was a scam." Rachel rolled her eyes. "Which is stupid because it's not Puremetics's fault I was up almost twenty pounds. Anyway, I plan to post pictures on my website to shut the haters up and prove I lost weight. If anyone assumes the transformation came from Puremetics's products, that's not my fault."

But will you tell them you had plastic surgery? Anna didn't need to ask the question. The answer weaved through Rachel's defensiveness.

"People buy from thin, beautiful women," Rachel said. "They want to believe their dream body is just a pill or body wrap away. And even if my customers never see the change they desire, they'll keep paying for products to keep that hope alive."

Anna leaned against the massage table as her brain tried to turn this puzzle into a picture she could understand. "It's just that you, of all people, could get to the top of Puremetics without all of *this*," she said, gesturing to the ice packs, pain meds, and ointments scattered on the table. "You are already gorgeous.

Surgery is costly, comes with risks, and requires recovery time. Why do it?"

Rachel pressed her lips together, her eyes suddenly drawn inward. She cleared her throat and spoke with an almost terrifying calmness. "Because, whether I like it or not, my beauty defines me." She sat a little taller as if lifted by a rising wave of secret rage. "My looks are the one thing everyone praises. *Oh, what a nice smile you have! Wow, nobody would guess you've had five kids! Rachel, you're so pretty, so thin, so perfect.*"

The mocking tone in Rachel's voice wasn't funny. It cut through the air like a million knives. She pulled further into herself with each word, retreating from their threat.

"Then I got pregnant with Sophie," she scoffed. "Growing a baby is hard enough but doing it for the sixth time in your thirties is a whole different story." Rachel shook her head, her eyes suddenly glistening with moisture. "Days after giving birth, my husband hinted that I should go to the gym. He eyed me anytime I took an extra serving of potatoes. Once Sophie stopped nursing, he made off-handed remarks about my love handles and flat, pancake breasts."

Rachel grabbed her chest, forgetting about the incision scars. She winced from the pain. "He doesn't care that these things nourished every one of his children. *It's not the body I fell in love with*, Paul said."

Anna wanted to look away, but Rachel's intensity trapped her.

"It doesn't matter how many sleepless nights I spent caring for sick kids. He doesn't appreciate the hundreds of meals I've prepped, the scraped knees I've kissed, the bedtime stories I've read." Rachel choked on her words and looked away. She tapped the prescription bottle beside her and chuckled. "My work—*my life*—is invisible to him. I'm only a body to be consumed."

Rachel took a slow inhale and closed her eyes. "I love my

children ferociously. I would gladly give my body for them. But since it's my only asset, I can't just let myself go."

The words suspended in the air like brooding storm clouds waiting to crack open the sky. Unsure how to escape the threat, Anna held her tongue, determined not to add to the building pressure.

"You're more than your body," Anna finally whispered.

Rachel looked up, meeting Anna's gaze. "Am I?" she asked, leaning forward. "Do you know what would happen to me if Paul ever made good on his threat to leave me for someone younger?"

Anna shook her head, trying to push away the image of her own husband fucking the graduate student in their bed. Her breath quickened as a familiar panic started to rise in her chest.

"I married Paul when I was twenty," Rachel said. "He convinced me to quit school and start a family. I have no education, no skills, and no work experience. If I were on my own, I'd be royally screwed.

"I built a massive following with my blog, but even that didn't pay a penny until I enrolled with Puremetics." Rachel fell back against the chair, crossing her arms. Her eyes grew narrow as her expression hardened into steel. "This isn't just a vanity project, Anna. And if I'm being honest, I *will* lie about the surgery if it means succeeding in this business. Puremetics is the only safety net I have."

Rachel's words stopped as if they had dropped off a cliff. As Anna followed them to the edge, she clung to the silence, hoping to avoid the inevitable fall. This was not what she signed up for. Rachel's despair hit too close to home. It was too raw, too exposed. Anna packed her things, saying only what was necessary to end the session and leave as quickly as possible.

If only it were as easy to run away from the pain.

As she drove home that afternoon, Anna wrestled with what to do next. Only one thing was sure: She would never mention

Puremetics to a patient again. The entire business thrived on poking holes in women's self-worth only to offer expensive Band-Aids for the gaping wounds it inflicted. There was no way to enroll anyone and keep her integrity.

But where did that leave her? Up until now, Anna had considered Gloria's plan a necessary treatment, like chemotherapy—painful but crucial. After talking to Rachel, though, Anna couldn't help but wonder how many other women saw this business as their only way out of a desperate situation. Was it possible to remove the cancer without destroying those who put all their hopes in a dream, unattainable as it may be? The whole cause felt hopeless, like an endless cycle of victims and perpetrators.

Anna turned onto Gray Street, and the tattered profile of Ghostly Manor came into view. The dilapidated house drew her in, beckoning like a bad omen. She drove past her apartment complex and pulled to the side of the road in front of it. The sagging snow-covered roof threatened to collapse. A large board covered in graffitied penises barricaded the front door. Even in its neglected state, Anna had believed in the building's potential. Maybe it was because she had seen herself in the structure's fragile, ragged state and wanted to believe broken things could be redeemed.

You're in over your head, the house taunted.

Anna knew houses didn't talk, even ones riddled with local folklore, but that didn't stop her from putting words into its mouth. The unsightly shack on Gray Street had inspired her to fight against Puremetics, to prove she had more fight left to give. Now, the house mocked her naive optimism, reminding her that some things were better left behind.

This was never going to end well for you, Anna.

The house was insistent. She imagined running with a sledgehammer and tearing the walls down herself, determined to shut it up, but she knew the moment it crashed, it would take Anna down with it.

After all, Anna had been swinging at Puremetics for months now. And the only thing ready to crumble from the impact was herself. She hit her head against the steering wheel, unable to see a path forward. If only she could go back in time and stop the business from forming. As it was, no matter what Anna did, someone was going to get hurt.

Give up, the house urged. *Stop now before the crash traps you in its rubble.*

Anna scoffed. "It's far too late for that."

17

JULY 1996

Gloria opened the glass door, analyzing the various jugs of milk. She couldn't remember what her mom was drinking these days, but it seemed like each time she came to visit, the fat percentage went down. Gloria placed a half-gallon of skim in the shopping cart and scanned her dad's list. There was a reason she hadn't been to her parents' house in months; they always sent her shopping when she did.

"Glo?" a familiar voice said from behind.

The hairs on Gloria's arms stood tall. She turned around and nearly dropped the shopping list when she saw the woman in front of her.

"Fi?" Gloria lunged forward and wrapped her arms around Fiona's slim frame. "Oh my god! How are you?"

Fiona's spine stiffened under Gloria's enthusiastic embrace. "I'm fine."

Gloria pulled back, pushing her salt-and-pepper curls from her face. "Sorry. Didn't mean to pounce."

It had been ten years since Gloria had seen her former roommate—a decade without a word. After a quick escape from the city, Gloria hadn't anticipated how hard it would be to move on. Life in a rural town made it easy to settle into the isolated seclusion of a middle-aged artist still hopelessly bound by unrequited love.

If only Gloria could say the same for Fiona.

The wedding invitation had been the only evidence of Fiona's existence, but it was a definitive statement of a person moving forward. Ten years was plenty of time for Fiona to build a new life unconnected to Gloria.

Was she happy? Was Chris taking care of her? Where did they live? Did they have kids? Was Fiona still going to church? Did she finish graduate school? The list of questions piled into Gloria's brain, one on top of the other, until they all melded together, and all she could mutter was, "Nice day we're having, isn't it?"

Fiona cracked a smile and took a step forward. "Glo, I need to apologize," she whispered. "I should have handled things better. It was cruel to leave the way I did."

Gloria pushed back the urge to grab Fiona's hand and run away. With a deep inhale, she rooted her feet and steadied herself. "It was a long time ago. It's okay. *I'm* okay."

It was the same speech Gloria had been telling herself for the past decade, hoping one day she'd believe it. She had come to terms with Fiona's beliefs and respected her decision to live according to them. But the wedding invitation with explicit instructions to stay away had fractured Gloria's heart. Fiona had made her feel like an evil temptation, a monster.

And still, Gloria couldn't help but push it all aside, more than willing to forgive at the first sight of the woman still stitched to her heart. After ten years of trying to move on, one chance meeting left Gloria feeling like a lovesick teenager again as a flurry of feelings overtook her rational thoughts. Her heart didn't care that she was forty-six or that Fiona was, most likely, still married. She couldn't help but hope this reunion meant something more.

"It's so good to see you! How are you doing?" Gloria asked, working extra hard to sound only casually interested.

Fiona smiled, albeit weakly. "I'm good. We're in town for the holiday to see family."

"In town? Where's home these days?"

"Boise." Fiona's eyes darted to the side like an animal checking potential predators.

Gloria followed her gaze, trying to read her nervous expression. "I hear Idaho is lovely. Are you here by yourself?"

"No," Fiona snapped back to attention, her smile a little brighter. "Chris is somewhere around here. We're grabbing a few things before heading to a Pioneer Day BBQ with his family."

"How great." Gloria forced a smile but couldn't hide the disgust in her voice.

Just thinking about Chris Blackwell sent hot prickles down Gloria's spine. She had only met him a couple of times, back when he and Fiona first dated, but it was enough. Manipulative and prone to angry outbursts, the only thing Gloria hated more than the man himself was that Fiona had ended up with him.

"He's buying some long-distance calling cards. Chris makes a lot of international calls these days," Fiona said, still hugging her sides. She rocked back on her heels, biting her lip.

Gloria didn't know what to say, especially because Fiona seemed equally lost for words. Neither woman dared move as some invisible link kept them frozen in the moment.

The hustle of people moving around the store filled the otherwise awkward silence. Squeaky shopping carts and the shuffle of feet against the linoleum floor provided a symphony to the unspoken words filling Gloria's mind. After years of considering what she would do if she saw Fiona again, Gloria couldn't summon a single thought. She just stared, surprised by how small and frail Fiona looked. Fi had always been petite, but now she looked like she could blow away with a tiny breeze.

"How's married life? Any kids?" Gloria finally asked, unable to bear the silence longer. But the look of pain that swept over Fiona's face at the question filled Gloria with instant regret.

"No," Fiona said, shaking her head. "We haven't yet been blessed with children."

"Oh, I'm sorry." Gloria quickly pressed on. "Are you working?"

"I'm helping Chris with this new business venture," Fiona said, cracking a small smile. "It's not really my thing, but he's very excited about it."

"Oh, Chris started a business?"

"He's launching next month." Fiona's gaze darted away again. She rubbed her arm, pushing her sleeve up and revealing a dark bruise.

"Oh my god, what happened?" Gloria asked, taking a step forward to inspect it.

Fiona quickly pulled her sleeve down, covering the black mark. "Oh, nothing. I just tripped."

Gloria looked closer, noticing a thick application of foundation and concealer under Fiona's left eye. Her hands balled into fists as her brain did the math. She lowered her voice. "Fi, is he hurting you?"

"Of course not," Fiona snapped. Her eyes grew wide as Chris walked around the corner into view. "There you are!"

Gloria panicked, wanting another minute—another lifetime —with Fi alone.

"Oh, my stars! Is that Gloria Wright?" Chris went in for a quick hug, slapping Gloria on the back as if they were lifelong friends.

Chris could be charming, which is what made him so dangerous. His all-American looks and dimpled smile perfectly matched his exuberant charisma. Combined with the pious devotion he loved announcing to the world, he fit in with the echelon of Mormon's best and brightest. Had Gloria not known his dark side and what he did to Fiona—and appeared to be doing *still*—she would never have suspected him of being an absolute monster.

"How the heck are you?" Chris said, cocking his head back. "I haven't seen you since—"

"—since I called the cops on you." Gloria smirked, folding her arms across her chest.

"Ha." Chris was clearly not amused. He clicked his tongue and nodded slowly.

Fiona squeezed his arm and met his gaze. "Let's not dwell on the past."

"You're right, sweetie. Water under the bridge." Chris took a small step forward and put out his hand. "I forgive you for involving the police in what was clearly a personal matter."

"You forgive *me*?" Gloria shook her head, her hand decidedly still tucked under her arms. "You harassed Fiona and refused to leave our apartment after she explicitly asked you to go."

"Glo, please," Fiona said, tensing even more.

"You always were spirited, Gloria. I'll give you that." Chris wrapped an arm around Fiona's waist, kissing her cheek. "This woman here is my everything. I wasn't about to let her go just because her roommate put some wild ideas in her mind, but I appreciate your intentions. I'm sure you thought you were doing what was best for Fiona, even if you misread the situation. Let's put the past behind us. What do you say?" He held out his hand again.

Gloria wanted to keep her arms folded in protest but caved when she saw Fiona's pleading eyes. She offered a quick, limp handshake.

Chris smirked. "Good girl." It took all of Gloria's strength not to punch him in the face. "There's not enough room for hate these days," he said, as if standing at a pulpit. "I'm focused on what I can do to improve the world."

"You don't say." The words pushed past Gloria's lips like razor blades.

"I'm launching an amazing new company guaranteed to empower and heal the world."

"That's a bold claim," Gloria said. "Starting a charity or something?"

"Essential oils," Chris said, pulling a business card from his pocket and stuffing it into her hand.

Gloria scoffed. "Essential oils?" Her eyes rolled so far back that she almost lost her balance. Chris didn't seem to notice.

"Trust me," he said. "This industry is ready to explode and change people's lives. And I'd be willing to let you join us on the ground floor."

"I'm not sure I'm ready to be baptized into the holy market of essential oils," Gloria said. "Nor do I have any interest in moving to Idaho."

"That's the best part!" Chris's eyes lit up. "You can earn a full-time income and be your own boss wherever you live. We're looking to establish our first batch of distributors who can share our amazing essential oils with their friends and neighbors."

"Like an Avon lady?"

"Much better." Chris was hyped up by his own marketing, not realizing how little he was actually saying. "This business could set you up for life, and it would make me so happy to see one of Fiona's friends on the path to living their dreams."

Fiona's *friend*. Did Chris have any idea what she and his wife had almost done—what they had meant to each other? He clearly didn't know Fiona the way Gloria did. How could he give his wife the life she deserved if he knew so little about her?

"I'm going to pass," Gloria said, handing the card back to him, "but thanks."

"You really should consider it. And if you don't want to talk to me, call Fiona. I just bought her a new Nokia." Chris pulled out a pen. He handed it and the business card to his wife. "Write down your mobile number."

Fiona's face went flush as her breath shortened. "Oh, I don't know. This is more your thing, dear."

Chris nudged his wife, his eyes forceful. Fiona took the pen and scribbled her information. He turned to Gloria. "I'm still working on getting this one to shine her light a little brighter. We've got good news to share, and like the Gospel of Jesus Christ, I want to spread the good word about the healing power of essential oils."

Fiona folded the business card in half and handed it to Gloria. Their eyes locked briefly, but Gloria saw a desperate supplication within that split second. She took the card, wanting to pause time as their fingers briefly touched.

"We got to run, sweetie," Chris said to Fiona before nodding Gloria's way. "It was nice running into you—a sign, I believe. I hope you take my offer seriously. Those who join early will undoubtedly reap the biggest rewards."

Gloria's eyes refused to look away from Fiona. "Good luck," she said. "I hope all your dreams come true."

Fiona smiled, blushing slightly at the comment.

"They will," Chris said as he dragged Fiona away.

As soon as they were gone, a rush of regret swept over Gloria as hundreds of unspoken questions suddenly found their voice. With so much to say, she didn't know if she'd ever have the chance. Her heart fluttered as she remembered Chris's card, realizing she finally had Fiona's contact information. Gloria unfolded the paper. Under the quickly scrawled digits were two little words. Her heart stopped as she read them: *Help me.*

18

"Do these body wraps really work?" a very pregnant woman asked as she picked through the basket of goodies in front of her.

"Absolutely. They are especially great for postpartum moms." Vicky crossed her legs, trying to remember if the woman's name was Katie or Kate. "When are you due, Kate?"

"Katie," the woman said. She smiled and patted her belly. "I'm hoping this little guy makes his big entrance next week. Heaven knows I'm ready!"

The other women chuckled.

Vicky scanned the eager group gathered in her living room. She was so thankful Becki introduced her to Stephanie back in February. Within two weeks of signing up, the therapist had enrolled six new people, proving she had a natural knack for the business and an impressive, untapped network. Still, Vicky didn't want to take any chances. With Convention only a few months away, she needed to build on Stephanie's momentum.

"Make sure you check out the stretch mark cream I threw in there. Great stuff."

Putting together goodie bags was just the beginning of Vicky's plan to conquer. With a closet full of Puremetics pills and potions—more than she could use in a lifetime—it cost her nothing to put together fabulous swag bags for Stephanie's friends. Still, Vicky knew freebies might attract customers, but they wouldn't ignite leaders. For that, she would need an emotional spark. Vicky sat back, waiting for the perfect moment to light the fire.

"How many children do you have?" Katie asked, the chattiest of the group.

"Four," Vicky said. And then, as if right on cue, Blaze burst into the kitchen with a blue-haired nuisance following close behind.

Jane.

The girl was more than a threat to her son's reputation and future. Jane was a constant reminder of all the time Vicky had wasted on Anna. Between the weekly mastermind calls, self-help books, new clothes, and even a personal introduction to Dr. Davis—Vicky had given Anna all the tools to succeed, and for what? She hadn't heard from the woman in weeks.

Blaze searched the kitchen for food while Jane scrolled through her phone. The two bantered a bit. Muffled laughter drifted into the living room while cabinet doors shut with heavy thuds. Vicky popped to her feet, excusing herself for a moment. It was time to mark her territory.

"Blaze, I'm kind of in the middle of something," Vicky said, purposely keeping her back to the girl. "Maybe it's best if Jane goes home."

"We're just grabbing a snack and heading up to my room."

A record scratched in Vicky's head. They had been over this a hundred times: No girls in the bedroom. "Food in the kitchen," she said. "You know the rules."

Blaze rolled his eyes. "Since when is that a rule?"

Since you started hanging out with Jane.

"It's fine," Jane said, inserting herself into the conversation. "My mom is coming to get me any minute. We'll keep quiet until she comes. Promise."

Vicky unclenched her jaw and smiled as she turned to Blaze. "Perfect. If you want a snack, get it quietly and eat at the counter."

"Whatever," Blaze said.

Vicky's heart wrenched at his callous response. She couldn't help but feel like her son was changing, becoming someone she didn't recognize. His moods were constantly fluctuating—angry one minute and sullen the next. He barely said two words about school or football anymore. But the major red flag was the amount of time he spent with Jane. So, of course, that's where Vicky put the blame. Yet, the more she pushed Blaze to hang out with his other friends, the more the girl showed up.

Blaze insisted they were just friends, but even if it were true, why *her*? He had always been popular. People clamored to be part of his inner circle. Why limit himself to someone so clearly below him?

Vicky pushed these thoughts aside, realizing now wasn't the time to dwell on them. She would not let Jane ruin tonight. She marched out of the kitchen and rejoined the party.

"So, Vicky, what's *your* favorite product?" Katie asked.

"Oh, that's like choosing a favorite child." Vicky laughed, tossing her hair over her shoulder. "Honestly, I use them all, all the time."

Stephanie chimed in. "It's only been two months, and I can tell the difference after using them." Her smile spread, taking over her entire face. "My skin is glowing; my energy is up. I'm not sure how I survived without these products."

Vicky beamed at this enthusiastic endorsement. Stephanie was a balm for Vicky's weary soul—an answer to her prayers after a challenging few months dealing with imposters. The two women continued praising the products while the group hung to every word. Seeing the glint in their eyes, Vicky knew it was time to light the match.

"The products *are* amazing," Vicky said as she stood, smoothing her blouse. "But my favorite thing about Puremetics isn't the supplements or skincare line. The best part about this company is what it has done to empower me and countless other women."

The doorbell rang, breaking the spell Vicky was carefully casting. She eyed Blaze, who read the urgent expression and went to investigate. Jane sat at the counter, sipping some water and quietly observing everything.

Vicky turned back to the group. The women sat poised, ready to be inspired. Their rapt attention eased Vicky back on track, filling her with purpose. *This is what you were made to do,* she reminded herself. *Focus on what matters and lead these women toward their potential.*

"Everyone here tonight has one thing in common. We're all moms." Vicky gracefully walked along the semi-circle of women, stopping in front of the very pregnant Katie. "Even if your child is not quite done baking."

A small laughter rippled through the group.

"And if there's one thing I know about moms, they'll do *anything* to give their kids the best life possible. And what could be better than being there for your children? Heavenly Father has consecrated motherhood. The home is our sacred dominion."

A small scoff echoed from the kitchen.

Vicky flinched, peeking at Jane through the corner of her eye.

"Some people might mock that holy calling," Vicky said, refocusing on the attentive crowd while trying to put Jane out of her mind. "Women of God know better."

The group leaned in, soaking up every word.

"Still, life is expensive." Vicky smiled, tossing her head back ever so slightly. "It can be hard to give our kids the opportunities we want, and that's why Puremetics is such a huge blessing. It's a company dedicated to helping mothers make money while providing a way for them to stay home."

Vicky glanced over at Stephanie, who shifted uncomfortably in her seat. Everyone knew Stephanie was a full-time therapist, mother, and devoted Mormon. It was risky to lean into the stay-at-home-mom angle, knowing Stephanie would be their direct upline. If Vicky pushed too far, she might offend Stephanie or scare away others from enrolling with her. Luckily, Vicky was skilled at dancing those delicate lines.

Besides, who's to say this wasn't a part of Heavenly Father's plan? Perhaps Vicky would inspire Stephanie to make her Puremetics business her *only* work, helping her leave the corporate world and return home. The idea energized Vicky. Her voice grew fuller and louder.

"Maybe you're just hoping for a little extra spending cash, or perhaps you'd like to earn enough to retire your husband—or yourself," Vicky said, smiling at Stephanie. "Imagine the whole family working toward one goal in the safety of your home." She paused, letting the idea sink in. "With Puremetics, it's all possible."

Katie raised her hand nervously. "But what if I'm terrible at selling? The idea of pushing products on my friends and family makes me feel uncomfortable." She looked around the group nervously.

"Tell me," Vicky said, undeterred by the question. "Have you ever tried a new restaurant or found a cute boutique you later raved about to your friends?"

"I mean, sure. Who hasn't?"

"Exactly," Vicky said with a smile. "Puremetics offers hundreds of products that can easily replace the ones you already buy. And these aren't the crappy, chemical-laden stuff sold at Target or even Sephora. Our products use the highest quality ingredients. Trust me, you'll *want* to tell the world about them. And unlike all those other times you raved about things you love, you'll get paid to talk about Puremetics."

Vicky could tell she had hooked the group. It was time to reel them in. She brought her hand to her lips, slightly bowing her head and waiting just long enough for the silence to magnify what she had already said. Vicky closed her eyes and imagined her own babies. She counted her blessings, recognized God's hand in her beautiful life, and summoned the Spirit to help touch the hearts of those willing to make a change.

"Heavenly Father designed you for this job," Vicky said, adding the tiniest catch in her small, sweet voice. She wanted the women to feel the emotional surge rising within her, hoping it would ripple into their hearts. "This is your chance to be with your kids. You can be a stay-at-home mom and contribute to the family finances without missing a precious milestone. And while you're doing the most important work at home, you'll also be helping other women do the same."

"Bullshit."

The word flew like an arrow from the kitchen, striking the group with perfect precision. Everyone's head flung back as their hands flew to gaping mouths. Vicky spun around, ready to kick Jane to the curb, but saw Anna standing there instead.

"This is absolute bullshit." Anna crossed her arms, armoring her chest as her eyes pierced like spears. "Puremetics is only interested in one thing: your money."

"Excuse me, ladies." Vicky's words seethed from her mouth as she barreled toward the kitchen. She snatched Anna by the shoulder and dragged her to the foyer. Jane and Blaze followed behind.

"What the hell do you think you're doing?" Vicky muttered

as she pushed Anna toward the front door. Even whispered, her words crashed against the walls with fury.

Anna dug her heels into the ground and flung a finger in Vicky's face. "No, what the hell are *you* doing? Are you actually using these women's beliefs to sell your shitty products?"

For a moment, Vicky felt an oppressive shame pressing against her chest at the accusation. She closed her eyes and shook her head, desperate to escape.

"I'm not sure what's worse," Anna said, not waiting for Vicky to respond. "Exploiting their faith or pressuring your leaders to get plastic surgery in an attempt to rank up."

"What?" Blaze flashed a scowl at his mother. "Mom, is that true?"

"I did nothing of the sort," Vicky snapped back.

Anna took a step closer. "What about Rachel Nelson? Ring a bell?"

The lump in Vicky's throat nearly choked her. She had only casually thrown the idea out to Becki back in January. She had no idea Becki ran with it. Vicky stumbled backward, grabbing Blaze's shoulder to steady herself.

"Is it true?" he whispered.

"You have no idea what you're talking about. I never said anything to Rachel," Vicky mumbled. She stood tall, facing Anna. "If anyone pushed the idea, it was Becki. Don't blame me."

"What about what happened in there?" Jane asked, pointing toward the kitchen. "You just told those women to join your pyramid scheme because—why? Because God expects them to be home, barefoot in the kitchen?"

"Oh, what do you know?" Vicky could barely contain her rage. "I will not apologize for sharing Puremetics as a means to living a righteous, Christian life. I'm sorry if I believe motherhood is sacred. Sue me."

Anna stood, tense and tight-lipped. "Jane, let's go."

"Gladly." Jane walked to the coat rack behind Vicky to grab her bag.

Blaze stopped her. "I'm so sorry about this," he said. "I'll call you tomorrow, okay?"

Jane half-smiled and nodded. She squeezed his arm and followed her mom to the door. Blaze scowled at his mother.

Vicky's heart plummeted, crashing to the earth with such impact that she wondered if it would ever be whole again. She stumbled backward as the world around her grew blurry. Throat tightening and temperature rising, Vicky tried to hide the uneasiness that threatened to knock her over. This was not the way it was supposed to go. She had built an empire and was adored by everyone. None of that mattered right now. A line was drawn. As her child crossed to the enemy side, it felt like the ultimate betrayal. Vicky was on her own.

"You're just jealous," she whispered.

Anna froze.

Jane whipped around. "How dare you!"

"Jane, it's fine." Anna turned, her solemn face inching closer with each deliberate step. "There is much to envy about your life, Vicky. Your house, your clothes, your business—it's all very impressive."

Vicky squeezed her eyes shut as her belly knotted and cheeks burned. A desperate desire to run away made it nearly impossible to stand still, but her feet were useless. Her heart was the only thing racing.

Anna's voice was calm and calculated. "At some point, you've got to ask yourself if it's worth it. Who did you have to climb over to get to the top? What lies did you have to tell?" She turned, followed Jane out the door, and slammed it shut.

Blaze stood stoic and unmoved with his eyes still set on the door. He shook his head and turned to Vicky. "I hope you're happy," he whispered before heading up the stairs.

Vicky watched as her son abandoned her, wondering how things could fall apart so quickly. She closed her eyes, feeling the anger, heartache, and embarrassment wash over her. Victoria Sterling was a lot of things. Happy was not one of them. Of course, that didn't stop her from slapping on a smile, marching back into her living room, and pretending nothing had changed.

19

"That was amazing!" Jane bounced in her chair, barely contained by the seatbelt, as they sped out of Splendor Springs.

"Not the word I would use." Anna clenched the steering wheel as her adrenaline continued to fire. She tried calming her nerves, steadying her breath as her eyes burned a path away from Vicky's house.

"Are you kidding me? Mom, you were fucking incredible!" Jane threw her head back against the seat's headrest. "The way you called Vicky out like that? Oh my god! So badass!"

The tiniest hint of pride struck Anna at this high praise. She quickly caught Jane's eyes and smiled. "It kind of was, huh?"

"Completely." Jane sighed as if reliving the moment. Her eyes drifted toward the evening sky. "I was worried you couldn't see what a dumpster fire Puremetics was. I'm so glad you're finally out."

Jane's words clawed their way to Anna's heart, pulling at the tangled mess of anger and fear that had strangled it for months. *Was* Anna done with Puremetics? That was the question she'd been wrestling with since February. If anything, her desire to see the company destroyed had only intensified over the last few months. The industry thrived on selling unattainable dreams and pushing products that capitalized on women's insecurities, fueling Anna's rage. But the more manipulation and lies she saw from its top leaders, the more she wanted to step back. She couldn't bring herself to play along, even if it were for a worthy cause.

Anytime Gloria asked for an update, Anna gave vague, evasive answers, hoping it would be enough to keep the OWLS from asking follow-up questions. She wanted them to assume things were on track while she figured out how to move forward without causing more harm. Despite her indecision, a part of her was still committed to seeing Gloria's plan through, proving she was up to the task.

Of course, Anna had no idea how that was even possible now. She was so far from the goalpost she wasn't even in the stadium. The only way back in the game was to sneak in another way. But how?

"I'm not sure I'm done with Puremetics," Anna finally said.

Jane turned. Her eyes were large with disbelief. "Are you serious?"

Anna's hands started to shake as panic filled her chest. She pulled over to the side of the road, trying to steady her breath.

"Mom, it's a fucking pyramid scheme."

"It's complicated. I can't—"

"—you can't *what*?" Jane's voice was unforgiving. "You've seen the way these rich, privileged women prey on vulnerable people. How much money have you spent on this thing? You know you'll never earn any of it back without ensnaring others."

"I know," Anna muttered.

"Then why the hell would you keep doing it?" Fear clipped the exasperated tone of Jane's voice.

A car zoomed past while they sat frozen. As the engine's roar diminished, the silence between Anna and Jane grew unbearable. Anna stared at her hands, frantically looking for a way to help her daughter see the truth without abandoning her promise to Gloria. As she sifted through a thousand potential responses, Anna realized there was no way to keep her commitment and not hurt Jane.

When put in those terms, the answer was simple.

"There's something you need to know." Anna paused, choosing her words carefully. She remembered her explosive confession to Lisa and hoped to approach this conversation more gracefully. But maybe that was the problem. Anna was sick of filtering her thoughts, tired of all the scripts. Perhaps radical honesty was a superpower worth harnessing. After all, things with Lisa turned out surprisingly well.

At that thought, an idea took root. Branches of inspiration sprung from Anna's mind, twisting their way to the light, suddenly revealing a path forward. Her heart raced as she double-checked her thoughts, unconvinced the answer could be so simple.

"That's it."

"What is?" Jane folded her arms. "What possible reason could you give to justify sticking with Puremetics?"

Anna smiled as she started the car again and set her GPS to Lisa's house. She merged back on the road, suddenly self-assured at the steps she needed to take.

The first one was to tell Jane everything.

"It all started when I showed up at the wrong house."

"I need a computer," Anna said, pushing herself past Lisa.

"Hello to you, too." Lisa stood beside her front door, noticing Jane still outside. "Hey, Jane. Come on in."

"You need to excuse Mom," Jane said, hurrying inside. "She's following a hunch."

Lisa laughed. "Oh, intrigue!"

Anna paced along the small but modern kitchen while waiting for Lisa to grab her laptop. She spent the last fifteen minutes catching Jane up on the Puremetics saga. As Anna anticipated, Jane licked up every juicy detail and was eager to join the cause. "You are so much cooler than I ever thought," Jane had said. Anna took the words to heart, hoping they would be enough to push her across the finish line.

Lisa returned with her laptop and handed it to Anna. She sat on the sofa and got to work without a word, typing frantically, hoping her idea had legs to run.

"Any clue what this is about?" Lisa asked Jane.

Jane smiled, bringing her fingers in front of her, tapping them like a cartoon villain. "Operation: Take Down Puremetics."

"Ah! I see your mom finally caved and spilled the beans." Lisa wrapped an arm around Jane's shoulder. "Good! Welcome to the club. I bet you'll have some tricks to help take down Christian White."

Anna looked up. "Jane, just because you know the plan doesn't mean I'm letting you get caught up in this mess. You stay out of trouble. Understand?"

"She said the same thing to me," Lisa said, shaking her head.

"Mom, I'm not letting you have all the fun!" Jane plopped down on the couch next to Anna. "Besides, who would suspect a teenager of sabotage? I'm like the best kind of secret weapon."

Anna hit *Enter* and watched the screen populate its findings. Her eyes lit up at the nearly endless list of results.

"What are you looking for?" Lisa asked, sitting on the other side of Anna.

"An army." Anna smiled, scrolling down the page.

Lisa shot a glance at Jane, who shrugged in return. "Explain yourself, woman."

"I can't believe it took me this long to realize my problem." Anna shook her head. "This whole time, Gloria told me to play by Vicky's rules. Follow her scripts. Be her clone. I was supposed to do whatever she said in hopes of building a downline big enough to get to the Leadership Gala."

Jane raised an eyebrow. "Yeah, and?"

Anna turned to her daughter, her hands gesturing with excitement. "The plan requires me to lie to people, to enroll innocent women in a toxic business. There's a reason Lisa is my only recruit."

Lisa laughed. "Yeah, because you're a horrible salesperson."

"And because you're not a predator," Jane chimed in.

Anna laughed. "Both are true, and that's why I've been spinning my wheels for *months* with nothing to show for it. So, I started thinking: Why not repeat the process that *did* bring me success?"

Lisa leaned back and chuckled. "Ambush your boss in the parking lot?"

"God, no," Jane said.

Anna shook her head. "If Gloria is right, this White guy has made a lot of enemies over the years. We know he has the money and influence to shove most of his problems under the rug, but he can't erase people's memories. There's got to be more people like Gloria who are desperate to see him taken down a notch." She locked her gaze on Lisa. "There must be more people like you. People willing to pay for a little justice."

Jane clapped her hands. "Oh my god! Yes!"

Anna pointed to the computer. "Look what came up when I searched *Puremetics, Christian White, scam,* and *revenge.* There are thousands of hits."

Lisa turned the computer toward her, reading the top results. "Most of these are talking about Puremetics's rapid rise in the market—hardly scandalous. Their PR machine has done a good job scrubbing the search results."

"But look further down the list." Anna scrolled. "There are plenty of articles pointing to problems. It's not all positive. Maybe I can reach out to some of these bloggers."

"I don't know. It looks like the same person writes a lot of these articles." Lisa clicked the mouse while her eyes danced across the screen. "And there doesn't seem to be an easy way to contact them. I like where you're going with this, but how will you find enough people to join your cause?"

"Wait." Jane grabbed Anna's arm. Her eyes focused intently on her phone. "Search for Aroma Harmony."

Anna typed the phrase. "Why?"

Jane sighed, shaking her head. She turned her phone, showing a post about Christian White. "Did you know Christian White used to be Chris Blackwell and that Puremetics was not his first business? Aroma Harmony was."

"Oh my god," Lisa said. "My mom got roped into Aroma Harmony years ago! She talked about the CEO—this Blackwell guy, like he was practically Jesus. It took over her entire life, even her personality. After she spent $10,000 and earned less than $200, my dad put his foot down. They nearly divorced over it."

Jane read aloud. "After Aroma Harmony failed, Blackwell legally changed his name to Christian White and relocated to Alpine, Utah, where he currently runs the company Puremetics."

Lisa leaned back in her chair. "Well, damn."

Anna peeked at Jane's phone. "Where did you read that?"

"It's some forum online. But there are pictures of both Blackwell and Christian. It's totally the same guy."

Anna rubbed the sides of her head, wondering what this all meant. Why hadn't Gloria mentioned any of this? She had to know, right? Anna thought about the woman from the mural—Christian's wife. Was that before or after Chris changed his name? How far back did Gloria's relationship go? If anything, Aroma Harmony's demise would strengthen a case against White. Was it possible Gloria didn't know any of this?

Pushing these thoughts aside, Anna continued down the rabbit hole. It only took a few minutes to understand Aroma Harmony's rapid rise and even quicker demise. Founded in

Idaho, the company grew to nearly a billion dollars within nine years of opening. They promoted their line of essential oils as the cleanest, purest products on the market. Third-party testing revealed White was cutting his oils with cheap ingredients, some of which caused severe allergic reactions and even a handful of hospitalizations. Business tanked after FDA regulations nearly shut the company down. Instead of course correcting, White jumped ship, leaving thousands of distributors high and dry.

Less than two years later, Puremetics was born.

Anna shook her head, amazed by the story unfurling before her eyes.

"Hey, check this out," Jane said, pulling up a link on the computer. "I think I found something."

It was a post from an online forum called *Aroma Harmony Justice*. Anna clicked the pinned post, dated five years ago, and read it out loud:

Warning: Puremetics
>   by AromaTruthUnveiled

Hey everyone, I can't believe I'm writing this, but I recently stumbled upon some unsettling news. Chris Blackwell has resurfaced in Utah and rebranded himself as Christian White. I thought I could finally put the nightmare of Aroma Harmony behind me, but Chris is launching a new MLM called Puremetics. It's like a sequel to a bad horror movie.

As most of you know, many former distributors tried to seek justice after Aroma Harmony crumbled. We filed complaints with the FTC, collaborated with consumer advocacy groups, and even considered a class-action lawsuit.

Our attempts to gather evidence against Chris were often thwarted. Documents mysteriously went missing, and witnesses were afraid to speak out, fearing retaliation. Moreover, Chris quickly hired high-profile lawyers who skillfully navigated legal loopholes. Every move we made was countered with a legal strategy that left us at a disadvantage. Even worse, White had the money to bury most of our work. Only the truly persistent would find any evidence of foul play.

Some of us received anonymous threats and warnings to stay silent. Chris wasn't playing fair, and the fear of personal harm silenced many potential whistleblowers. Then, Chris cleverly dissolved Aroma Harmony, making it difficult for any meaningful accountability. On top of it all, many hard-working distributors lost much-needed income while everyone else was left with useless products worth thousands of dollars.

It's disheartening to see our hopes for justice dwindle. Many of us have given up the fight, feeling defeated and exhausted. Chris has learned to manipulate the system, leaving us powerless against his schemes.

So, if you hear whispers of Puremetics and a certain Christian White, be wary. We may never get the closure we hoped for, but at least we can warn others about the dangers lurking behind these MLM schemes.

Stay vigilant, my friends.
   - AromaTruthUnveiled

Hundreds of comments followed. Most expressed concern over this news, voicing their desire to protect others from Chris's unethical practices. A few replies were from old distributors who had joined different MLM companies, trying to recruit people to their new gig. And there were the odd outliers who added little to the conversation beyond a few crazy conspiracy theories. Anna's personal favorite was the guy who insisted Chris was an alien. Reading through them all, Anna felt the rage of injustice simmering inside. But one comment stopped her dead in her tracks.

"Listen to this reply," Anna said, her eyes wide with disbelief. She inhaled sharply, afraid to give the words a voice as if reading the comment would legitimize it. "Has anyone else wondered about the mysterious disappearance of Blackwell's wife? It's like she vanished into thin air."

Jane leaned over, reading the response underneath. "Was it foul play, or did she run away? Why is there no information about her?"

Anna felt her stomach drop.

"Whoa," Jane said. "It just keeps getting worse."

Lisa pushed the computer away. "Don't believe everything you read online. It's a pretty wild claim on an anonymous website with no proof to back it up. There's enough evidence to prove White's a garbage human being without having to sensationalize crazy rumors."

"Yeah," Anna said, hoping Lisa was right. Swirls of color filled her mind until it felt like Gloria's mural was right in front of her. The upward lift of Fiona's chin. The pained expression on her face. The phoenix rising from the ashes. What if the rumor was true?

Anna felt a chill as she realized Gloria might be motivated by revenge.

"This is promising!" Lisa's bright voice snapped Anna back to attention. "You can direct message people inside the forum."

A twinge of hope rose in Anna's belly as she sidestepped the unsettling questions piling at her feet. She grabbed the computer and clicked on the forum's home page. "The community has over three thousand subscribers."

"But the most recent post is more than two years old," Jane said, pointing to the date. "Are any of these people still around?"

"There's only one way to find out." Anna returned to the pinned post, clicked on AromaTruthUnveiled's profile, and tapped the private message link. A smile crept along her face as she began typing a message.

"What are you doing?" Jane asked.

"Enlisting our army."

20

The steady stream of water on the other side of the wall drowned out Vicky's thumping heart. Blaze could easily spend twenty minutes in the shower—giving her more than enough time to skim his texts, but that didn't calm Vicky's nerves as she scrolled through hundreds of messages. Perched on the side of his bed, she hunched over his phone like a raccoon digging through a garbage can.

There had to be something to prove Vicky wasn't crazy. A confession of love, pressure to do drugs, requests for nudes—she would take anything to give her a reason to ban Jane from Blaze's life once and for all.

Justifying this blatant breach of privacy was easy. Vicky only wanted what was best for her son, and it's not that she didn't trust Blaze. He was a straight-A student, captain of the football team, and an active member of the seminary council. Prying into his personal life only became necessary when he met *her*. Removing the blue-haired cancer was the only way to get her sweet, once-loyal son back.

How else could Vicky explain the traitorous look from earlier that night? Blaze had landed his sympathy on Jane instead of his own mother, even though Vicky was the true victim. Anna had embarrassed her in front of her friends and ruined her sales pitch. It was unthinkable that Blaze would choose their side and cast Vicky as the villain.

Jane had undoubtedly corrupted her son, turning him against his family.

It was only a matter of time until he abandoned his faith.

The thought made Vicky's toes curl. Determined to intervene before that happened, she had no choice but to investigate. She waited for Blaze to shower. The moment the bathroom lock clicked, she dove into action. Vicky snuck into his room, unlocked his phone, and scrolled to the very top of a long thread of messages, ready to be shocked—and vindicated.

She started at the beginning of their back-and-forth exchange. There was little proof of foul play. Messages were short, with days or weeks in between new ones. Questions about biology exams and information about football games made Vicky question her sanity. Maybe Jack was right. Perhaps she made this whole story up in her mind. Was it possible she had overreacted?

The conversation picked up speed further down the timeline. As November rolled into December, signs of a genuine friendship emerged from the blue and gray bubbles. At one point, the texts transitioned into an array of movie quotes. After a while, the letters morphed, becoming a sea of emojis. Vicky rolled her eyes, trying to decipher any subtext among the icons. But as far as she could tell, there still was no indication of romantic feelings or inappropriate interaction.

That was good, right? She wanted Blaze to be safe, and by all accounts, he was.

But as disappointment settled in, Vicky was forced to face the truth: If there was no foul play, the problem wasn't with Jane. It was with *her*.

Vicky gripped the phone, her fingers turning white from the pressure, determined to keep digging. After a few more lines about biology, a string of bad dad jokes, and a handful of ride requests, the conversation took an abrupt turn.

> Hey, can I tell you something?

Of course

> It's kind of personal

Oh? That's ok. Hit me with it.

> I'm gay.

Vicky's heart stopped as she read the last line. Then everything stopped. The world crashed into her, knocking the air from her lungs. She gasped as she reread the two words that turned everything upside down: *I'm gay.*

She cupped her hand over her mouth, keeping her insides from leaping out of her body. This wasn't the proof she wanted. Where was the text of Jane confessing her feelings? Or the one where Blaze asks for more pot? Vicky had prepared herself for those possibilities, not this.

Anything but this.

I'm gay. The words grew bigger and bigger, consuming her whole. They chewed her body and spit her out. Still, Vicky couldn't shake them. The line repeated over and over and over. *I'm gay. I'm gay. I'm gay.*

It couldn't be true.

I'm gay.

Blaze was straight. He liked girls. Vicky remembered him talking about his former crushes: Paige or Sage or something like that. It had been so long ago that she couldn't remember. Denial dripped into Vicky's brain, trying to wash away this stain that was spreading by the minute. Her precious, beautiful child was supposed to go on a mission and get married in the temple. He could *not* be gay. That was not the plan. This is not how his story would go—not the life she had worked for.

Vicky's hand shook as she scrolled the conversation forward, praying it was all a joke. It had to be! Her heart jackhammered against her chest, and she read on, waiting for the punchline.

> Wow. I'm not sure what to say other than I think you're amazing, and it means a lot that you'd share this piece of you with me.

> Nobody else knows.

> You can't tell anyone.

> Never!

> But if it's who you really are, why hide it?

> Aren't you hiding something, too?

> What do you mean?

> I heard rumors.

> That you're a lesbian.

"I knew it!" Vicky punctuated her words with a swing of her fist. Jane *was* the problem. She was the outsider, the outcast, the one who had put these crazy thoughts in Blaze's head. This confirmation gave Vicky hope that she could still save her son. He wasn't lost, just confused. Vicky could remind him who he really was.

With a quick flick of her finger, Vicky pressed forward, eager to see Jane's response.

> OMG. People are stupid.

I know I don't fit the mold around here, but I promise there are actual lesbians at this school who look exactly like your typical Mormon girl.

So, you're not?

No. I'm not into the ladies. Honestly, I'm not really into anyone.

Wait, is that why you're telling me your secret?

No!

Maybe.

I just figured you'd understand. It doesn't matter. I trust you. You make me feel like I can be myself. So, thanks.

Anyway, I just needed to tell you. To tell someone. My parents would flip if they knew.

Your secret is safe. Promise.

"Mom!"

Vicky spun around, dropping Blaze's phone on the floor with a loud whack.

Blaze stood, wrapped in a robe, his hair dripping on the carpet. "What the hell are you doing?" He lunged forward, snatching the device from off the ground. "Were you snooping?"

"What? Of course not!" The words flew from Vicky's mouth despite the blatant lie.

Blaze unlocked the device, his eyebrows furrowed as he read the screen. Anger quickly morphed into fear. The color from his cheeks drained as his face turned a ghostly white. He looked up, mouth gaping, chest retreating. "Did you read this?"

Vicky nodded as tears welled in her eyes. She didn't know what to say—or how to feel, for that matter. She had been caught red-handed, but so had Blaze. His secret was suddenly, forcefully, out in the open, and neither knew what to do with it.

A million thoughts raced through Vicky's mind. How could this happen? Were there signs she missed? Could she have prevented it? Had he acted on his feelings? All the questions spun, picking up speed, and settled into one fear: that she would lose her son—forever.

There was no way around the truth. If this was who Blaze was, his eternal salvation was at risk. Could he be fixed? Would he be willing to live alone? Live a lie? Have a righteous family? Fulfill his covenants? Or would he give in to temptation, removing any chance for a celestial life?

It was too much. Vicky's heart wasn't just broken; her entire world had shattered.

The two stood, staring at one another as if looking away would untether them both. Downstairs, Ryker and Tymberlee were fighting. Music blared from Jaelyn's room across the hall. Jack yelled from his office, telling the younger two to keep it down. Evidence of their once ordinary life crashed against Blaze and Vicky as they stood unmoved.

There was no way to undo it. But maybe, Vicky hoped, they wouldn't have to move forward if they both stayed still.

"Are you going to tell Dad?" Blaze finally whispered.

Vicky opened her mouth, unsure what to say. Of course, Jack needed to know. This matter was far too important to ignore, and Jack was the spiritual head of the house. If Blaze was struggling with these feelings, the sooner they stepped in to help, the better.

But the look in Blaze's eyes forced Vicky to shake her head.

"I won't tell him until you are ready," she said, terrified by her low, shaky voice. Where was the confident woman who always knew what to do? More to the point, where was God in all of this? She blushed with shame just thinking about how abandoned she felt.

Blaze nodded. "Do you hate me?"

Vicky wanted to yell, *No!* She wanted to wrap her child in her arms like when he was little, but all she could picture was having him ripped from their eternal family. Scraped knees and baseballs through windows were easy to fix. Vicky had always known how to comfort her son, but she didn't know how to deal with *this*. There was no easy answer, no guidebook. Layers of beliefs and doctrine shrouded her maternal instincts, keeping her feet planted instead of propelling her to comfort her child.

Of course, Vicky loved Blaze. Nothing would change that. But as the weight of this news slammed down, she felt trapped. So, she did not answer his question. She did not run into Blaze's arms or smother him with the reassurance of her love. Instead, Vicky ran away, stuffing the truth so far down it might as well be buried six feet under. It was the same thing she did the last time her salvation was on the line: She pretended nothing had happened.

21

A blast of wind rushed past Gloria as she fumbled through her purse. She zipped her coat and tightened the scarf around her neck. Thankfully, it hadn't snowed yet, but the temperature had dropped considerably since arriving at the bus station.

Her fingers, red and nearly frozen, dug into the bottom of her bag. She exhaled with relief when they touched the cold metal of a coin. She pulled out a quarter, smiled, and hurried to the pay phone.

Gripping the coin with one hand, Gloria reached for the business card in her back pocket and turned it over. The desperate *help me* scrawled on the back in Fiona's handwriting always made her stomach plunge no matter how many times she read it. When Chris handed Gloria the card back in July, she had no idea what journey it would initiate or the months of planning required to get her here in Payson, Utah, waiting for shuttle number 604.

The card with Fiona's secret message had pushed Gloria into action. She called Fiona that same night. And then the next day

—and the one after that. There was no response for nearly a week, filling Gloria's imagination with horrible possibilities. She couldn't sleep, had lost her appetite. Fueled by terror and a knowledge of Chris's abusive manipulation, Gloria was determined to keep calling until she heard Fiona's voice.

Finally, that moment came.

"Are you okay?" Gloria's words slammed into the phone like a wrecking ball. "What do you need?"

"Gloria! What a pleasant surprise." Fiona's airy tone moved right past the wreckage.

Gloria frowned, flinching her head back slightly. There was a flutter in her stomach as she pressed her sweaty palm against the back of her neck, trying to escape the sudden heat rising from within.

"Chris will be so happy to hear you've considered his offer."

Gloria closed her eyes and shook her head as she tried to make sense of the stilted pleasantry coming from the other side of the phone. *Help me,* the card had said. Not *join me* or *grow a business with me.* Fiona was in trouble. There was no other way to interpret it. The single thought had consumed Gloria over the last few days, tunneling her vision until all she saw was Fiona.

Had she misread the situation?

A million doubts threatened to knock Gloria down as she steadied herself against the wall. After planning for every worst-case scenario, it seemed unthinkable that Fiona was only interested in selling an opportunity.

"I'm calling about the message on the card," Gloria said. She banged her head against the wall as her shoulders drooped forward. "I thought you were in trouble."

"That's great! I'd love to tell you more about the business. Give me a second, and I'll get that information for you. Hold on."

Gloria stood dumbfounded. What the hell was going on?

A few muffled moments later, Fiona's voice returned through

the receiver. "Sorry, Glo. Chris was standing next to me. I needed an excuse to get away."

"Oh my god, Fi. Are you okay? What's going on?" Gloria's body buzzed with adrenaline. The only things keeping her from combusting were a drive for answers and a desperation to help.

"I'm fine," Fiona said, lowering her voice so quiet it cracked. "I mean, I'm not fine. I need out, Glo."

"Out of what? Your house?"

"Out of my house, this marriage, this church. I can't take it."

"Are you safe? Are you in immediate danger? Is Chris hurting you?" Gloria's brain was running faster than her mouth. "I can come get you. I'll hop in the car. Boise is, what? Six hours away? That's nothing."

"It's not that simple." Fiona paused, amplifying the choppiness of her breath.

Every second of silence felt like a threat. "What do you mean? It's not a problem. I can come. I'll do it."

"No." The response was firm, unyielding. "I can't just leave without a plan. Chris will figure it out and bring me back."

Forget a plan. Gloria was ready to fight. She could take Chris. Her rage demanded justice; the consequences be damned. She sighed, shaking off the urge to attack. The goal was to help Fiona, not get revenge. "So what then?"

"I need a whole new life—a clean break." There was a catch in Fiona's voice. She cleared her throat and spoke as if she only had seconds to get the message out. "I must ensure Chris can't trace anything back to me. This phone? He checks my records. He'll see that we talked. Do not call this number again. I'll email you. I set up a new account I only use from the library. What's your address?"

Gloria focused on her breath, trying to see a path forward. Fiona was right. For this to work, they needed to be thoughtful, careful.

"My email is GloriaWright50@hotmail.com."

"Perfect," Fiona said. "I'll message you in the next few days. I'm going to need your help."

"Of course. I'll do anything."

Gloria closed her eyes as one compelling question lingered behind. She was unsure if she wanted to ask it but certain she'd regret not knowing the answer. "Where will you go?" She braced herself against the wall, knowing it was unwise to put her hopes on the line just yet. "You can always stay with me."

There was another long pause. The silence seeped into every crack of Gloria's heart, threatening to burst it open.

"I don't know," Fiona barely croaked out.

It wasn't the answer Gloria wanted, but it still made space for hope. She exhaled, releasing the pressure in her chest. "That's okay. I just want you to be safe, Fi. I hope you know that. Safe and happy."

"I know, and I appreciate it. I'll be in touch soon."

It was the only phone call between the women. True to her word, Gloria waited for an email. Together, Gloria and Fiona worked out every detail of Fiona's escape. The plan was to slowly stow away necessities: clothes, money, and essential documents. Fiona created a separate checking account, updated passwords, and discussed filing a protective order with a lawyer. It all had to be done discreetly, unsure who Fiona could trust. Chris wasn't just well-liked. He was extremely well-connected. One false step and it could end badly.

Now, nearly four months later, Gloria feared the worst had happened.

Fiona's shuttle had come and gone with no sign of her. Gloria held on to the possibility that she had taken a later bus, but after more than two hours of waiting, that hope was fading fast. The best-case scenario was that Chris suddenly changed his schedule, forcing Fiona to try again next week. But it was also possible Fiona had changed her mind—or worse, that Chris had figured out the plan and ended it.

That was a thought Gloria didn't want to dwell on. Not yet.

The coin stood ready to drop in the phone's slot when Gloria snapped it back into her hand. No matter how much she wanted answers, calling Fiona's mobile phone was a surefire way to mess things up.

"Give it a few more minutes," Gloria muttered, trying to keep her spirits up. "She'll be here soon."

She stuffed the quarter and card in her pocket and sauntered back to the bus stop, grateful for its tiny enclosure as the first signs of flurries appeared in the sky. Three shuttles and six local buses had come and gone, dropping off or picking up only a few passengers. The small stop just outside Payson, Utah, was hardly a popular destination, which is why Gloria chose it.

"Do you think we'll get a lot of snow tonight?" a man asked as Gloria sat beside him. His wool cap, thick scarf, and knee-length coat made it impossible to know his appearance or age.

"Looks like it," Gloria said, not particularly in the mood to chat. She leaned back, counting the lines of the tiny roof overhead.

"Heading anywhere fun?" The man's words were light and conversational, but his tone was meaty and pointed.

"No. I was supposed to pick up a friend, but it looks like her bus is running late."

"Buses do that. How long have you been waiting?"

Gloria pushed back the sleeve of her parka, noting the time on her watch. It was even later than she thought. "Almost three hours."

The man guffawed. "Where is she coming from? The moon?"

"Out of state," Gloria said flatly. She didn't want to talk anymore. With every passing minute, she worried something had gone wrong. But there were other contingencies they had planned for, including later shuttles. Gloria had orders to stay put until Fiona stepped off the bus.

After waiting ten years, Gloria could wait a few more hours.

The squeaky breaks of a north-bound shuttle pierced the air. The man got up, brushing off a couple of snowflakes from his wool coat. He was taller and broader than Gloria expected. His eyes latched on to her as he pulled out an envelope.

"Be careful out there," he said, leaning closer and handing her the package. His voice went low. "I'd hate for you to get hurt."

Gloria sat frozen in her seat as her heart tried to jump from her chest. The man boarded the bus and moved to a center seat. He shot one more menacing look at Gloria before the vehicle pulled out.

When the bus was out of sight, Gloria ripped open the envelope and unfolded the paper inside. Her hands shook, crumpling the note as she read.

Gloria,

I appreciate your concern, but I've changed my mind. Please know I am happy and well. While I value your friendship, it would be best if we never talk again.

Sincerely,

Fiona

Gloria had memorized every curve and slant of Fiona's terrifying *help me*. She reached for the business card in her pocket to confirm what she already knew: The handwriting on this note was not Fiona's.

22

"Mom, why are you crying?" Tymberlee whispered, tugging on Vicky's sleeve. The organ played *The Spirit of God* at the same tempo as Chopin's *Funeral March*. The congregation's voices lagged as the organist struggled to pick up the pace.

"I'm fine," Vicky whispered as she pushed away a tear and continued to sing.

Her eyes drifted toward Blaze, sitting on the other side of his siblings. He slumped over, elbows on knees and head nestled in his hands. As if sensing Vicky's watchful eye, he turned, catching her gaze for only a second before they both snapped their attention forward.

It had been over two months since Vicky learned Blaze's secret. Two months since the image of her perfect family shattered, leaving her cut and bleeding as she tried to put the pieces back together. She hadn't spoken to Blaze since that night in his bedroom. Not really, at least. Both pretended nothing happened. Vicky would ask him to put away the laundry or to pick up

Jaelyn from ballet. Blaze would remind her about his sports camp fees or say he needed more shampoo.

This attempt to uphold their normal routine while quietly denying anything had changed did little to numb the pain. Vicky knew these small, meaningless interactions only widened the gap between her and Blaze. He spent more time away from home, usually at Jane's. Despite her uneasiness toward the girl, Vicky was glad that somebody supported her son—it was more than Vicky could apparently do.

What kind of parent stood idly by while their child suffered?

Vicky pressed her eyelids shut, hating the answer that echoed back: The same kind who would give one of His precious children this ungodly cross to bear.

True to her word, Vicky hadn't said a thing to Jack, although she almost divulged the secret a few times. The first was when Jack suggested Blaze ask out one of the Sorenson girls who moved in down the street in May. The twin sixteen-year-olds had been hanging around the house since they first saw Blaze. When Jack mentioned it, Vicky watched her son fumble for an excuse, and she almost intercepted by spilling the truth.

The other two times were late at night, when Vicky and Jack were tucked in bed, lights off. Protected by the cover of night, Vicky considered letting the secret slip, hoping the responsibility of bearing it alone would give way. But each time she parted her lips to say the words, nothing came.

Vicky wanted to believe it was her integrity that kept the secret guarded. After all, she had promised not to say anything until Blaze was ready, his pleading eyes convincing her to stay silent. But really, Vicky kept quiet because she hoped the truth would eventually die if left long enough in the dark.

In the meantime, she focused on keeping the house sparkling, her figure trim, and her business thriving, foolish enough to believe keeping busy would somehow turn back time.

If she worked hard enough, they could go back to the way things were.

It was an act she could almost believe. Almost.

All it took was seeing Blaze, slumped over at the other end of the pew to crack the facade. Her sweet, precious firstborn was gay, and it felt like Vicky's world had compressed inward.

There was a time when the Church rejected the idea that anyone was born this way, and pockets of members held on to that old belief. Vicky knew better. She believed her son was who he said he was, which is what made this so hard. There was no way to change or fix him. Blaze had to choose between living a lonely life or sinning against God, between temporary happiness on earth or the joy of eternal salvation. No matter how hard Vicky tried to find a way around those doctrinal truths, she kept hitting a wall. She found herself grasping for air as the weight of his confession continued to crush her.

Vicky wiped another tear and suddenly realized she had missed the opening prayer. As the congregation said their solemn *amen*, she sat taller, hoping nobody noticed.

"Dear Brothers and Sisters," Jack said as he adjusted the pulpit's microphone. "I have been asked to read a letter from the First Presidency."

Rustling papers, inaudible whispers, and the constant shifting of bodies all stopped. While not uncommon, direct counsel from the church's top leadership garnered more reverence than the typical Sunday announcements, even if the message came via form letter.

Jack cleared his throat. Vicky couldn't help but notice there was a catch in his voice. His typically broad posture was sagging ever-so-slightly as if he was wrestling with his own demons. Did he know about Blaze?

He took a moment before reading the letter. "Enclosed is a statement by the Council of the First Presidency and Quorum of the Twelve in response to the recent Supreme Court decision legalizing same-sex marriage in the United States."

A sob escaped Vicky's lips as a swell of emotion caught her off guard. The world had been buzzing with the recent news. She had overheard people discussing the implications of the court's decisions at the grocery store, at PTA meetings, and everywhere online. It was all salt on an open wound. Church was supposed to be her sanctuary. Vicky grabbed Tymberlee's hand and squeezed it hard.

"Ouch, Mom!"

"Sorry, honey," Vicky whispered, quickly releasing her daughter's hand. Her unrelenting heartbreak was momentarily replaced with embarrassment as Tymber's yelp echoed through the chapel. Vicky took a tissue from her purse, wiped her nose, and squeezed the wad of paper in her palm as if her life depended on it.

Jack continued reading the long letter. His voice was forced and cautious. "Because of the recent decision of the United States Supreme Court and similar legislative actions in a number of countries that have given civil recognition to same-sex marriage relationships..."

A mixture of emotions battled in Vicky's heart. The growing acceptance of the LGBT community eased her mind anytime she thought about her son's safety. But the opposing dread about Blaze's eternal salvation was hard to subdue. It kept throwing punches, threatening a total knockout. The Church's stance on homosexuality was unmistakable. If Blaze chose to marry another man, he would not be fit for the Celestial Kingdom. He'd be lost to his family forever.

"The Church of Jesus Christ of Latter-day Saints restates and reaffirms the doctrinal foundation of Church teachings on morality, marriage, and the family," Jack continued to read. "Marriage between a man and a woman was instituted by God and is central to His plan for His children and the well-being of society."

Vicky couldn't shake the feeling that Jack knew something. He seemed conflicted as he read the words to the congregation, which was atypical for a man who never strayed from doctrine. She wanted to see how Blaze was reacting but couldn't bring herself to look in his direction; afraid eye contact would be her undoing.

Jack continued. "A family built on the marriage of a man and a woman is the best setting for God's plan of happiness to thrive. That is why communities and nations generally have encouraged and protected marriage between a man and a woman, and the family that results from their union, as privileged institutions." He paused, taking a moment to settle the growing emotion in his voice. "Sexual relations outside of such a marriage are contrary to the laws of God pertaining to morality."

His eyes lifted from the page and locked with Vicky's, and she suddenly saw the cross he was bearing. It had nothing to do with Blaze and everything to do with her. Their son might have been struggling with feelings of attraction, but he hadn't broken the law of chastity yet. He hadn't acted on his inclinations.

Vicky and Jack had.

Eighteen years ago.

In the back of Jack's car.

Vicky's hands shook, just like they had that December night in 1996.

"We're going to get married anyway," Jack had said after zipping his pants. "We love each other. It's not the end of the world."

Two weeks later, after a faint pink line appeared on the plastic pregnancy test, it felt like the end to Vicky. At just eighteen, she wasn't ready for marriage. Despite being told the right place for any righteous woman was inside the home, Vicky dared to see herself doing something else. She loved science and math in high school and had considered pursuing both in college. Before chaining herself to a house and kids, she wanted to attend graduate school, travel, and maybe even start a career.

Sure, Vicky wanted a family. She understood the importance of motherhood. Her testimony of God's plan was strong, but she didn't see why she couldn't explore her options and live a little for herself before sacrificing it all for the next generation.

That was before she met Jack.

He was Vicky's first serious boyfriend and a returned missionary, placing him head and shoulders above those high school boys she dated. But more than that, Jack was an actual catch. He was cute, clever, and working toward law school—all of which made him an attractive prospect. And sure, Vicky had occasionally caught herself daydreaming about a future together, but she was barely out of high school. The two minutes it took to conceive Blaze seemed hardly worth giving up her dreams, let alone her eternal salvation.

When Jack called the next day, he acted like nothing had happened. "Wanna grab a bite?" he had said. "I've been thinking about growing my hair out."

The fact that they had committed the second most serious sin didn't seem to bother him. When Vicky told him she was pregnant, he seemed eager to get out while he still could. It was a conversation that lived rent-free in Vicky's mind for eighteen years.

"You said you loved me," Vicky had said.

"I do, babe," he had replied.

"You said you wanted to marry me."

"Yeah, and you said you wanted to wait."

"Well, that was before you knocked me up. So, are you going to do the right thing, or do I need to call your Bishop?"

Finally, a flicker of fear danced across Jack's face. "No. You can't do that. My parents would kill me."

"What do we do?" Vicky asked, terrified of the answer.

"We'll get married. Over Christmas break."

Plans for the perfect dress, invitations, and carefully selected colors suddenly vanished as their parents threw together a secret shotgun wedding in three weeks. With every rushed decision, Vicky waited for someone to call her out. Surely, someone would figure it out. Her mom, his dad—somebody. Nobody plans a last-minute potluck dinner in the cultural hall and calls it a proper wedding unless they are hiding something.

No one would believe it.

But everyone did—or, at least, they pretended to.

As soon as Jack proposed, the couple acted like they had done nothing wrong. Not once did they bring it up, not even to each other, not for eighteen years. The silence between them widened as thousands of ordinary moments slipped into a familiar routine. It wasn't a bad life, but it also wasn't the one Vicky had envisioned. She didn't even finish her freshman year. Instead, she committed herself fully to this new role of wife and mother, hoping in doing so, she'd eventually be free of this anchor pulling her down to hell.

As Jack finished reading the letter, Vicky finally saw the regret in his eyes. And she wondered. Did he feel the same burden she felt? Or was his disappointment tied to something else? To her, maybe. She always assumed they had a happy marriage, that despite the path they took, they would have eventually ended here anyway.

Right now, she wasn't certain.

All Vicky knew for sure was that the secret had taken its toll. The shiny facade they built to hide their flaws had kept Vicky and Jack at arm's length. The lie of perfection had built a wall around her heart. And now, with Blaze's secret, it felt like history was repeating itself.

As Vicky listened to Jack read the prophet's counsel, all she could think about was breaking free. She was sick of playing a character and exhausted from trying to prove her worth. As her tears filled her eyes, Vicky wondered if she'd ever get to stop pretending that everything was okay.

23

The front door squeaked open. Anna slid through the crack, late and out of breath. It didn't help that she had to park halfway down the street. After tiptoeing past the small entryway, she dropped her bag on a side table and scoped out the usual crowd of activists in Gloria's living room. Standing front and center, Gloria smiled as Anna snuck her way to the back.

Emily did not offer the same warm welcome. Sitting with her stick-straight spine, she glared as Anna scurried to an empty seat. Emily placed the half-eaten shortbread cookie on the small plate beside her and brushed the crumbs from her fingers. "I think it's time to consider a new plan."

Anna's heel caught the edge of a large rug and stumbled. Trying to catch herself, she knocked over a bowl of plastic lemons on the console behind the couch. She bounced to her feet, fumbling to put everything back in place as heat radiated up her neck.

Emily didn't flinch. "I've said it from the beginning: We don't need a confession. The video we've put together will get the job done. All we've done is waste time and money trying to get someone on that stage."

Even without mentioning names, Anna could tell the OWLS were discussing her, the scowl across Emily's face being the biggest clue. Anna wasn't surprised. For months, she had done nothing to earn their confidence. Anytime the OWLS asked for an update, Anna would meander around the truth, hoping to distract them with vague talks about potential instead of focusing on actual enrollments—which was still only one. Nevertheless, despite not doing the work, a tiny voice inside Anna's head told her to wait things out, that something would eventually fall into place. And it finally did.

Today, Anna was ready to talk numbers.

"Facts don't change people's minds," Gloria said. Her tone was reminiscent of a mother nagging a child for the hundredth time. "No matter what damning information gets published, the Puremetics PR machine manages to deny or spin the truth to their benefit. The distributors don't realize they're victims because it's a damn cult. The only way they'll listen is if Christian betrays himself. We need a confession."

Gloria removed her ruby-red glasses and rubbed the bridge of her nose. "Besides, we're getting ahead of ourselves. We haven't even heard from Anna yet." She turned, placing her spectacles back on, and smiled. "Would you care to tell us how it's going?"

Emily scoffed. "Yes, by all means. Give us one of your impressive updates, Anna. Let me guess: You've magically jumped four ranks since we last chatted. We're saved!" Everyone eyed Anna as Emily tore into her with unfeeling sarcasm. A few whispered while others giggled at the jab.

Anna tried not to let it rattle her. This was the moment she'd been anticipating for days. She puffed her chest as she inhaled sharply. "As always, Emily, you're right on the money."

A smug smile spread along Emily's face. "Don't be too hard on yourself. It was a big ask." She shot Gloria an *I-told-you-so* nod.

"No," Anna said, trying not to let her voice shake. "I'm saying I did jump four ranks since we last talked."

Emily huffed. "Be serious."

Anna sat up straight, interlacing her fingers across her lap like the CEO in a board meeting. "I am serious." She pulled out her phone, showing the room her Puremetics dashboard. "See? Right there: Sapphire Executive."

Gloria's mouth dropped. "Holy Hell. How did you do it?"

"It's a bit of a story," Anna said, moving to the front of the room. "In all your research of Christian White, did you ever come across a company named Aroma Harmony?"

Gloria's lips formed a tight line. Her shoulders tensed.

Emily stood up, inserting herself between Anna and Gloria. "Of course we have. What does that have to do with this?"

"Everything." Anna crossed her arms, matching Emily's defiant stance. "Aroma Harmony was run by Chris Blackwell, who, as it turns out, is Christian White's real name. After that company failed, he changed it and founded Puremetics."

Murmurs rippled from the other women in the living room. Wide eyes and whispered chatter suggested this was news to most of them. Anna noted it, still trying to understand why Gloria would withhold this information.

"I'm aware of all of this," Gloria said, taking a seat. The sudden shift in her energy was palpable. She didn't look mad, just worn out.

"Why didn't you say something?" Anna asked quietly. "It would have made my job easier if you had given me all the details upfront."

"How? Chris's background didn't matter to your mission," Gloria shot back with a twinge of defensiveness. "I'm not sure why you felt compelled to go snooping around the past. All you had to do was join Puremetics and replicate Vicky's success."

"But that's the problem!" Anna's cheeks turned red as months of frustration spilled over. "You know how manipulative and toxic Puremetics is, yet you had no qualms sending me into the lion's den, knowing the only way I could survive was by being just as manipulative and toxic."

Gloria leaned against her chair and dropped her head. "You're right. I'm sorry. If there was any other way..." She sighed and looked up. "I told you before, sometimes we get our hands dirty if the cause demands it."

"It wasn't *your* hands getting dirty, though." Anna cleared her throat, realizing she might not be cut out to be an OWL after all.

"No." Gloria sighed, running her fingers through her silver curls. "And I'm guessing yours are filthy now that you've hit rank."

A smile spread across Anna's face. "That's just it. I only started seeing success when I stopped telling lies."

Emily cocked her head. "What do you mean?"

"Well, once I discovered Christian White used to be Chris Blackwell, former CEO of Aroma Harmony, I did some digging." Anna hated using the word *I* as she told the story. Lisa and Jane had been instrumental in this discovery, but she didn't want the OWLS to know about their involvement just yet. "After Aroma Harmony failed, Chris left a lot of distributors high and dry. And that was on top of all the other shitty stuff he had been doing."

"We know all this," Emily said, even though it was clear that by *we*, she meant Gloria and herself. The other ladies sat with bated breath, hanging onto every word. "Please get to the point."

"The point is the man has a lot of enemies." Anna shifted from one foot to the other, wishing Emily's scowl wasn't so effective. "Over the past six weeks, I have been quietly reaching out to some former Aroma Harmony distributors who are just as eager to take him down."

Gloria's eyes lit up. "Oh my god! You've convinced them to enroll under you! Why hadn't I thought of this before?"

"But is it enough?" Emily asked, always the pessimist. "Even if you got a hundred people to sign up, you're still asking each of them to spend like $2500 a month to get the numbers necessary to hit rank."

Anna locked eyes with Emily, as a smug smile consumed her face. "Actually, I personally only enrolled eight people."

Emily rolled her eyes. "Then how did you—"

"I hand selected the top contributors of a forum dedicated to airing Aroma Harmony grievances." Anna tapped on her phone and then showed her Puremetics report. "Each of those women have, on average, enrolled one hundred and fifty people. Altogether, my organization is over one thousand strong."

"Holy fuck!" Gloria's hand flew to her mouth.

Emily dropped her arms as her lips curled upward in an unfamiliar smile. "I must admit. I'm impressed."

That admission alone ignited Anna's confidence.

Gloria clapped her hands. "This is brilliant, Anna! Absolutely brilliant."

"But are you sure you can trust these people?" Emily asked, second-guessing her initial praise. "You just gave away the entire plot to a crowd of strangers. What's to keep them from leaking something and ruining everything?"

Anna inhaled slowly, trying to maintain her conviction. She had thought this through. She had been careful. "I didn't reveal the entire plan. All these women know is I plan to speak out on stage against Christian. They don't know about the OWLS, the video, or the confession."

"Okay, then." Emily relaxed ever so slightly. She nodded, taking her time with her response. "In that case, good job."

A wave of relief washed over Anna as she exhaled.

Gloria flipped the paper of a giant sketchpad—their makeshift whiteboard—and began writing. "Jesus. So, this is happening? You will walk across the stage at the Leadership Gala. We're going to get our confession!"

Anna smiled. "What do you say? Are you ready to take down Christian White?"

Gloria clapped her hands. "Abso-fucking-lutely."

Anna reached for a muffin off the plate Gloria had set in the middle of the coffee table. The rest of the OWLS had left an hour ago while Emily stayed behind to help prep Anna for her role at PureExpo 2015. While the steps seemed simple enough—pin the microphone to Christian's lapel—the convoluted details of the Leadership Gala were anything but.

"Wait," Anna said. "What exactly is the Gathering of Gifts?"

"That's what they call this idol-worshiping part of the gala." Gloria blew away the steam from her cup of tea. "It became an official event last year, although the tradition started three years ago when one of the first Royal Diamonds decided to use her two-minute speech to kiss the boss's ass."

"Wait. What?" Anna said, her mouth full.

"It's true." Emily rocked in her usual chair with her usual scowl. "Instead of thanking those who helped her hit rank, the woman gave Christian a pair of diamond-studded cuff links, making everyone else on stage look like ungrateful schmucks. So, the next year, not wanting to look stupid, everyone in the Leadership Gala showed up with a gift."

Gloria shook her head. "Christian ate it up like a Thanksgiving Feast. The gala was supposed to be a leader's chance to shine." She took a slow sip. "Now, it's an official part of the celebration—one more ego-stroking indoctrination."

Anna cringed, imagining it. "So, what am I supposed to do?"

"During the Gathering of Gifts, you will give Christian this." Gloria leaned forward and pulled a ring-size box from her cardigan pocket. She placed it on the table and opened the lid, showing off a sophisticated gold-plated lapel pin featuring the Puremetics emblem. "But you can't just give it to him; you need to pin it on him."

"Right," Anna said, picking up the box and inspecting the item. The pin was small, less than an inch across. The Puremetics logo was engraved into the metal: a scripted P and a swirl that wrapped around a small, purple gemstone. "Is this really a recording device?"

"The amethyst is covering the microphone," Emily said. "It was my idea."

Anna handed the box back to Gloria, afraid to break it. "Impressive."

"When it's your turn to give your gift, say something about how Puremetics will always be close to your heart," Gloria said.

Emily sat tall, lifting her hand to heart, speaking like a royal on parade. "Or how through Christian's shining example, you've learned that the only way to succeed is by pinning the things that matter most to your heart."

"Oh, that's good, Em," Gloria laughed. "Speak to the man's ego!"

Anna tried to laugh along, but the more she considered her role in this task, the more her nerves rattled. "How many people will be at this thing?" She looked at Emily, who always seemed to have a handle on the numbers.

"Last year, there were 8,000 attendees. It's expected to be close to 10,000 this year."

The answer hit Anna in the throat, knocking the wind out of her. She bent over, holding the sides of her ribs as she gasped for air. "I can't do this!" Her chest heaved, laboring for oxygen. "I thought you needed me to be your eyes and ears. You said nothing about having to give a speech in front of a stadium full of people!"

Gloria scooted her chair closer, leaning in. "You've got this, Anna. It doesn't need to be a long or spectacular speech. Two or three carefully crafted sentences are plenty. We'll help you write it and practice. The important thing is that you pin the brooch on Christian."

"Aim for the heart," Emily said without batting an eye.

The scene played out in Anna's mind. She imagined herself awkwardly trying to stick the pin to Christian's lapel, only to press so hard that blood trickled from his white-pressed shirt. Anna would stumble backward, tripping over a microphone cord and somehow bring the entire stage down. Sweat pooled under her arms just thinking about it. "What if I mess up?"

"Then I can finally prove we never needed you in the first place," Emily said with a sly smile as she sipped her tea.

Anna chuckled nervously, choosing to believe Emily's sarcasm was friendly banter.

Gloria patted Anna's knee. "I know it sounds scary, but your part will be quick. The less memorable, the better. You don't need to worry about anything else."

Anna's stomach twisted into a pretzel as she tried to untangle her thoughts. She had known from the beginning that her only objective in hitting rank was to make it to the Leadership Gala. And while the idea of having to approach the man himself was sending her toward another panic attack, she tried to endure the stress and remember that she was part of something bigger.

"What is the rest of the plan?" Anna asked.

"There are two parts," Gloria said. "The video and the confession. We have a connection with someone on the AV crew who will play our video during the closing session."

Emily leaned back, nodding. "The video is good. Even without a confession, I still think it will do enough damage to encourage a mass exodus of distributors that will cripple the company."

Knowing the entire mission wasn't resting on her shoulders made Anna feel a little better. "And what about this confession? If I'm planting the microphone during the Leadership Gala, when—and who—is getting Christian to talk?"

Gloria and Emily exchanged glances as if this was a sore subject.

"I'm going to approach him," Gloria said. "After the gala, Christian will turn the time over to the VP of Products to unveil their new lineup for the year. I'll approach Christian offstage and drill him with questions he can't evade. The microphone pin will be synced to Emily's phone, who will be recording off to the side."

Emily sighed. "I sound like a broken record, but I still think it's a bad idea. The guy is too smooth, Gloria. And your complicated past with him makes it risky. I should be the one to do it. He doesn't know me."

"And as I've told you a hundred times," Gloria said, setting her cup down, "I know how to get under his skin. This is too important, Em. Now that Anna has come through, I'm not giving up this chance to catch him red-handed."

"Fair enough," Emily said, throwing her hands up. "Consider the matter closed. And, of course, I support you. Now, we still need to discuss the video's ending."

As the two women debated, Anna couldn't help but smile at their odd but loyal friendship. She fell back against the couch's cushions, ready to call it a night. Just as she went to check the time on her phone, it rang. Anna excused herself and headed to the porch while Emily and Gloria continued to argue.

"Hello?"

"Is this Anna Price?" an unfamiliar voice asked.

Anna stood a little taller. "It is."

"This is Tammy Wilson, otherwise known as GiantSlayer."

"Oh my god! From the Aroma Harmony forum!" Anna perked up. "You are one of my new enrollees."

With the help of Lisa and Jane, Anna sent dozens of messages to the forum's most active users, earning her eight recruits, who went on to enroll hundreds more. She only knew them by their usernames: AromaTruthUnveiled, DisHarmony34, Justice4Harmony, and other altruistic-sounding names. When Anna looked at her Puremetics report, there was no way to decipher their legal identity from their online alias.

User GiantSlayer was an outlier who only posted once but whose words ignited a fire. Her single thread was the most read, commented, and quoted post on the forum. Drawing on an analogy from *Jack and the Beanstalk,* her words encouraged others to help her take down the Giant, Christian White. Anna was thrilled when she agreed to join the fight.

Hearing Tammy's voice made the whole thing that much more real.

"I'm so excited to talk to you," Anna said.

"Likewise," Tammy replied. "As I mentioned in some of our messages, I am grateful to see someone taking on this task. I know I'm not alone. Several of us have bought convention tickets and are going to Salt Lake next month to watch the magic happen."

"Oh, wow." Anna tried not to let this information rattle her. "That's amazing. We could not have made this work without all of you. I hope we can meet up in person sometime."

"That's why I'm calling. When I get into town, I'd like to treat you to dinner, meet you face to face, and hear more about your journey."

A wave of emotion rushed up Anna's throat. "I'd love that."

"Great, I'll email you the details when it gets closer. I look forward to it."

"Perfect," Anna said, practically lifting off her seat.

"Oh, and Anna?" Tammy paused, her voice suddenly growing quiet. "Thank you. I'm not sure you know what this means to me and so many others. The work you're doing? It matters."

Anna ended the call and looked up at the night sky. A well of pride and excitement swelled within. Talking to Tammy, building this army—this journey had given Anna the courage to see herself as more than a screwup. Real women were cheering her on, people who were eager for justice. She felt a second wind and readied herself to return inside and finish preparing for the big event.

As Anna drove home that night, her mind buzzed with all the details of a plan finally coming together. After parking her car, her eyes drifted toward Ghostly Manor like they always did. She hugged her purse and walked along the neglected sidewalk until she was standing in front of the building. It stood against the moonlit sky, mysterious as ever.

"You were wrong about me," Anna said in a rare but growing sense of confidence. "This is going to work."

Ghostly Manor stared back, its empty windows gazing into Anna's soul, but said nothing. Anna nodded, turned on her heels, and headed home. She took the house's silence as a good sign.

24

Gloria always considered email a nuisance. The bulk of her messages were not-so-funny forwards, inspirational quotes, and a handful of conspiracy theories forwarded by her mother. It was challenging tending to the actual needs among the weeds. So, when Mom's latest email landed in her inbox, Gloria had her finger prepped to delete it, giving the message only seconds to prove it shouldn't be pruned.

But apparently, some emails weren't just weeds. They were bombs.

Subject: Not sure you saw this

To: gloriawright50@hotmail.com

From: joannewrightisright@yahoo.com

A friend sent this to me. Didn't you know this couple? Hugs and Kisses, Mom

Hands shaking, Gloria clicked on the attached link and immediately felt the impact of its explosion.

Blackwell's Disappearance Stumps Investigators

Eric Orton, Staff Writer, *Boise Beacon*, Oct. 9, 2008

Fiona Blackwell, wife of Aroma Harmony CEO Chris Blackwell, went missing under suspicious circumstances in September of 2007. Following an exhaustive investigation, law enforcement officials have regrettably been unable to unearth any conclusive evidence despite initial suspicions of foul play.

Blackwell staunchly maintains his innocence, asserting he was not involved in his wife's departure. He contends her disappearance prompted the closure of his essential oil enterprise. Blackwell has temporarily withdrawn from public life, citing the need for personal healing and reflection.

In contrast, former distributors express vehement criticism, attributing the downfall of Aroma Harmony to Blackwell's purported mismanagement of product quality, internal discord, financial irregularities, and allegations of sexual harassment. These challenges culminated in the company's bankruptcy filing and subsequent closure.

Boom.

Beads of sweat gathered around the base of Gloria's neck. She struggled to breathe as she reread the article. *Suspicions of foul play?* Her stomach turned. If Fiona disappeared a year ago, how was this the first Gloria had heard about it? Why wasn't the world demanding action? Where was the justice?

Where was Fiona?

As the news sunk in, Gloria's stomach revolted. She flew to the bathroom, violently forcing her lunch into the toilet. Wiping her mouth, Gloria leaned against the tiled wall, its cool touch shocking the back of her neck. She stumbled to her bedroom and rifled through the nightstand drawer until her hand pulled out a crinkled business card. She turned it over, rereading Fiona's handwriting for the thousandth time: *Help me.*

Gloria had tried. She had waited three hours at the bus after spending months covertly planning to help Fiona escape, but Fiona never showed. Instead, Gloria received an envelope and a not-so-veiled threat. For weeks—months, years—she waited for a message, an email, a phone call. She kept her eyes peeled for the tiniest hint of a signal telling her to rush in and do something.

She reached into the drawer and pulled out the envelope handed to her by a man bundled beyond recognition. Gloria pulled out the note within it. *I've changed my mind,* it read. *It would be best if we never talked again.* Fiona's name was signed at the bottom, but Gloria knew it wasn't her handwriting. She always suspected Chris had interfered, but now she knew it.

Thick, heavy tears dropped on the paper, smearing the ink. Gloria crumpled the note, screaming until her throat burned as she threw it against the wall. She should have gone to get Fiona when she had the chance—she should have fought harder.

Gloria curled into a ball on the floor, holding the business card to her heart. It was the only thing she had of Fiona's. Those frantically scrawled words were all that was left. *Help me.*

Gloria had tried.

Help me.

She should have tried harder.

The next few hours were a blur. Gloria couldn't recall how she ended up in her living room wearing only overalls, a sports bra, and her simmering rage. She didn't know how all the furniture ended up pushed against the side wall, draped in old sheets. It didn't matter. She swung the paint can, splashing vivid reds on her wall like blood splatters. Guttural grunts and heaving sobs filled the air, a soundtrack to her frenzied ritual. Her hands, not brushes, smeared the color from baseboard to ceiling. Gloria sobbed as she created. She screamed, yelled, and cried some more, allowing her tears to paint her face as she covered the wall in her living room.

Hours later, Gloria gasped for breath as she focused on the details. She layered textured lines among the chaos of color. Desperate to keep her alive, Gloria memorialized Fiona in the heart of her home. Working only from memory, she pulled out the cobalt blue of Fiona's eyes, the sharpness of her cheekbone, and the soft curls of her hair.

As Gloria stood back to inspect the result of her outburst, she cried again as she considered what was lost. Chris had ruined Fiona's life, killed her spirit, and maybe more. Gloria didn't care what the investigators had said. She knew the man well enough to know his charm and money could sweep anything under the rug, even a crime so heinous it took Gloria's breath away.

The painting memorialized the pain, creating a memory of the woman Gloria loved. But it did more than that. Emerging above Fiona's profile, Gloria had painted a phoenix rising from the ashes, igniting hope for a second chance. She held onto this idea, not as a reminder to let go of her rage—but to *use* it. Before there could be a rebirth, Gloria would first need to light a fire. Maybe it was too late to help Fiona, but it wasn't too late to strike a match.

Chris Blackwell would pay for what he did.

25

13 DAYS UNTIL CONVENTION

The phone vibrated against the smooth walnut wood of the coffee table. Vicky reached for it, but the gap between her fingers and the device might as well have been the distance between her and the sun. With her body fused to the couch, no call could summon the energy required to answer.

As the phone finally gave up, Vicky held back her tears, wondering what was wrong with her. It was more than just Blaze's situation—even more than her trying to reconcile her past. Vicky suddenly realized no matter how hard she tried, perfection would always elude her. After years of attempting to control and force her way into the life of her dreams, she found herself tripping on all the very flaws she was trying to hide.

If perfection wasn't attainable, what was the point?

On the surface, Vicky looked like she was doing fine. Masking her slow-motion descent was imperative, so she did enough to go unnoticed by Jack and the kids. Food always managed to make its way to the table. The house was clean. If anything, dialing her efforts to the bare minimum only proved how little people noticed her hard work. The only time Jack asked if something was wrong was when she faked a headache last Thursday to get out of having sex.

It was even easier to disengage with Puremetics. Yesterday, instead of jumping into her usual end-of-the-month push, Vicky told her downline she was sick. She had accepted that hitting Royal Diamond wouldn't happen in time for Convention. As disappointing as it was, Vicky had moved on— or given up, as it were. Watching her dream slip through her fingers was too much. So, Vicky let things coast, knowing she'd keep her current rank and paycheck even if she checked out for a while.

The phone buzzed again, this time for just a quick second. Suddenly worried that someone was hurt, Vicky summoned her strength to stretch her hands the extra six inches necessary to make contact. Her fingers grasped the device and tapped to open the new voicemail.

"Victoria, this is Jennifer Gray from the Puremetics Distributor Relations Division. I wanted to chat about a member you enrolled, Anna Price. There has been some unusual activity on her account over the last few weeks, and we just wanted to make sure she was within policy standards. We're thrilled to see anyone succeed, but for legal reasons, we like to investigate when someone's organization grows more than a thousand new members in a month."

Vicky gasped. A thousand members? She jumped to her feet, her energy suddenly bursting from the seams.

"Based on our internal investigation," the voicemail continued, "everything seems legitimate, but we always check in with the direct upline when any red flags pop up. Anyway, if you are aware of any violations, please give me a call back as soon as you can. Thank you."

The laptop screen flung open as Vicky took a seat at her desk. She logged into her Puremetics account and waited for the sales report to load. With everything that had happened since April, Vicky had given up on Anna months ago.

"Oh my gosh," Vicky said when the report finally populated. Her mouth dangled open as her hands jumped to her lips. She couldn't believe what she was seeing. Anna's organization was suddenly Vicky's second-strongest leg with 278,050 OGV. Anna had reached Sapphire Executive. How was it possible?

Vicky clicked on Anna's name, eager to see the thousand people she had supposedly enrolled, but when the list came up, there weren't even a dozen names.

"She enrolled, what—" Vicky said, counting to herself, "— eight new people. That's it?"

It was hardly noteworthy, so Vicky dug further, clicking on the first recruit on the list. A string of names ran down the screen. She repeated this with each new distributor directly under Anna, expanding Anna's suddenly robust organization. Each of her eight new people had hundreds of recruits, each having only enrolled within the last two or three weeks.

Vicky stared at the screen, dumbfounded. None of this made sense.

The front door slammed with a heavy thud, but Vicky barely heard it. Blaze walked in, carrying a crystal vase with purple, long-stemmed roses bursting from within. "These were on the front porch," he said, placing the flowers on her desk.

Vicky's eyes landed on Blaze. The pull of a hundred questions tugged at her heart: *How are you doing? Are you happy? Are you safe?*

Blaze moved across the kitchen. Vicky was desperate to bridge the chasm between them, eager to pull him close, but fear was ruling her life these days. Worried about saying the wrong thing and accidentally pushing him further away, she kept her son at a distance, mumbling a weak "Thanks."

He didn't hear or just chose to ignore it. Blaze grabbed an apple and cut his teeth into its flesh, keeping his eyes downward.

Before Vicky could venture another word, he was gone. She dropped her head into her hands, hating herself a little more each minute she stayed silent.

Vicky pulled the card nestled inside the bouquet and read the note from her upline, Clara:

Fastest Royal Diamond in company history!! You are the golden child of Puremetics. So proud of your success, babe! xoxo - Clara.

A smile flickered from the corner of Vicky's lips like spring's first glimmer of sun after a long, harsh winter. *Fastest Royal Diamond.* It only now struck her that with Anna's sudden surge, Vicky had reached her goal. She shook her head, not knowing whether to laugh, cry, or scream. She wanted to believe she had earned this place at the top, but that meant accepting Anna's ascent, and Vicky wasn't sure she could do that.

The doorbell rang. Still lost in her thoughts, Vicky opened the front door, surprised to see Becki standing on the porch.

"Rock star!" Becki flung her arms around Vicky's neck. "I don't care if you're still contagious. This is incredible, babe! You did it! Royal Diamond!"

"How did you know?" Vicky asked, her mind still racing at this unexpected news.

Becki pulled back with an incredulous stare. "Just because you were sick didn't mean your people would let you down. A bunch of us got together yesterday to make sure you crossed that finish line. Clara orchestrated the whole thing when she realized how close you were to hitting rank." She pushed her way past Vicky, letting herself into the house.

"I must admit," Becki said, tossing her keys on a small side table. "I didn't think Anna was up to the task, but apparently, you were right about her."

"You don't think it's suspicious? Her sudden climb to Sapphire Executive?"

"She hit Sapphire! Dang." Becki shook her head. "Clara didn't give us the numbers. I assumed she had recruited just enough people to push you to the top." She whistled. "Sapphire Executive? Really?"

The two women plopped down on the sofa. Vicky scratched her head, unwilling to believe any of this was happening.

Becki leaned back, crossing her legs. "Maybe Anna contacted some bloggers or online influencers. As you already know, people with a platform could build a base of customers quickly."

"Maybe." Vicky didn't believe it. What were the odds that Anna knew that many high-profile people?

"Anyway, it doesn't matter how she did it. You hit Diamond, baby! You are officially Puremetics royalty!"

Vicky smiled weakly, wishing Becki's enthusiasm could lift her spirits. A part of her wanted to believe Anna had come through, but it didn't make sense. "Compliance called me," she said. "Anna's rapid rise got them suspicious. They wanted to make sure everything was legit."

Becki barely flinched at this news. "Really? Huh. Did they find evidence of cheating or something?"

"No. They said everything looked okay on their end but wanted to check in with me just in case I knew something."

"I mean, it is weird. You know what I thought of Anna. She's not exactly leadership material."

Vicky agreed, but it was more than that. Anna had been so angry that night back in April, her accusations still fresh in Vicky's mind. When Anna and Jane stormed away, Vicky assumed that was the end of Anna's Puremetics journey. What prompted this sudden turnaround? It didn't add up.

"So, how do you plan on celebrating?" Becki asked, clearly ready to move past the Anna issue.

"Celebrating?"

Becki let out an exasperated sigh. "Yes, woman. You just hit the ultimate milestone. How are you going to mark the occasion?"

The question smacked Vicky in the face. This was supposed to be her big moment. Instead, this achievement came as a shock. A threat almost. Vicky never would have guessed anyone could make the impossible jump needed to send her to the top, especially not Anna Price. It wasn't supposed to be this easy for someone like *her*.

"I hadn't given it much thought," Vicky muttered.

"Girl, you must be sick. I'm going to let you get some rest, but as soon as this bug is gone, we are going to party! You hear me?" Becki stood. "Get better, okay? Convention is less than two weeks away and we need you feeling and looking radiant for your big moment."

Vicky smiled, touched by her friend's support. "Thanks."

Becki let herself out as Vicky sat, dumbfounded—questioning this moment she had worked so hard to achieve. Could she accept this outcome? Was it possible to bask in the glory of this dream and wrap herself in the accolades that came with it, knowing Anna was the one who had handed it to her? Heaven knew Vicky had worked her butt off in this business. She deserved to reach the top but hated that Anna had tarnished what was supposed to be a shining moment.

It was impossible to say *thank you* and move on. It was impossible to accept Anna's success, just like it was impossible to talk to Blaze, work out past sins, let the scale creep up, or ignore the growing lines around her eyes. Vicky felt compelled to dig her heels and hold onto the vision of perfection she had committed to living even as the world became more forgiving and accepting—perhaps because of it. Victoria Sterling was not ready to believe that life was messy and chaotic because doing so would destroy the very idea of the woman she tried to be.

Vicky needed to figure out what Anna had done to manipu-

late the system and finally rid herself of this pebble in her shoe
—even if it meant losing her rank in the process. Instead of
letting an imposter tarnish her inevitable rise to the top, Vicky
would happily wait a few more months to reach Royal Diamond
the *right* way.

Opening a new browser, Vicky wasn't sure what she was
looking for, but that wouldn't stop her from searching every
corner of the internet. There had to be something buried online
proving Anna didn't deserve this moment in the spotlight. In
Vicky's mind, there was only enough room for one shining star.

26

CONVENTION: DAY 1

Anna stuffed her key card into her purse and hurried toward the hotel elevators. After driving into Salt Lake City late last night, she had slept through her alarm and was running late. The flurry of activity within the hotel had died down considerably. Still, as soon as she exited the lobby, she found herself running against streams of crowds as she dashed toward the Salt Palace Convention Center.

Nearly everyone on the streets wore Puremetics purple—official branded merchandise or their own color-coordinated outfits. Glittery gold lanyards hung from participants' necks with multi-colored ribbons cascading below their name tags. Walking arm in arm, women grouped off into little factions. One group wore cowboy hats and boots; another had opted for matching bomber jackets. Anna felt transported to some strange world where *High School Musical* and *Mean Girls* collided in a battle of cliques. She braced herself against the streams of crowds, nearly toppling into a wall of women posing with a selfie stick.

"PureExpo 2015!!" the women yelled as they pouted their lips.

Registration had opened hours ago, and Anna hoped the lines wouldn't be long as she ran up the stairs to the Salt Palace. Large decals featuring the Puremetics logo and its top products covered the windows of the iconic metal tower that marked the building's entrance. Anna pushed through the doors. Light spilled from giant skylights and walls of windows as she walked into the massive lobby. The loud hum of a crowd filling the space dashed Anna's hopes for a quick in and out.

Six lines extended behind signs organized alphabetically. Anna made her way to the back of the "O - R" group and caught her breath. She pulled out her phone and checked the time. Vicky was throwing a leadership lunch for her downline at a restaurant down the street, and at this rate, Anna would be late. Again. She quickly texted Gloria: *It's a madhouse here!* And another one to Jane: *How's everything at home?* Anna tucked her phone into her pocket and moved another few inches up the line.

Giant posters and signs filled every empty corner of the convention center. Smiling, photo-shopped women showed off popular products and hinted at new ones being announced over the next two days. Balloons, banners, and corners dedicated to snapping images for social media made the event seem bigger than Anna had anticipated. But it was the rabid fandom that truly surprised her.

All around her, the word Puremetics rippled through the crowds like an anthem. The excitement was palpable. With every passing moment, Anna felt herself getting more rigid as their energy pressed against her chest. There were so many people. Thousands of them. And they were united in a delirious devotion to a company Anna was determined to help take down.

She swallowed hard as she finally made her way up the line. The woman in front of Anna hugged a huge packet against her chest as the staff member handed her a lanyard. Like the others Anna had seen on the street, this woman's badge had nearly a half-dozen ribbons cascading down from the plastic sheath, each one inscribed with gold letters: *First Time Attendee, New Rank Achieved, Jamaica Trip Winner, Leadership Retreat Winner.* The woman donned the gaudy nametag, smiling at Anna as she skipped toward the market expo.

"Hello! Welcome to PureExpo 2015!" a staff member wearing a Puremetics Purple t-shirt said in a voice far too cheery for someone who had been doing this for nearly six hours. "What's your name, hun?"

"Anna Price." It was hard to match the woman's energy. Anna had only been waiting in this chaos for thirty minutes and was already eager to head back home.

"Hmmm... I'm not finding you on the list. Oh, wait—" The woman stopped, reading something handwritten next to a crossed-out name. "Right, uh." She shook her head, suddenly devoid of the uppity energy that had greeted Anna. "There's a small problem with your registration. You must report to Customer Service in Meeting Room 258, just over on the other side of the main entrance."

"How could there be a problem? I signed up online. The funds went through weeks ago." Anna felt her pulse speeding up at the thought of things falling apart at the last minute.

"I'm sorry, ma'am. There's nothing I can do. They'll help you in 258." She scribbled the room number on a sticky note and passed it to Anna.

"Okay." Anna rubbed the sides of her face, scrunching the note between her fingers. Her phone rang; it was Gloria. She debated sending it to voicemail when the staff personnel cleared her throat loudly.

"Sorry, ma'am. Would you mind scooting to the side so I can help the next person?"

"Of course," Anna said, her face turning red. She tapped the accept button as she made her way toward the exit. Her voice cracked as she answered. "Hey, Gloria. What's up?"

"Are you registered yet?"

Anna smoothed out the sticky note as she balanced the phone between her shoulder and ear. "Yeah, all set." She figured it would be confirmed soon enough. "I gotta run to Vicky's little luncheon. I'll call you when I'm done, and we can make sure we're all set for tomorrow."

She hung up and switched to her message app, hoping Jane had responded. No such luck. Stuffing her phone in her pocket, Anna looked at the sticky note and swallowed hard. It had to be a simple mix-up. She'd take care of it after lunch. With a sharp inhale, Anna braced herself to face the crowds, working her way to the restaurant three blocks away, still wishing she was back home.

The place was packed. It was good that Vicky had reserved the entire restaurant, not just the party room like last year. Even though only twenty percent of her organization had made it out for Convention, it was still more than enough people to fill the space.

Hand-crafted centerpieces dotted the tables while place settings instructed the women where they belonged. It was all according to rank: The top leaders were front and center, while newer recruits and those who had barely moved the needle sat on the outside. Chatter filled the restaurant, and Vicky stood in front, trying to recreate the enthusiasm that had come so easily at last year's convention after her rapid rise to Presidential Emerald.

This luncheon was as much about celebrating Vicky's success as it was about spotlighting her people's achievements. For months, she went over every detail to make the event perfect, knowing her reputation was on the line. Vicky hated faking a smile for what should have been a defining moment.

She dinged her champagne flute filled with sparkling cider. "Ladies, if I can get your attention for a few minutes before lunch is served."

The conversation died down. Chairs screeched along the floor as women turned to face Vicky. Goosebumps ran up her arm as the group's energy and smiles flowed toward her. Through all the drama with Blaze and Anna, she had forgotten about the excitement of Convention. The vision of building an empire had carried Vicky from the starter package to the company's top rank in just two years. Because of her, several women in this room had tasted the sweet success of hard work.

Of course, this opportunity wasn't only about the money. Most people in the restaurant hadn't made back their total investment in dollars and cents, but Puremetics offered these women a chance to be something special—more than a mom, a cook, a cleaner, or a chaperone. The company lived and breathed off the backs of women who wanted to be more than housewives. It had given them a taste of independence, a chance to feel like a boss.

Gratitude flooded Vicky as she remembered what this business had meant, giving her hope that the old Vicky would soon be back, ready to keep growing.

"I am so honored to be with you today," she said, choking on the growing emotion in her throat. "The fact that you're here, committed, speaks volumes of the kind of leader you were born to be."

Vicky could tell she wasn't the only one moved by the moment. A few women brushed away tears, while others continued to beam from ear to ear, snapping dozens of photos as if they could capture the moment with their phones.

"Whether you've hit a new rank this year or even encouraged just one person to join this revolution of health, sisterhood, and empowerment—you are doing God's work. I am so proud of each of you and know that it's only up from here!"

The room erupted in applause but was quickly interrupted by a loud thud. Vicky snapped to attention as Anna fumbled in the back of the room, having knocked over one of the massive posters Vicky had set up.

"I'm so sorry," Anna whispered as she picked it up. She tiptoed to the side of the restaurant, looking for an empty seat— a seat Vicky knew didn't exist.

A rise in blood pressure and a sudden breathlessness overtook Vicky as she followed Anna with her eyes. She laughed nervously, stumbling on her words. "Sorry, what was I saying?"

The kitchen doors swung open, and a dozen servers walked in with trays of food.

"Ah! Lunch," Vicky said, grateful for the distraction. "I hope you enjoy this meal. It's my way of thanking each of you for showing up like the absolute rock stars you are."

Applause and delightful *oohs* and *ahhs* gave Vicky the moment she needed to recalibrate. She quickly shuffled through the crowds, making her way to Anna and whisking her off to the side.

"What are you doing here?" Vicky hissed.

"What do you mean?" Anna said, trying to squirm out of Vicky's grasp. "I got a million email reminders about this event. You invited your entire downline, and now that I'm one of your highest-ranked leaders…" her voice trailed when she saw the look on Vicky's face.

"No, I mean, what are you doing here, at Convention?"

"What are you talking about?"

Vicky grabbed her phone from her back pocket and opened her email, muttering as she scrolled through messages. "Corporate told me they were taking care of this." A few women sitting nearby had put down their forks and leaned in to listen. "Ha! There." Vicky shoved her phone in Anna's face.

"What is—"

"Just read it," Vicky said, cutting her off.

Anna sighed and began reading. "Dear Ms. Sterling, we appreciate you bringing this alarming news to our attention. Given the evidence you have supplied, it seems only fitting to terminate Anna Price's account as she is not upholding the Puremetics standards that we require of our distributors..." Her voice trailed off as she shook her head. "What the hell is this, Vicky? What have you done?"

"Oh, there's more." Vicky snatched the phone back and finished reading the message. "Our compliance department will issue a refund for Ms. Price's convention ticket and ensure that she is not allowed in the event center. We agree that protecting the company's reputation is of the utmost importance."

"You see!" Vicky's voice was now at full volume. The room had gone silent. All eyes were on her and Anna. "Corporate said they had handled it, and yet here you are! It's bad enough you went and recruited a thousand trolls, but then you dare to show up here?"

Anna stumbled backward, her eyes darting back and forth. "I don't... what exactly..." She buried her face in her hands, muffling a scream. It was unclear if Anna was enraged or embarrassed, but a rawness seemed to rip her usually subdued demeanor.

Vicky scoffed and moved in closer, lowering her voice. "What did you think would happen after enrolling a bunch of hate-filled losers? Did you really believe their stories? Did you think you were doing something noble by convincing them to join you in some desperate attempt to shame the company? Or were you just eager to prove you aren't as pathetic as everyone thinks?"

The room stood silent. Fingers gripped forks tightly as everyone collectively held their breath. Nobody dared move or knew what to say until Anna finally took a clue and marched out the door, slamming it against the wall with a deafening thud that echoed in Vicky's chest.

Anna's fists pounded against the door. After running from the restaurant to the hotel, she tried to catch her breath. The hexagon pattern on the hallway carpet twisted and swirled, making it even harder to stand up straight.

The door swung open, and Gloria's face fell. "Anna? What's wrong?"

"I've ruined everything!" Anna yelled, pushing her way into Gloria's hotel room.

"Whoa, hold on." Gloria followed Anna, who plopped face first into the bed. "What happened? Are you okay?"

"They kicked me out." The words were muffled by the thick bedding.

Gloria turned Anna over. "Oh, dear. That doesn't sound very good, but let's not jump to conclusions. I'm sure it's all just a misunderstanding."

"No!" Anna sat up, her voice frantic. "Vicky found out. She knows everything!"

Actually, Anna wasn't sure what Vicky knew. There was a chance Vicky had only learned about the secret recruits—at least, that was what Anna hoped. She leaned into Gloria, who wrapped her arms around Anna's sobbing body. Her chest heaved as each blubbering exhale dropped her closer to the earth. Soon, even Gloria's tender embrace wasn't enough to keep her upright. Gravity pulled Anna toward the mattress again, curling her into a ball of despair.

"Can you tell me what happened?" Gloria's voice was tender with a hint of worry. She rubbed Anna's back. The air conditioner suddenly erupted with a clang, blowing air into the stuffy hotel room. One door down, an occupant's off-key singing drifted through the walls. Gloria sat silent, letting the warmth and weight of her hand secure Anna.

It didn't help. Anna was untethered.

"They terminated my account," Anna said, her voice weak as she drew into herself even more. "Vicky must have discovered our plan somehow, or at least she knew the people I enrolled were looking for revenge."

"Shit," Gloria muttered.

Anna sat up, her eyes puffy and red. She wiped her nose with her sleeve just as Gloria handed her a tissue box. "I'm so sorry, Gloria. I ruined everything. I always ruin everything. All your hard work and Emily's and Claire's and Dottie's and—" Anna's face pinched inward as she choked on the words. Another burst of sobs pushed her chest upward as she tried to speak through the hurt. "Everyone was counting on me, and I ruined it all."

Gloria sat silent, her eyes bouncing back and forth in a way that made Anna hope she was formulating some new plan. Her phone buzzed, and she picked it up, reading an incoming text. "Dammit."

"What is it?" Anna asked.

"When it rains, it pours," Gloria said. "Emily is not coming."

Anna held her breath as a series of messages buzzed in rapid succession. "Is she okay?"

Gloria sighed, tossing the phone on the bed. "She'll be fine. She fell chasing some kids off her lawn. Broke her leg and is heading to the hospital to get it set."

At any other moment, Anna would have found this image of Emily hilarious. Instead, it just felt like a doubling down of lousy luck. "Doesn't she have the video? Is the whole plan falling apart?"

"Simmer down," Gloria said. "We have multiple copies of the video on several devices. The plan isn't ruined, but this does make things tricky."

Despite the dozen OWLS who had helped implement the

plan, Gloria insisted on a bare-bones crew in case things went sideways as they had last time. That meant Gloria, Emily, Anna, and the mysterious AV mole were the only ones attending the event. With Emily gone and Anna kicked out, things were looking grim.

"I need to make some calls," Gloria said, suddenly in business mode. She softened her gaze as her eyes met Anna. "Everything is going to be okay. Do not beat yourself up over this but do get some rest. I'll call you later this afternoon, okay?"

Anna nodded, grateful for Gloria's kindness. She let herself out and made her way down the hall. As she turned the corner, Anna froze as she watched Jane exit a room. "What are you doing here?"

Jane turned just as the door behind her clicked shut. Her eyes widened as she saw Anna. "Mom?"

A flurry of panic lit Anna's nerves on fire as she ran through a list of potential disasters that would justify Jane's sudden appearance. "Is everything okay? What's wrong?"

"Mom, I'm fine. Nothing is wrong." Jane stepped closer. "God, you look awful. What happened?" She rushed over and threw her arms around Anna's still-shaking frame.

Fighting to regain her composure, Anna wiped away the tears and forced a laugh. "Oh, you know. Just messing things up again." She hated being like this in front of Jane. Her daughter had been through enough these past few years. The last thing she needed was a mom who couldn't get her shit together. "But seriously, why are you here? *How* did you get here?"

The door opened again, and Blaze stepped into the hallway. His spine stiffened when he realized the teens had been caught.

"Blaze drove," Jane said.

Anna smiled at the boy but wasn't about to let Jane get away without an explanation. "But why? What are you doing here?"

Jane leaned back and smiled. "Did you really think I wasn't going to come watch your epic takedown? No way!"

Anna shook her head, wanting to be angry. It felt like the appropriate parental response, but instead, she threw her arms around Jane. "You're too good to me, kid." She looked over at Blaze. "So does that mean he knows?"

She asked the question innocently enough. Who was Anna to point fingers when she had revealed the secret herself? But as soon as the words left her lips, she realized Blaze may have been the one to tell Vicky. She held her breath, ready to rage, depending on the response.

"He knows, but he hasn't said a word," Jane said as if she could read Anna's mind.

"Are you sure?" Anna asked, still on high alert. "Because Vicky just got me kicked out of the convention. The plan—or at least my part—is off."

"I swear I didn't say anything! My mom has barely said two words to me in the past three months." Blaze huffed. "It's just like her to ruin everything." He pressed his lips together, frozen by the truth of his statement. His whole body stooped by the weight of its meaning.

Right. That. Jane had told Anna about Blaze's situation. Seeing such a kind, level-headed kid suffering simply for being himself broke her heart. Even with Vicky's flaws, Anna never expected her to turn her own son away.

Anna reached out and gave Blaze a bear hug. "It will get better. I know it."

He softened into the embrace as if starved for motherly attention. "Thanks."

"Sorry to interrupt this tender moment," Jane said, "But I still don't understand what happened. They kicked you out of Puremetics? Can they do that?"

Anna nodded, her eyes all out of tears but not regret. As awful as it was letting Gloria down, Anna hated disappointing Jane even more. This child had been to hell and back, offering her undying support and quirky take on life in a way that had kept Anna going when she wanted to stop. "I screwed up, kid. Again."

"No. This is not on you." Jane tenderly squeezed Anna's shoulders. "And I refuse to believe it's over. There's got to be a way around this."

Anna wanted to believe her daughter and find a way out of this mess, but she had hit a dead end. There was no clear path to Christian, no way to make it on the stage, no chance of planting the microphone. As far as Anna was concerned, her usefulness had officially run out.

27

"I'll be there in fifteen," Vicky said, ending the call. She fell back on the bed and smiled. After all the drama at the luncheon, she hadn't expected the day to turn itself around so suddenly.

"Who was that?" Becki asked as she pulled on her suede boots.

Vicky wasn't thrilled about sharing a room at Convention, not with all she had going on these days, but Becki was insistent they roomed together. That had been the plan since last year. Becki had been Vicky's first and closest friend since moving to Splendor Springs, and she was also her most dependable leader in her organization, but cohabiting meant putting on an act. Vicky was sick of pretending to be okay.

Plus, it turned out Becki was not easy to live with. As soon as they checked in yesterday, a million irritating habits suddenly burst to the surface, threatening to change how Vicky thought of Becki forever. The way she smacked her gum, her constant complaining about the softness of her sheets, the number of pillows on the bed, or the lack of amenities in the bathroom—it had all worn Vicky down within the first twenty minutes of arriving.

The only reason Vicky was willing to miss the market expo was because she needed a break from Becki's constant *I told you so* attitude about Anna Price. When Vicky mentioned heading back to the hotel after lunch, she didn't expect Becki to join her.

But not even Becki could pop this bubble lifting Vicky's spirits. After a series of disappointments and setbacks, she was finally getting what she deserved.

"That was Evelyn Davenport," Vicky said, sitting up with a satisfied smile.

"Wait. As in Christian White's personal assistant?"

"Yep." Vicky bounced to her feet and grabbed her makeup bag. She analyzed herself in the mirror and pulled out her favorite lipstick. "Christian wants to thank me for getting to the bottom of Anna's shenanigans."

Becki rolled her eyes. "I've met Evelyn. She's not the type of person to use the word shenanigans."

Vicky laughed. "Okay, I'm paraphrasing. But she did say Christian was impressed with my research and grateful I uncovered the disturbing behavior before it spread further in the company."

"Nice," Becki said, slipping on her lanyard. "Clara was right. You really are the golden child of Puremetics. So happy for you, babe."

"Eh, I'm sure it's their way of softening the blow of not reaching rank."

"So, they finally came to a decision about all of that?" Becki clicked her tongue. "I can't believe they won't make you a Royal Diamond. It's not your fault all of Anna's recruits were frauds."

Vicky shrugged. There had been no official announcement, but she assumed the company had no choice but to revert her to Presidential Emerald.

"Well, I'm still impressed." Becki wrapped her arms around Vicky and squeezed tightly. "I'm sure you'll rank up on your own in no time."

Vicky melted into the embrace, surprised by how much she needed it. "Thank you."

"You're meeting him in fifteen minutes?" Becki said, throwing her bag over her shoulder. "Back at the Salt Palace? You better get going."

"Actually, he's here in the Marriot."

Becki paused, pursing her lips. "He's invited you to his hotel room?" She shook her head, and a half-smile crept along her face. "You go, girl."

"Stop it," Vicky said. "It's not like that. He's set up a makeshift office up there. He's a busy man with a company to run even during Convention. Besides, Evelyn is up there with him."

"Whatever you say." Becki winked at Vicky as she opened the door. "Go get 'em, tiger."

Vicky ran her fingers through her blonde beach waves and ensured her purple silk blouse was perfectly half-tucked into her dark wash jeans. Her more formal business attire hung from the closet door, ready for tomorrow's leadership meetings. Vicky wondered if she should change into something more professional, but glancing at the clock, she saw there wasn't time. She pressed her lips, blending her freshly applied lip color, and made her way to the hotel's top floor.

Every step amplified Vicky's nerves as she walked down the long corridor. Stopping to take a deep breath, she tried one last time to calm herself before knocking. Christian's assistant opened the door and welcomed Vicky inside. Always the picture of professionalism, Evelyn stood poised and impossible to read. Her hair was pulled back in a high bun, delicate golden hoops dangled from her ears. A crisp white buttoned blouse tucked into a heather gray pencil skirt gave her a feminine authority that Vicky admired.

"Victoria, thank you for coming. Mr. White is looking forward to speaking with you."

Evelyn gestured for Vicky to follow her toward the balcony, where she could hear Christian talking on the phone. The room was bigger than Vicky and Becki's standard accommodations. A small sitting area and desk were next to a king-size bed. But it was the high-rise view that caught Vicky's attention. Between the sprawling city below and the mountains kissing the blue August skies, Vicky understood why he chose to do his business from the balcony instead of inside a stuffy hotel room or crowded convention center.

"Mr. White will be with you shortly." Evelyn gestured toward a small sofa beside the glass doors. Christian, still chatting outside, turned briefly to catch Vicky's eyes. He winked with a dimpled smile. A lump formed in Vicky's throat as Evelyn exited the room. As the door closed behind her, Vicky felt her muscles tense.

The rabbit hole that led to this moment reopened in Vicky's mind. The initial shock of Anna's sudden rise had forced her to dig for answers. After a week of dead ends, Vicky finally found a loose thread from an old forum about some failed MLM. Amidst a sea of hideous accusations about the company's CEO, Chris Blackwell, one post tried to tie Christian to this dead business. Vicky read through hundreds of comments, rolling her eyes at the insane lies people were willing to believe. One person honestly thought this Blackwell guy was an alien. These were not intelligent people.

Of course, rumors like this weren't new. All successful businesses and people dealt with detractors—hateful trolls and their outlandish gossip. Part of Vicky's initial training was learning how to deal with people's objections and the constant stream of lies typical of network marketing. She had always been told not to let these fake claims cloud the truth about Puremetics's mission.

Vicky knew propaganda when she saw it, and this forum was nothing more than bitter conspiracy theories from people who refused to take ownership of their failures. She sent screenshots and a summary to the Distributor Relations Division, which took decisive action. Of course, the triumph of sniffing out Anna's plan came with the risk of losing her new rank, but Vicky didn't care. After everything that had gone wrong recently, there was satisfaction in preserving the sanctity of Puremetics.

But now, as she sat nervously in Christian's hotel room, a budding doubt grew in Vicky's mind. What if all those rumors were true? What if she was putting herself in danger?

Christian held up one finger as he finished his phone call, letting Vicky know he'd be done soon. Vicky quickly pulled out her phone and hit record as she propped it against her purse on the desk. "Just to be safe," she whispered as her hand shook. But as soon as she sat back down, her heart jolted her to reconsider. It was stupid to worry about someone like Christian White. Vicky quickly grabbed the device and stuffed it in her pocket just as Christian opened the glass door.

"Victoria! Always a pleasure when our paths cross." He straightened his tie before reaching his hand out to Vicky. Despite his age, the man's gray hair and broad shoulders gave him a distinguished air. "Thanks so much for meeting with me today. I'm sure you'd rather be mentoring your leaders or checking out the new product teasers. I can't wait to reveal what we're releasing this year."

All the muscles in Vicky's body relaxed as she tried to hide the wave of relief that washed over her. Christian's professional demeanor and genuine excitement about the business pushed her back into her right mind. This meeting was about the company and its mission. There was no reason to get caught up in crazy schemes.

"Thank you for inviting me," Vicky said. "It's very exciting anytime I get to connect with Puremetics's leadership. You and your executive team do so much to make this company the family it is." She was delighted to hear her words flow easily despite her roller coaster of emotions.

"It *is* a family. I'm glad you recognize that. There's nothing more important to me than family, which means nothing is more important than this company."

Vicky smiled, trying to figure out what to do with her hands.

"Well," Christian said, sitting down and offering the seat next to him, "I didn't ask you here to tell you things you already know. I wanted to congratulate you and thank you."

"It's always nice to be noticed." Vicky sat on the sofa beside him, trying to keep a professional distance.

"I heard you stumbled on some disturbing information," he said, shaking his head. "One of your enrollees somehow signed up hundreds of online trolls—for what reason exactly?"

"I'm not entirely sure." Vicky shrugged, wishing she had more facts. "I saw a couple of comments on a post littered with ridiculous claims. Most of them had nothing to do with Puremetics and were years old, but a few new comments mentioned an absurd plan about enrolling with a Puremetics distributor who wanted to walk in the Leadership Gala. From the context, they were clearly talking about Anna Price, which makes sense since she suddenly gained a thousand enrollments in one month after nearly a year of failure."

Vicky took a deep breath, realizing her mouth was running a mile a minute. She steadied herself, trying to calm down. "I don't know exactly what Anna was planning to do. Frankly, the woman isn't the most bold or outspoken person. She probably would have embarrassed herself more than the company, but one thing was clear: Whatever the final plan, Anna Price was working to shame Puremetics publicly."

Christian clicked his tongue. "Some people. Imagine what they could do with all that time and energy if they put it toward something good. It's such a shame."

Vicky nodded.

"Well, I'm sure their plan would have failed even if this Anna person had made it to the stage, but we are still grateful you nipped it in the bud before it happened. Thank you."

"My pleasure," Vicky said, feeling quite proud.

Christian smiled, his hand landing softly on Vicky's knee. "And now to congratulate you. I hear you're our newest Royal Diamond and the fastest distributor to reach the top. Impressive."

Vicky carefully moved her leg, releasing it from Christian's grip. "Thank you, but I'm not sure I qualify anymore now that Anna's account has been terminated."

"Actually," Christian said, leaning in with a smile, "when someone's account is closed, their entire downline moves under their upline. Ms. Price had several qualifying legs, which means you still reached rank."

"But those women only signed up to harm the business."

Christian laughed, throwing his head back. "True. I can't imagine they'll keep their accounts active for long, although you'd be amazed how many people forget to turn off their auto-ships when they decide to walk away. Their money is still good. More than a quarter of a million dollars came through. As far as Puremetics is concerned, at least for now, you are a Royal Diamond."

He leaned forward again, his hand back on Vicky's knee. "And even if you have a temporary setback as those imposters fade away, with your drive, your skill, your beauty—" Christian paused, moving his hand further up her thigh. "—you'll be back on top in no time." His eyes lingered on Vicky's lips as he slowly leaned in toward her.

"Stop," Vicky said, pulling back. Her heartbeat quickened as her mouth went dry. She could barely process what was happening. The muscles in her body tensed, firing off like an alarm that made it impossible to think.

"I can't stop when I see something I want." Christian pushed himself toward Vicky, trapping her against the corner of the sofa. His hands ran up her waist toward her breast.

Vicky kneed him away, pushing with all her force. "I said *stop.*" She ducked under his arm and stood, but Christian grabbed her wrist, pulling her back down. She could feel her pulse in her mouth as her heart tried to barrel out of her chest.

"Don't act like you don't want this. Why else would you be so eager to come to my hotel room?"

"What the hell are you talking about?" Vicky twisted her hand, breaking free from his grasp. "I want nothing to do with this!" She grabbed her purse and bolted toward the door.

"I can make your life hell," Christian said, his voice so calm and calculated it pierced straight to her heart. "Remember that, my dear. This empire you think you've earned?" He snapped his fingers. "I can make it go away with one phone call."

Running into the hallway, Vicky let the door slam behind her. Down the hall, Evelyn stood, staring out a window. Still poised and unalarmed, she turned to face Vicky. Catching the tears streaming down Vicky's face, Evelyn looked away—as if it were her job.

Vicky's fingers pressed the elevator's button a dozen times, her fingers turning white from the strength of her pressure. She prayed for a quick escape. The ding of the elevator's arrival offered the tiniest hint of relief. Vicky threw herself into the metal box when the doors swung open, not waiting to let anyone off. She buried her head in the corner and sobbed.

"Mom?"

Vicky turned, shocked to see Blaze and Jane standing four feet from her. Without a thought about why they were there or what they had seen, she flung her arms around her son's neck, refusing to let go as if he was the only thing that could keep her from drowning. "I'm sorry," she whispered as her tears washed his neck. "I'm so so sorry."

28

"Mom?" Blaze pulled back, pushing the hair out of Vicky's face. "Are you okay?"

Vicky wiped her nose, shaking as if her body could slough off the memory of Christian's touch. Her eyes met her son's gaze, finally registering his unexpected appearance in this place. "What are you doing here?"

"Hey, Mrs. Sterling." Jane stood awkwardly in the corner and waved before stuffing her hands into her pockets.

It was hard to understand what was happening. Finding Blaze in this particular elevator in a hotel more than sixty miles from home only added to the shocking string of events that had nearly pummeled Vicky.

"Jane needed to see her mom and didn't have a car," Blaze said. "She asked for a ride."

"From Splendor Springs?" Vicky straightened herself up, smoothing her hair with her fingers and tucking in her shirt. She sniffed, trying to reclaim some form of composure. "That's nearly an hour's drive. I thought you had work."

"I got someone to cover for me. Mr. Graft said he didn't mind."

The elevator dinged, and the doors opened on the fifth floor.

"I'm going to give you guys some space," Jane said, carefully stepping into the hallway. She smiled at Blaze. "Text me when you're ready."

The doors closed, and Vicky instinctively tapped the button, desperate to get further away from the scene of Christian's assault. She couldn't bring herself to meet Blaze's eyes. Whatever impulse had driven her to his arms was now drowning in shame and disappointment.

The elevator stopped, letting them off onto the third floor. Vicky dragged her feet to her room, praying Becki was nowhere near the hotel. Blaze followed, quiet but with a desperation in his face that made Vicky feel safe but guilty.

As soon as they entered the room and confirmed they were alone, Blaze broke the silence. "Tell me what happened, Mom. Are you okay?"

Vicky shrugged, biting her lip.

"Whatever it is, you can tell me." Blaze blinked, pushing back his own tears. "I'm here for you. No matter what."

A hiccup of emotion bubbled from the back of Vicky's throat at this statement. She felt unworthy of such love—specifically now, especially from Blaze. As his mother, she was supposed to be comforting *him*, and she had failed countless times to fulfill that role over the past few months.

As the floodgates opened, Vicky covered her mouth, trying to hide her muffled sobs. She ran into the bathroom, locked herself inside, and fell apart. Terrifying sounds moaned from deep within her throat. Vicky's tears drenched her face as she sat on the tiled floor. Blaze knocked, begging her to open the door. Unable to give him even that, Vicky sunk further, wishing she could collapse into herself like a dying star.

Eventually, she slowly stood and splashed water on her face. Vicky was surprised by how quickly she had drained herself of tears, but it wasn't enough to fix the pain. Her red, puffy eyes and pale, sullen skin made her reflection in the mirror unrecognizable.

"Mom, we need to talk about this," Blaze said, knocking on the door. "I need to know you're okay."

The last thing Vicky wanted to do was tell Blaze what happened. What would he think? Would he blame her? Had Vicky done something wrong? Her mind replayed the scene from Christian's hotel room, filling her with questions. Had she led him on? Did she inadvertently flirt? Had she not said *no* loud enough? Tears streamed down her face again, pooling in the corners of her mouth and leaving a salty taste on her lips.

Vicky thought about staying in the bathroom forever. Hiding was the only way to keep pretending everything was okay. After years of burying her mistakes under layers of shine and success, Vicky's past had found a way to the surface. Christian must have seen it, must have sensed her sins. She frantically looked for a way to make the hole inside her bigger, hoping to hide this new shame along with all the others. But the more Vicky dug, the more she realized she was only burying herself. If she wanted to break free, she'd have to start by uncovering her secrets. She wiped her tears and opened the door.

Blaze jumped to his feet when Vicky came out of the bathroom. "Mom! Please, talk to me!" Ashen-faced and with searching eyes, his breath was erratic as his pupils bounced back and forth, trying to read Vicky's face.

"Sit down, sweetie." Vicky perched on the edge of her bed; Blaze joined her. Vicky tried to find a starting point—a way into the conversation that wouldn't be too painful, unsure how Blaze would see things once she laid everything at his feet. She started at the beginning.

"Your father and I had to get married." The words surprised Vicky. She had sworn to take this sin to her grave, hoping a lifetime of regret and commitment to her family would be enough to be granted forgiveness in the next.

Blaze did not look surprised. His gentle, puppy-dog eyes offered the grace Vicky didn't feel she deserved.

"I love your dad. We had talked about getting married before —" Vicky paused. "Well, before it was our only option. And while I will always be disappointed and angry with myself for letting it happen, I will never regret the person who resulted from those actions. My mistake does not mean you're a mistake."

"I know," Blaze said softly. "And I kind of figured it out a few years ago. I mean, I was eleven pounds at birth, but supposedly a month early? I can do basic math." He chuckled softly. "It's not that big of a deal."

Vicky scoffed. "I broke the Law of Chastity. You know how serious that is."

"Second worst sin next to murder, supposedly," he said with a sullen expression. "I've heard the Sunday School lessons plenty of times. Do you really think one small moment, especially one shared with someone you care about, deserves a lifetime of regret and shame?"

"What if I'm still broken?" Vicky asked, her voice barely audible.

Blaze was quiet for a minute as his eyes turned inward. He shook his head and sighed. "I don't believe people are born broken or that we need saving. Why can't we just accept that being human is hard, and that we're all just trying our best?"

More than anything, Vicky wanted to release this burden she'd been carrying, but hearing these statements from her son made her wonder how far he had drifted from Church Doctrine. Suddenly, the question Vicky had feared asking slipped through her lips. "Do you still believe in the Gospel? In Heavenly Father's plan?"

"I don't know," Blaze said calmly. "I've struggled with many questions over the past few years and don't know where I stand. If there is a god, and he truly loves us, I can't imagine him wanting his children to spend a lifetime feeling broken or ashamed."

"You're not broken," Vicky said, wishing she had said it months ago. "I hope you know that."

She looked at her son. In the past year, the last lingering remnants of her little boy had disappeared, transforming him into a man. When Blaze was little, Vicky often pictured his wedding day, wondering what woman would be worthy of her firstborn. That's when she realized she had been raising her children as if they were characters in *her* life's story, scripting their world to fit her desired ending. *No more.* Vicky was done trying to control the narrative, especially because she knew what it was like to give up your dreams to make someone else happy.

"I'm so sorry I've been so distant," Vicky said, tears flowing again. "I never should have betrayed your trust by snooping on your phone." Her body flinched just thinking about it. "You needed reassurance and love, and I ran away. It was cruel."

Blaze looked down as he nervously twisted a loose thread on his shirt. "It's okay."

"No." Vicky's voice caught. "It's not. I was horrible. I love you, Blaze. Nothing will change that. I've been wrestling with this news, not because it changes how I feel about you, but because it threatens some pretty stubborn beliefs of mine."

He looked up, catching Vicky's gaze. Tears swelled in his eyes. "You think I'm going to hell."

Vicky reached for his hand and squeezed. "If that's true, I'd rather go to hell with you than change who you are. You are a beautiful soul, and you are not broken. You don't need to be fixed. The world needs you just as you are, and I'm sorry it's taken me so long to figure that out. I want you to find whatever and whoever makes you happy." She choked on her words, desperate to get them out. "Can you forgive me?"

Blaze wrapped his arm around his mother. She nestled her head into his chest, unable to believe the day had come when he was taking care of her. "I forgive you," he whispered, holding her tighter. "And I hope you can forgive yourself."

The two sat, silently crying in each other's arms. Vicky inhaled her child like she did when he was little. It was hard letting him go, her love so entangled with every piece of him, but she knew Blaze's freedom would keep him closer than trying to cage him forever.

Blaze pulled back and kept his eyes steady on Vicky's face. "Now, can you please tell me what happened?"

"I had a meeting with the Puremetics CEO," Vicky said, steadying her breath. She closed her eyes and exhaled slowly. "He asked me to come to his room to thank me, but then—" she paused, still trying to make sense of everything. "He tried to…" The words wouldn't come, but the image of it was fresh in her mind. She shook her head, trying to get rid of it. "I pushed him away…"

"What are you saying?" Blaze jumped to his feet. "Did he assault you?"

Vicky's hands flew to her face as she nodded.

"Mom, you need to call the police!"

"You don't understand, honey. Christian White has money and power. All I have is my word against his. Trust me. As someone who has lived in this world as long as I have, there's very little I can do."

Blaze slumped back down on the bed and pulled Vicky in close. "I'm really sorry, Mom. It's awful, and it is not your fault."

"Are you sure?" Vicky said, pleading for an answer she could believe.

"Absolutely." Blaze clenched his fists. "Now I hate this Christian guy even more."

"Even more? What does that mean?"

Blaze sighed. "Mom, since we're being honest with each other, you should know I didn't just come here so Jane could see her mom. I mean, I did, but that's not the whole story."

Vicky sat tall and cocked her head. "I don't understand."

"I'll explain everything, but only if you promise not to get mad. It's about Jane's mom and her mission to take down Christian White."

"Oh," Vicky said, suddenly conflicted. She had been instrumental in getting Anna kicked out of Convention, but after what happened with Christian, Vicky was beginning to regret that decision. Was it possible Anna had been right all along? She sighed. "I know about Anna's plan. It's not going to work. I stopped it."

A slight grin lifted the side of Blaze's mouth. "Trust me. You don't know everything."

29

Anna pulled the keys from the ignition and exhaled slowly. The large windows framed a cozy scene of friends and families gathered inside the restaurant, but Anna did not feel its warmth. She was consumed with relenting heartache, still reeling from her embarrassing dismissal at Vicky's luncheon. After disappointing Gloria, Anna wasn't in the mood to disappoint anyone else.

Yet, that was what she came to do.

Her phone buzzed. Anna opened the text message from Lisa, eager to procrastinate a few seconds longer: *Just got off work and saw your message. Can't believe they kicked you out! I told you Vicky was the devil. Hang in there. It will be okay. Can you talk now?*

Anna tapped out a reply. *Can't. Have to break the news to Tammy. Let's chat later.*

She had almost forgotten about the dinner plans with Tammy, one of the people she had enrolled from the Aroma Harmony forum. Their phone conversation a few weeks ago had meant so much to Anna. It reminded her that she was finally doing something right with her life, something meaningful. Now, she had to inform this woman, who had traveled hundreds of miles to watch Anna defeat their giant, that their mission had already failed.

"You okay, Mom?" Jane asked. "We're already late. We should probably get inside."

"Yeah, you're right." Anna sighed again as she reached for her purse. "This was supposed to be a happy meeting."

Jane patted her mom's knee, offering a sympathetic look. "We talked about this. Gloria hasn't given up on the plan, and neither should you. We're going to figure this out—together."

"Thanks, kid." Despite the constant disappointments that seemed to bombard Anna's life, she couldn't help but feel lucky to have such an incredible daughter by her side through it all. She sat tall, pulled her shoulders back, and opened the car door. "Okay, let's do this."

They entered the restaurant. Anna's eyes drifted along the crowd until they settled on a petite woman sitting alone. Immediately, Anna knew it was Tammy, although she didn't know why—she certainly didn't look like a giant slayer. Tammy sat upright with an assured posture. Her silk blouse and feminine pixie cut reminded Anna of an older Audrey Hepburn.

"I think that's her," Anna said as she moved into the dining room, trying to figure out why the woman looked familiar. She reached out to shake her hand. "You must be Tammy! I'm Anna. Sorry, we're late."

"I just sat down." Tammy smiled, revealing laugh lines around her eyes. A waitress stopped by with a glass of red wine, hinting to Anna that Tammy had probably been waiting longer than she let on. "It's nice to meet you, Anna."

"This is my daughter, Jane." Anna stepped aside. "She's equally excited to meet you, so I hope you don't mind her tagging along."

"Of course not! Hello, Jane." Tammy straightened her spine and folded her hands in her lap. "I'm just so happy we could meet before tomorrow's big event. From what I understand, at least a hundred of us made the trip to watch this all play out. We have our own group chat and have been taking bets on Christian's reaction when it all goes down. I'll add you to it."

A hundred people? Anna's stomach turned.

"About that," she said, taking a seat. The sooner Anna pulled off the Band-Aid, the sooner this awful day would end. "I'm afraid you may have come all this way for nothing." The familiar swell of regret filled her chest. She pushed it down, trying to be brave.

"Oh?" Tammy's face fell ever so slightly—enough to show her disappointment. "What happened?"

"It seems my direct upline found evidence of this plan of ours. She informed the company, and they terminated my account. I just found out a few hours ago." Anna glanced down at her fingers twiddling in her lap. "I'm so sorry to waste your time. It seems like the army we assembled invested in a failure."

"Mom," Jane said. "This wasn't your fault."

Anna shook her head, still unable to believe it had all come to this. She tried to read the expression on Tammy's face, hoping to determine just how angry or upset this news had made her. The woman maintained a bright, polite smile, but Anna could tell it wasn't sincere. Tammy's eyes couldn't hide the disappointment.

Jane's phone buzzed. Face pulled down, she tapped out a handful of messages.

Tammy chuckled. "Teens and their devices."

"It's not just teens," Anna said. "I've accidentally photobombed at least a hundred group selfies today. The Puremetics huns are constantly documenting every moment." She took a sip of water as soon as the server set it on the table. "Anyway, I'm so sorry you came all this way for things to fall through at the last minute."

"It's not hopeless, Mom." Jane's face was still buried in her phone until a small whoosh sounded, releasing her attention so she could focus on the group again. "Gloria will come up with something. I know it."

"Gloria?" Tammy asked. She leaned forward as her eyes grew serious.

"She's the one who really put this whole thing together. Well, her and her little group of misfits." Anna laughed, tucking her hair behind her ear. "They needed me to enroll and rank high enough to get on stage as part of a bigger plan they've been putting together for a year or two, maybe longer."

Tammy's eyes drifted downward as her body froze. She shook her head, drawing her delicate fingers to her lips. "Gloria Wright?"

"Yeah. Do you know her?"

"No." Tammy folded her arms in her lap, still transfixed on her thoughts.

Anna squinted in the restaurant's dim light. "Where are you from, Tammy? You look so familiar."

"Salt Lake, originally. Well, Murray," Tammy said, her mind clearly focused on something else. She closed her eyes and refocused. "I lived in Idaho for a bit—that's where I got wrapped up in the Aroma Harmony disaster. After all that went down, I decided I hadn't seen enough of the world. I've been traveling a lot the last eight years, but Santa Barbara is the closest thing to home these days."

"I guess you just have one of those faces," Anna smiled, taking another sip. She leaned back and cocked her head. "Something about your smile."

Tammy shrugged, the tension in her shoulders growing. She grabbed her wine and took a sip.

Anna's eyes grew wide. "Oh, my god. You're the woman from the mural."

"The what?"

The mural. The woman's profile. A phoenix overhead. Anna

nearly fell out of her chair. "You're Fiona—Christian White's wife."

"No," Tammy said, lowering her voice. "I think you are mistaken."

"Oh my god, oh my god, oh my god!" Jane's mouth ran full speed ahead. She dropped her phone and leaned forward. "You're the missing wife?"

Tammy's eyes darted around the restaurant as her hands began to tremble. "I'm sure I don't know what you're talking about."

"Yeah, there are all kinds of crazy rumors online about the mysterious disappearance of Fiona Blackwell. Some say her husband killed her. Others wondered if she had been drugged and dropped off in Mexico." Jane fell back in her chair, smiling from ear to ear. "And here you are! I'm so glad you're not dead!"

Tammy leaned forward, catching her head with her hand while the other lifted her wine to her lips. She took one giant gulp and swallowed hard. "Do you think we can talk about this somewhere else?"

Anna nodded, not waiting a second before offering an arm for support as the three women hurried out of the building. They piled into Anna's car, Tammy sitting shotgun.

"Is it true? Are you Fiona?"

"Yes," Tammy said, her breath erratic. "But you can't say a word. As far as anyone knows, my name is Tammy Wilson. Can I trust you two to keep this secret?"

"Of course," Anna said.

"Does Gloria know you're here? Does she know you're alive?" Jane was bouncing in the back seat, hyped up by this revelation.

"No. I had no idea Gloria was a part of this." Tammy rubbed the sides of her head, looked up, and sighed. "Although, it makes perfect sense. That damn woman and her unconquerable sense of justice." A faint smile crept along Tammy's face before sinking back into panic.

Tammy locked eyes with Anna. "You can't tell Gloria. It would be too much for her to handle right now. I will talk to her when the time is right, and *only* if this plan to take Chris down works. If things go sideways and he discovers that Gloria is behind things, he might..." her words drifted away, unable to finish the sentence.

Anna's imagination filled in the blanks. Her heart rate spiked, and she wondered what new mess she had created by reaching out to Tammy in the first place. "Is it safe for you to be here? Why come back now after all these years?"

Tammy inhaled slowly, biting her lip. "No matter how many times I showed up at my parents' house with bruises or a black eye, they told me to make things right with God and that it would magically fix things. I stayed with Chris much longer than I should have because I didn't believe I had a choice, and then I ran away for the same reason."

"But how did you escape?" Anna asked.

"It wasn't easy. Gloria and I worked together on a plan for months, and it ended poorly. The lawyer friend I was working with ratted me out to Chris. Chris doubled down, monitoring every aspect of my life, threatening anyone who might want to help me. It took me another seven years to break free, and I had to do it alone. Gloria was the only one I trusted to have my best interest in hand, but she was also the one with the largest target on her back. I had to bide my time, cut off all connection with her, and make sure my escape had no strings attached to Gloria whatsoever."

Anna drank the words in, horrified by their implications. "If it's that important to keep your secret, why did you go along with my plan after finally breaking free?"

"Because I'm not free. I'm always running, always hiding. I am sick of feeling like a coward." Tammy balled her hands into tiny fists as her chest rose and fell with heavy breaths. "When some strange woman messaged me out of the blue, fighting *my* fight, I knew I couldn't sit still." She smiled at Anna. "You inspired me."

Jane nudged Anna's arm. "See, Mom! You're amazing."

"You are," Tammy said, squeezing Anna's hand. "And I'm here, hoping to siphon a smidgen of your bravery to give my story a better ending."

No one had ever called Anna brave, but the memory of sending messages to groups of strangers, trying to sell them a different kind of Puremetics opportunity, had felt like a courageous act. More than anything else, Anna wanted to feel it again. It was a shame everything was falling apart. "I'm sorry to let you down just as we approach the finish line," she said.

Tammy smiled. "I think it's too soon to give up hope."

"Me, too," Jane said with a decisive nod.

Anna twisted her purse strap, wrestling with it as her mind fought for an answer. "I just wish I knew what we could do. Gloria insists we need a distraction to make this work, but there is no way I can get on that stage now."

"I might know a way," Jane said, holding up her phone and revealing a long string of text messages. She smiled as her eyes drifted to the side of Anna's window and pointed.

Anna turned, surprised to see Blaze and Vicky standing outside her car. Vicky knocked on the glass, and Anna rolled down the window.

"Anna," Vicky said, her voice low and sincere. "I want to help."

30

CONVENTION: DAY 2

"Here, put this on." Vicky handed Anna a Puremetics lanyard as she entered Vicky's hotel room.

"Who is Gigi Burton?" Anna asked, reading the nametag.

"No clue. I found it in the hotel lobby. Bad news for Gigi, good news for you." Vicky moved into the bathroom to change, keeping the door open as she talked. "It will give you access to the event. You may not be on stage for the Leadership Gala, but at least you'll be in the arena."

Anna slipped the badge over her head, letting it dangle from her neck, trying to imagine how Gigi Burton might stand or talk. She checked her reflection in the mirror by the TV, cringing at the bags under her eyes. Despite her exhaustion, Anna's mind was on high alert. The past few days had felt like a never-ending roller coaster—each second, there was an unexpected turn.

Last night's twists had been particularly jarring. Meeting Tammy and discovering her true identity filled Anna with a dreadful sense of responsibility. More than anything, she wanted to tell Gloria to ensure both women found the closure they deserved. But of all the secrets Anna had been hoarding over the last eleven months, this one seemed imperative to keep safe.

Then there was Vicky's sudden turnaround, setting the plan back into action and proving there was still at least one more climb on this crazy ride. Gloria and Anna were hesitant to let Vicky help but eventually agreed after Jane convinced them it was the only way to get the confession. Vicky would give Christian the lapel pin with the recording device, allowing Anna to take Emily's place as the backstage videographer. It was perfect.

Anna's body was dragging after a late-night planning session with the new crew—a group far more eclectic now that Jane, Blaze, and Vicky were standing in for Emily and the other OWLS. Nobody would think they were a knitting group or book club, but maybe their odd-ball lineup would make them even more inconspicuous.

Everything seemed primed for success, but Anna couldn't shake the feeling that they were heading for another dive, that something would go wrong. Could they really trust Vicky? Was Vicky emotionally up for the task? Anna didn't know all the details of what happened in Christian's room but could see the scars left behind in Vicky's eyes. It was a trauma too many women shared.

"Are you sure you're okay?" Anna asked as Vicky walked out of the bathroom. "You know you don't have to do this."

"Actually, I do," Vicky said in her usual assured manner, turning her back to Anna. "Now, help me."

"It's just that I'd understand if you wanted to back out." Anna zipped Vicky's dress, admiring the emerald gown she had chosen for the leadership gala. Light bounced from the tiny sequins, making Vicky look like a mermaid.

Vicky turned, grabbing Anna by the shoulders. "As I said last night, I *want* to do this. I realized I was wrong... about a lot of things. When Blaze told me what you guys were doing, I knew this was my chance to help make things right." She turned, fiddling with a small jewelry box. "I'm tired of pretending things are okay when they're not, and for once in my life, I'd like to push back against the system instead of always trying to find my place inside it."

Anna nodded, her face still covered in doubt.

"Don't worry about me." Vicky tousled her hair one last time and checked her lipstick. "Stay focused. There's not a lot of time."

The hotel door buzzed before swinging open. Jane and Blaze walked in, looking like a pair of zombies.

"Hey," Anna said, helping Vicky with her necklace. "Did you guys get any sleep?"

Jane rubbed her eyes. "A little. After you guys left Gloria's room, we stayed behind to test all the files and microphone." She shook her head. "Gloria is all set to go."

Vicky smiled, placing her hands on her hips. "Good job guys!"

"What about you, Mom?" Jane asked. "Are you sure you know what you're doing?"

Anna rolled her eyes, catching the subtext of her daughter's words. "I think I know how to hold a phone and hit record."

Jane lifted an eyebrow. "It's a little more complicated than that. You need to make sure to sync the microphone to your device."

"Yes, you've shown me a million times. I got it."

"It's just that you're even less technically savvy than Gloria," Jane said with a smirk.

Blaze and Vicky chuckled. Anna wanted to be annoyed, but it was true. She had a history of technical blunders, and this high-pressure situation wouldn't make things any easier.

"Blaze and I could record the confession, you know." Jane plopped down on the bed.

"No," Vicky said, reapplying her mascara as she leaned

toward the mirror. "I told you last night. I'm only willing to do this if you and Blaze are nowhere near the arena when everything goes down."

Blaze crossed his arms. "What do you think will happen? We're sharing video footage not showing up with a bomb."

Anna leaned against the desk, her body begging her to lie down. "There will be a ton of people, and we don't know how this will end. It's safer for you guys to be away from the crowds. We'll keep you updated on everything in the group chat."

"Fine," Blaze said, getting up and moving to the bathroom.

Vicky shook her head as he closed the door. "It's still hard to believe you kids have been plotting against me this whole time."

"Just the last few weeks," Jane teased, stretching her arms over her head and yawning. "Blaze only learned about any of this a few days ago, and he actually defended you several times."

Vicky cleared her throat and smiled.

"Now, Mom, on the other hand." Jane whistled. "She's been undercover from the beginning, undermining your every move."

Anna blushed, even though she knew Jane was mostly kidding. "I was never plotting against you, Vicky. Just Puremetics."

Vicky dropped her head and sighed, taking a quiet moment before looking up and catching Anna's gaze in the mirror. "Christian is a horrible human being and deserves to have his empire ripped away, but you need to know that this work means so much to so many women. I poured my heart into this business. I worked for this success."

"And sometimes," Jane said, crossing her arms, "you did it at the expense of others. I think it's important to take responsibility for that."

Vicky straightened up. "I promoted wellness products. I wasn't holding people hostage or intentionally lying to them."

"No, but you pressured me into a twelve-hundred-dollar purchase," Anna said, surprised that she dared to push back.

"The OWLS told me they would cover the payment, but I had no guarantee. All I could think about were the bills I might have to skip to pay off some stupid, overpriced vitamins."

Vicky nodded, biting her lip. Taking a deep breath, she walked over and touched Anna's shoulder. "You're right. I'm not blameless, and I'm sorry." She glanced at Jane. "To both of you."

Anna squeezed her hand. "And I'm sorry I lied about my intentions. Even if I was doing it for a good cause, it doesn't change the fact that I manipulated people to get ahead, just like you."

"Damn capitalism," Jane said.

Anna pulled her daughter in for a hug. "And I'm sorry I kept the truth from you for so long. You were so upset with the whole Puremetics thing. I had no idea what you'd think when you learned the actual truth."

"I was upset because I know you can succeed at whatever you put your mind to," Jane said, "and I hate Puremetics."

Anna laughed.

"But this thing you've been doing with Gloria? I'm one hundred percent on board." Jane smiled. "Even if you fail, which is always possible, wouldn't you rather fail at something important? Something good?"

Pulling Jane in for another hug, Anna could barely contain her love for the kid.

"Alright, ladies. Hugging time is over." Vicky clapped her hands. "Anna, we've got to go. You'll need to find a seat, and I need to get to the pre-gala orientation."

"Break a leg!" Jane said, smiling at her mom. She turned to Vicky. "But not, like, literally."

Anna laughed. "Yeah, Emily already did that."

I'm backstage ready to go. The gala is about to start. Vicky sent the message, trying to stay focused as her nerves kicked in.

> ANNA:
>
> You got this.
>
> BLAZE:
>
> Good luck, Mom!
>
> GLORIA:
>
> Stick it to him!
>
> JANE:
>
> Right in the heart!!

Vicky chuckled. These last few wishes for luck would need to sustain her until she finished the job. She stuffed her phone in her purse and dropped it in the bin with everyone else's belongings. Her fingers wrapped around the one item she'd carry with her on stage: a small velvet box with a lapel pin inside.

A black curtain separated those backstage from the rest of the audience, so Vicky couldn't see the crowd as she stood in the dark half of the stadium. But the audience's chatter conveyed the event's enormity. Enthusiastic distributors from all over the world packed the Energy Solutions Arena. Vicky wondered what everyone would do when their hero came crashing down.

Becki waved from the front of the line. Like Vicky, she was being lauded as a leader of Puremetics, having reached the rank of Presidential Emerald. Vicky smiled, wishing she could delight in the moment more. She and Becki had talked about walking the stage together ever since Becki started pushing the business. As Vicky looked at these women in their dazzling gowns, she couldn't help but see the cracks in what was supposed to be a perfect moment for each of them.

A small monitor mounted on a table gave Vicky a view of the action happening on stage. She cringed as Christian White walked toward the microphone. The audience erupted in applause. Even from where Vicky stood, behind all the action, it was a deafening wave of enthusiasm. Her chest throbbed from the noise as it pressed against her.

Christian's voice boomed through the sound system. "This is perhaps my favorite part of convention: The Leadership Gala." Even on the tiny screen, his presence loomed large. He paused, waiting for the noise to settle. "The amazing thing about Puremetics is that anyone can achieve unthinkable dreams through a compensation plan unlike any other. What other company is structured in a way that lets people earn this kind of success?"

The women backstage exchanged nervous smiles as they smoothed their hair and plumped their lips. Standing at the end of the line, Vicky went over her speech, determined to see this plan through to the end. Still, she couldn't help but mourn the loss of a dream she had worked so hard to achieve. The vision of her empire shattered, but she was determined to make something meaningful from the pieces left behind.

White continued. "The Leadership Gala is when we celebrate those consistently putting in the effort, earning their way into our top earner's positions. The ranks of Sapphire Executive, Presidential Emerald, and Royal Diamond represent our best and brightest."

The applause was never-ending. The man could barely get one sentence out before rabid cheers interrupted him.

He pressed on, his demanding presence slowly quieting the crowd. "Any of you can achieve this greatness. As we celebrate these twenty-three women today, I want everyone in this audience to think about what it takes to get to this point. Next year, I want to see even more of you on stage. Commit to reaching your dreams. Think about who you can share this opportunity with. Push yourself to keep spreading this light even when someone says *no*—even when they *keep* saying *no*. I guarantee the women you're about to see in just a moment have heard the word *no* more times than they can count. But they were persistent. That is the key to success."

The roar from the crowd pierced Vicky's brain. A staff member motioned for the line to move forward as she held the curtain's edge, ready to lead the first group onto the stage. Inspirational music swelled from the speakers. Vicky couldn't look away from Christian's face on the monitor. His smile grew with every second until it consumed his face.

"Ladies and gentlemen," Christian said, "I am pleased to present this year's lineup for the Leadership Gala. Please help me first welcome the fourteen women who reached the rank of Sapphire Executive."

Fourteen people. Vicky counted them as they disappeared through the curtain. *Just fourteen?* Knowing there were more than ten thousand people at Convention alone, how could so few have earned this promotion? What had once felt like a distinct honor now stunk of ignorance. Clearly, this level of success was the exception to an unspoken rule. Most people failed at this business. Vicky knew this from her own experience but had always blamed the struggling distributors, never the system so obviously flawed.

"First up is Lindsay Romero from Austin, Texas. Lindsay joined Puremetics three years ago and has continued to influence thousands of women as she shares the Puremetics opportunity through her popular blog, Wellness Warrior."

Applause rippled through the stadium with a small pocket of enthusiastic cheers from one corner of the audience. Vicky watched from the monitor as Lindsay's eyes squinted against the spotlight. A woman in a gray pantsuit handed Lindsay a bouquet of roses. She took the microphone, not missing a moment of her twenty seconds in the spotlight.

"I want to thank my husband for his steadfast support, my downline for believing in this incredible opportunity, and, of course, Christian White. Without him, none of this would be possible." Lindsay took off the lei she had been wearing and solemnly placed it around his neck. "This lei represents the first trip I earned through Puremetics: The Hawaii Getaway in 2012. On that trip, I vowed to make it to the Leadership Gala. Thank you, Christian, for making it happen."

Lindsay leaned in to hug Christian, and Vicky felt her stomach knot. A rush of heat washed over her as sweat began kiss her forehead.

"You okay?" a staff worker nearby asked.

"Fine," Vicky said, steadying herself against the table. She smiled, trying to regain her composure. "Just nervous."

The woman grabbed a nearby folding chair and offered it to Vicky. "It's a big day. Take it easy. You still have some time."

Vicky thanked her, sat, and focused on her breath as she watched the other thirteen Sapphire Executives take their moment. Each offered their thanks, ensuring that Christian White got the most praise. Small gifts of gratitude, a tradition that had only begun a few years prior, took center stage as the leaders moved on and lined up in the back.

Christian removed the lei from his neck, added it to the pile of gifts, and carried on with the presentation. "Now it's time to celebrate the newest Presidential Emeralds. First up is Becki Young."

Vicky couldn't help but smile as her friend took her moment in the spotlight. She knew how hard Becki had worked to get here. How hard all these women worked. Was there a better opportunity out there? Was the whole industry, as Gloria put it, a stinking hot turd? Vicky wanted to believe there was a way to spark this kind of fire in others without all the baggage, but it seemed impossible. So, for the moment, she quietly cheered her friend from the sideline, trying to savor the rush one last time.

Waiting through the other presentations was nerve-wracking. Vicky's heart felt like a jackhammer trying to break open her rib cage. The group of women backstage slowly got smaller as she watched these new leaders take their moment in the spotlight. Summoning all her courage and squeezing the small jewelry box, she prepared for her turn.

"And finally, it's time to bring out the Royal Diamonds." Christian waited for the applause to die down again. "With only three new ranks this year, it's easy to see what a distinction this honor is. These women will join an elite fourteen others from the last five years who have made the climb to Royal Diamond. It is no easy task, but it is possible for everyone here today."

Vicky waited as the staff pulled the curtain back, welcoming her and two others onto the stage. The crowd jumped to their feet, their applause sounding more like a jet engine than praise. Sweat ran down the back of Vicky's neck as Christian introduced the first two leaders. Their bios were longer, the praise more embellished, and unlike the other ranks, these women got two minutes to speak to the crowd. With every word, every accolade, Vicky felt like she might pass out.

"Last, but certainly not least, is Victoria Sterling." Christian shot Vicky a look of warning that made Vicky's spine curl.

"Victoria has the distinction of being the fastest-growing leader in Puremetics's history."

Cheers swelled from the crowd.

"Her influence has reached millions, using her popular blog and online status to share Puremetics far and wide. And yet, she proved you don't need millions of followers to make this opportunity work, as every one of Victoria's qualifying legs lives within a ten-mile radius from her home in Kinderhook, Utah. A love for her neighbors and community has pushed Victoria to greatness."

The executive handed Vicky her bouquet of red roses. A staff member led her to the microphone. Taking a deep breath, Vicky felt her practiced speech slip from her mind. Her lips parted, but nothing came. Panic flooded her body as her nerves took command. Only when her eyes landed on Anna and Gloria standing in the audience did she find her way.

"My dear, Puremetics family. It is an honor to be with you today." The audience cheered, and Vicky took advantage of the moment to breathe. "I have dreamed of this moment ever since my first convention, which was only a year ago—" she said lightly. Laughter rippled through the crowd. "But a lot can change in a year. In a month. In a moment. When an opportunity presents itself, and you feel your whole-body light on fire, you know you must act."

Vicky looked at Christian, his dimpled smile hiding the secrets Vicky could never forget. "Like everyone else, I wouldn't be here without a tremendous team of support. My family, my downline, my faith—it takes a community to thrive." She pulled out the velvet box and pointed to Christian. "But of all the people who have paved this path, this man stands alone."

Christian smiled, waving at the audience as they rang out with devotion. His eyes seemed to soften as Vicky approached him. "I'm glad you've come to your senses," he whispered. "I was worried you'd do something foolish."

As Vicky pulled the pin from her box, she considered pressing it into Christian's heart but smiled instead as she pinned the brooch to his lapel. "It was a miscommunication, I'm sure," she said quietly. "Besides, who would believe me if I said anything."

Christian wrapped his arms around her and moved his lips to Vicky's ear. "Exactly." He squeezed her shoulders and pulled back, winking before returning to his adoring fans.

Vicky snapped the velvet box with a satisfying click.

31

Every cell in Anna's body stood at attention as Vicky pinned the brooch to Christian's tie. Time didn't just stop. It expanded, pulling every moment, every person into its own universe. Anna tried to understand how she became a part of this strange reality. Christian's smug smile, Vicky's knowing glance, Gloria's grip on Anna's shoulder—each story unfolded, revealing an unlikely connection between each character.

And there was Anna, standing at the crossroads of it all.

"She did it," Gloria whispered, breaking the spell and sending life back into motion. Her hand continued to press into Anna's arm like a conduit, pulsating with an unnerving determination. "We're in business." Gloria lifted her chest with a determined inhale and exhaled slowly. "Ready for part two?"

Anna nodded despite the sudden urge to run away. In theory, her new task as the videographer was more straightforward and far less public than what Vicky had just accomplished, but that didn't stop Anna from silently freaking out. Breathing deeply, she ran through a mental checklist of her duties, determined not to screw things up.

The first step was to find a good hiding spot. The large black curtains that cut the stadium floor in half would provide ample nooks for cover. *Check.* Next, Anna needed to ensure the microphone was connected via her phone's Bluetooth. She drilled that step with Jane last night. *Check.* Finally, Anna needed to record everything while keeping Christian in the frame and Gloria out of it. *Easy enough.* Laid out in this simple one-two-three, Anna breathed easier until she remembered Vicky's final warning: *Don't get caught.*

"Shit," Gloria whispered, looking at her phone.

Anna felt her heart jump into her throat. "What? What's wrong?"

"Shit, shit, shit!" Gloria's entire body clenched, screaming without making a sound. "Our AV person says the video file is corrupt. It won't open."

"But you have a backup, right? You have multiple copies on several devices—that's what you said."

Gloria frantically typed out another message. "She's saying all three versions we gave her show the same error."

"We know the files work on my laptop. I could text Jane to bring it here. Is it possible to hook the whole computer to their system in the AV booth?"

"Maybe." Gloria removed her glasses and rubbed the bridge of her nose. "I wish Emily were here. She's the techy one." With a huff, Gloria threw her head back. "Okay, you know what? It's fine. Text Jane. It's better than doing nothing, and we have bigger fish to fry and less than twenty minutes to corner Christian."

"Right." Anna stood tall, trying to shake off her nerves as she sent a quick message to the group chat: *Video file won't open. Jane, bring the laptop to the arena. We'll figure out how to get you inside when you arrive.*

Gloria locked eyes with Anna. "We need this to confession more than ever. We have to make this work. Do you know what to do?"

Anna closed her eyes, the pressure mounting on top of her. "Yes? I think so. Yes! Yes, I'm ready."

They waited for the perfect moment to slip behind the curtained wall. The VP of Products, an overly polished woman in a purple pantsuit, was pitching a new energy drink onstage. Her over-the-top, syrupy voice was giving Anna a headache.

"Pure-Vigor is more than just a boost of energy. This unparalleled elixir is designed to rejuvenate your spirit and elevate your vitality. Infused with a synergistic blend of ethically sourced superfoods, rare botanical extracts, and a touch of enchantment, Pure-Vigor is set to revolutionize your productivity."

The woman turned to the giant screen behind her as a video testimonial played. "I was dragging my feet every day, feeling like total garbage," said the woman in the video, another blonde beauty who had been with Puremetics since the beginning. "After three weeks of Pure-Vigor, I feel like a new person!"

Gloria rolled her eyes. "Each year, it's the same thing. It's unbelievable how fast these women go from barely surviving to suddenly thriving anytime a new product comes out, forgetting that last year's product had supposedly already cured them. It's like they can't keep their own stories straight."

Unlike Gloria, the crowd fawned over the news, their roars so loud Anna could barely hear her thoughts. Fortunately, their cheers were the perfect distraction as Gloria and Anna snuck behind the black dividers. Anna relaxed as soon as they were out of view of the audience, but her muscles fired when Gloria quickly pushed her toward a fold in the curtain. "Someone's coming. Hide!"

Cloaked by the heavy fabric, Anna's eyes bulged as Christian White approached. He yelled, his voice barely audible over the crowd's never-ending applause. "This is a closed event. Who let you back here?"

Gloria stood tall, pulling down the hem of her zebra-striped blazer. "Hey, Chris. Long time no see."

Anna fumbled with her phone, frantically trying to unlock it and open the appropriate app. Her hands shook as she tapped the record button and checked the audio input.

Stepping closer, Christian squinted his eyes in the poorly lit corner of the stadium. "Gloria Wright? Are you kidding me? What the hell are you doing here?"

"I feel like I could ask you the same question," Gloria said, leaning in closer. "Shouldn't you be in jail?"

Christian cocked his head back. "For what? Creating a company that helps thousands of women live their dreams?" His voice dripped with sarcasm as he thrust his wrists together in pretend handcuffs. "Such a crime! Lock me away!"

Anna's heart thumped violently against her chest. She was unconvinced Gloria was going to get anything useful out of this man.

"How about murdering your wife?" Gloria shot back.

Christian's eyes grew wide. "Excuse me?"

As surprised as he looked, it was nothing compared to Anna's shock. Did Gloria think Christian murdered Fiona? If so, it would explain her unceasing determination to trap Christian with his own words, but if this were the big reveal Gloria had anticipated, a confession would never come. Anna should know. Fiona wasn't just alive—she was in the building, sitting in the audience as Tammy Wilson.

"I loved Fiona." Christian folded his arms and tossed away any feigned pleasantries. "Her disappearance nearly destroyed me. To have you come here, infiltrate this celebratory event, and accuse me of something so heinous is disgusting." He snatched Gloria by the wrist and tapped a button on his barely visible earpiece. "Security, we have a trespasser. Near door R. Please secure and detain her for further questioning."

Anna watched in horror as two men came, grabbed, and dragged Gloria away. Gloria didn't fight, didn't even glance in

Anna's direction. She clearly didn't believe the man's words and was still convinced he had done it.

Christian was unmoved. He straightened his tie, the golden pin still neatly in place, and walked toward the stage. In a few minutes, the closing session would begin. The confession was a no-go, but there was still a chance to get the video out.

A million concerns collided as Anna tried to think of a plan. She stared at her phone, desperate for an answer or, at the very least, a way to talk to Gloria. She finally opened her messages and quickly texted Vicky: *Where are you?*

A response came seconds later. *Still backstage. Becki won't shut up!*

Checking to ensure nobody was around, Anna crept along the backside of the stage, making her way until she saw Vicky talking to a handful of women. Becki's hands gestured with over-the-top motions. Vicky caught Anna's eyes and excused herself.

"What are you doing back here?" Vicky whispered, grabbing Anna's shoulder and moving further away from the others. "You can't let Becki see you. She knows who you are and, more importantly, that you shouldn't be here."

"We have a problem."

"The video won't play. I saw the group chat." Vicky sighed. "Jane is coming, and she'll probably bring Blaze. It's fine. I'm sure they'll figure it out."

Anna exhaled sharply. "Gloria was taken away by security. She did not get the confession."

"What?" Vicky blurted out. She blushed, looked over her shoulder, and lowered her voice. "Is she okay? Do we need to find her?"

Anna shrugged. Her phone buzzed with another update. "Jane and Blaze are at the fifth level entrance." She looked at Vicky. "Are we making a mistake by pulling them into this?"

"Let's be honest," Vicky said, shaking her head, "they probably would have shown up on their own anyway."

Anna chuckled, having thought the same thing. As much as she wanted to protect Jane, she had come to rely on her unfailing support, and it seemed wrong to do this without her.

"We need a contingency plan." Anna rubbed her forehead. Visions of Security carting off Gloria kept popping into her mind, along with a hundred other things that could go wrong. "Even if the kids get a new file to the AV crew, it's too easy for someone to shut us down. How much of the video will play before security turns the whole system off?"

The presentation on stage was still blaring overhead. The speaker's voice combatted Anna's thoughts, blocking any chance for a creative solution.

"And for our final new product line," the VP of Products said, "we've saved the best for last. What you're about to see will change the game." The woman paused as more cheesy music filled the gap. "Introducing PureScents: Puremetics's first line of 100% pure premium grade essential oils."

"Essential oils?" Vicky scoffed. "Isn't that the product that destroyed Christian's first business?"

A smile crept along Anna's face. "Yep."

Vicky shook her head as she pressed her fingers into her temples. "I always thought the man was a genius, but he's really just an overconfident lying bastard, isn't he?"

Anna couldn't help but laugh.

"So, what do we do?" Vicky's eyes landed squarely on Anna.

Was she asking Anna for advice? Anna had been following orders this whole time, doing whatever Vicky or Gloria had demanded. Between the two of them, Anna had felt comfortable sitting back as they led the way. How could this possibly all be resting on her shoulders?

Because you see things others don't.

Anna almost didn't recognize the voice in her head. She was used to the kind of self-talk that kept her feeling small, like the voice that had mocked her as she stood before Ghostly Manor, telling Anna she was destined to fail. Or the one blaming her for Dale's infidelity or the one trying to convince her she deserved her shitty job, her crappy apartment, her lonely life. Anna had always been her worst critic, so this new voice startled her.

You know what to do, Anna. Trust yourself.

The lightbulb in Anna's head clicked, illuminating a scene so vivid and complex it took a minute to see it all. Like a storyboard sketching the ending in her mind, Anna saw a new plan unfold. She knew what needed to happen—the people, timing, and positions necessary to make it all work.

"Essential oils didn't take Christian down," she whispered. "That's our job." Anna pulled out her phone and began typing furiously. "I know how to save this. It will be tricky, and we've got to move fast."

"Okay." Vicky stood tall, matching Anna's energy. She leaned forward with an earnest expression. Her whole body stood ready to act, except this time, she waited for Anna to lead the way. "Tell me what to do."

32

The crowd roared as Christian took the stage one last time. Vicky couldn't help but notice the CEO stood a little less self-assured than he had during the Leadership Gala. There was tension in his shoulders and nervousness in his eyes. Perhaps Gloria's confrontation hadn't been entirely useless. The man looked rattled.

Good.

Vicky checked her phone, scrolling through the onslaught of messages that had populated over the past fifteen minutes. Anna's instructions were still coming in fast and furious. Vicky had never seen her so composed, directing everyone like a conductor gearing up for the concert that would make or break a career.

Anna's new confidence didn't just surprise Vicky; it ignited her. The sudden transformation instilled a willingness to follow the woman into whatever battle awaited them. Vicky stood by the stage as directed, praying everything would fall into place.

"Wow, what an incredible new lineup!" Christian said, turning toward the audience. "How excited are you to share these products with the world?"

Loud cheers drowned out Vicky's pounding heart.

"I tell you; this convention has been unlike any other." Christian paced along the front of the stage. "The speakers, workshops, and unmatched products prove Puremetics only gets better each year, and that success comes to those who never give up."

Vicky rolled her eyes as the audience hooped and hollered after every cliché platitude that dripped from Christian's mouth. The man could announce his plans for a Jonestown reenactment, and they'd probably cheer themselves into a Kool-Aid frenzy. And she should know. Up until yesterday, she had bought into the lies. It was a devotion that made Vicky unsure this plan —or *any* plan—would work. Could anything get these people to see the truth?

She shuddered when she remembered what had finally opened *her* eyes.

Christian raised his arms, gesturing for the crowd to quiet down. "Still, it hasn't been a year without its challenges. The more we strive to heal the world, the more our detractors work to bring us down. For every award and praise we get in the press, someone is spouting lies online, hoping to see us fail. But we never will!"

Vicky checked the time, knowing these closing remarks wouldn't last much longer. She texted the group: *How's it going?* Her heart continued to drum as she waited for a reply and sped up when three dots bounced at the bottom of her screen. The responses came in bursts, one right after the other.

JANE:

We have the laptop, almost to the AV booth.

ANNA:

J & B, I'm heading your way now.

BLAZE:

There are two security guards right outside.
What do we do?

ANNA:

The diversion I've planned will get rid of them.
I'm sending the signal now.

As the information poured in, Vicky tried to keep steady. She knew only the highlights of Anna's plan and wasn't sure what to expect exactly, except that she was supposed to keep her eyes on Christian at all times. *Do not lose track of that man.*

As if on cue, a loud voice boomed from the audience. "Christian White is a fraud!"

Standing near the stage, Vicky looked over her shoulder, trying to locate its origin. Not too far back, a woman raised her arm high, waving her phone like a flashlight. Those around her snapped to attention, hoping to catch a glance at the sudden outburst. She yelled again, louder. "Christian White is a fraud! Christian White is a fraud!"

The CEO stood centerstage, squinting into the crowds. "What?" His tone was more confused than angry, but Vicky welcomed his distracted attention while the audience groaned, trying to figure out what was happening.

"Christian White is a fraud! Christian White is a fraud!"

The woman continued her battle cry, getting louder and more confident each moment.

A security officer ran down from the stadium's lower bowl to the floor where the woman stood. Their flashlights illuminated her face, revealing a satisfied smirk as they removed her from the crowd. A few people cheered as she was led up the stairs, only to be interrupted by another outburst.

"Christian White is a thief!"

The voice was quieter only because it came from higher up

the seats, nearing the mid-tier section. Again, necks turned as chatter buzzed from the audience.

"Christian White is a liar!"

This third voice came one row behind Vicky, and by the look on Christian's face, he now realized what was happening as he tried to take control of the situation.

"See? What did I tell you? There will always be people fighting those who dare to stand out. Don't let the trolls distract you!" Christian's dimpled smile tried to lift, but the fear in his eyes pushed it back down. The voices of dissent multiplied. Scattered throughout the crowd, more women stood and shouted their grievances, adding to the disruption and drowning out any pleas for order.

"Christian White belongs in jail!"

"Christian White stole my money!"

"Christian White broke the law!"

"Christian White is not who he says he is!"

Anna's army was ready to fight.

Vicky laughed. Anna had mentioned that a hundred or so of her enrollees had made the trip to Convention. It was a brilliant move to use them as a distraction. As each new woman shouted, the crowd became increasingly restless. Some pushed back, screaming counter-remarks. Security officers yelled for staff members to help as the detractors quickly outnumbered them.

Taking it all in, Vicky kept her eyes glued on Christian. The CEO turned off the mic, said something into his earpiece, and vacated the stage. Vicky crept along the sidelines, watching in delight as the man slowly unraveled as he stood in the wing.

A security officer yelled into his radio as he jumped off the stage and ran up the stairs. "All staff members should report to the arena immediately. We need all hands on deck." Garbled sounds buzzed from his device. The man continued to yell, taking two steps at a time. "I don't care if you're saving the Queen. I need all staff inside the venue immediately!"

Vicky smiled as she sent a message to the group: *It's working.*

From where Anna stood, the stadium noise was nothing more than a muffled hum. Huddled next to Jane and Blaze in a small nook around the corner from the AV booth, the only signs of trouble she could hear came from the security officer's walkie-talkie. She peeked around the corner. The device buzzed with life, giving her a hint of what was happening inside the arena.

"All staff members should report to the arena immediately. We need all hands on deck!"

The man reached for the device, his feet still planted. "Hatch and I are stationed outside AV. Evans told us to stay put after someone found a questionable video in the files."

As soon as his thumb released the button, static garbles blared from the speaker until the first voice pierced through the noise again.

"I don't care if you're saving the Queen. I need all staff inside the venue immediately!"

"You heard him," the second officer said, taking off down the hallway.

Anna pressed her back against the wall, hoping the two men wouldn't notice her as they rushed toward the stadium entrance. Her phone buzzed, and she quickly read Vicky's text.

"Go now!" Anna whispered with an urgency that propelled all three of them into action. They moved quickly and quietly around the corner until they reached the AV room's door and peeked through its small window.

"There are three people inside," Jane said. "How do we distract them?"

Anna wrestled for a solution, trying to size up the enemy on the other side of the door. "I'm not sure. They look young. Maybe twenty, possibly teenagers."

"Look," Blaze said, opening a small supply closet door nearby. He pulled out a box of neon security vests. "I've got an idea. Put these on." He handed them out, slipped one over his head, and moved to the front of the trio.

Anna couldn't help but admire Blaze's confidence. He was a lot like his mother, even if his bravado was more understated.

Blaze knocked. "Let me do the talking."

An acne-faced teen pulled the door open. His annoyed grimace quickly changed to a nervous smile as he read the shiny silver letters that read *Security Officer* along Blaze's chest. "Uh, is there a problem?"

Was this the guy Gloria was working with? It seemed unlikely. Anna tried getting a better look at the other two workers inside the booth, wondering if there had been an actual problem with the video file or if Gloria's mole had gotten cold feet. These were the types of questions Anna needed to figure out if this plan was going to work—and *fast*.

"Yeah, there's a problem," Blaze said. He furrowed his brow and leaned in. His six-inch height difference worked in his favor. "All staff have been ordered to help with the developing situation in the arena. That means *everyone*."

The kid stuttered, his knees shaking. "B-but... we're in the middle of a session!"

"And we're in the middle of a crisis." Blaze pointed out the large glass window in the AV booth that looked over the entire stadium. "All staff have been ordered to help. Do I need to spell it out for you?"

A woman with a sagging ponytail pushed back from the giant light board, her chair spinning toward the door. "We can't just leave!"

"I'll keep things running," a third woman said as she stood up from the shadows. Her eyes narrowed when she spotted Anna standing behind Jane. She was old enough to be the other two workers' grandmother, but her confidence and authority were undeniable. "After all, I'd probably break a hip if I tried to help. Seth and Jessie can go. I'll stay."

"But—" the young man began to protest.

"But nothing," the woman said. "I've been doing this for longer than you've been alive. I can handle a few light changes and music cues on my own. Go!" She put her hands on her hips, pulling back her cardigan just enough to show off an owl brooch pinned to her shirt.

Anna caught the pin's golden shimmer and smiled.

"Lead the way," the ruddy kid said to Blaze.

Blaze hesitated, glancing toward Jane. "Right, uh—"

"You need a tour guide?" Jane yelled. "Run down the hall and take any of the hundred doors to the arena. Help gather the disruptors. We've got a few more people to round up."

The two young AV workers hurried away. Anna took a timid step forward. "Are you with Gloria?"

The woman smiled. "Name's Harriet. Nice to meet you. Hurry and close the door." She moved her chair over, making space. "And lock it."

"We have a new video file," Jane said after checking that the door was locked. "You said something was wrong with the original one?"

"Yeah, something must have happened when I uploaded it. No matter what I do, I keep getting the same error message."

"That's not good," Anna said.

"Honestly, I think it worked in your favor." Harriet leaned back, shaking her head. "A supervisor saw the files and got suspicious but couldn't open them either. If he could, none of you would be here right now."

Jane unhooked the laptop bag from her shoulder and pulled out the computer. "If we have the right hookups, we should be able to play the video from our laptop. Is there still time?"

Harriet laughed, pointing out the window. "Have you seen

the chaos out there? My girl Gloria knows how to make a spectacle."

"That's actually my mom's doing," Jane said, nudging Anna.

Anna sighed. "Gloria was taken by security. We don't know where she is, but we think they might have confiscated her phone. She hasn't responded to any texts."

"Oh dear," Harriet said. "I hope she's okay, but she might be safer away from this mess. Look at it."

Anna peered over the edge, trying to adjust her eyes so she could make sense of the chaos unfolding within the hordes of people below. The bright yellow security vests were swarming in every direction, spread too thin among the groups of women scattered throughout the crowd, waving their arms and taking a stand. She shook her head, watching it all unfold.

It was a strange scene, but even stranger was Anna's pride, knowing she had started it all. For a woman who had been afraid to live big and bold, this felt like a defining moment. Anna hadn't just sat back and waited for things to happen. She deliberately raised chaos, riding on the simple hope that by breaking things down, something better would take its place.

"The video is ready to go. Just tell me when to hit play," Harriet said.

Anna stood poised, as if holding a match that would set the world on fire. "Now."

Vicky held her breath as the *PureExpo 2015* logo on the Jumbotron went black. She could almost feel every eyeball turn toward the screens hanging overhead as if they were suddenly coming to life. Dramatic music drowned out the chaos, quieting the crowds.

This was it.

"Meet Christian White, the mastermind behind Puremetics, a

company built on deceit and the exploitation of dreams." The narration boomed through the speakers as a black-and-white photo of Christian filled the screen, followed by a montage of images from company retreats, leadership cruises, and past conventions. "He promised beauty, prosperity, and financial freedom, but underneath the shiny facade were layers of lies, fraud, and abuse."

A woman appeared on the screen, her face blurred from recognition. "After getting sick from PureLife vitamins, I had the product third-party tested. Not only did it contain ingredients not listed on the package, but several unlisted ingredients were known allergens. You shouldn't have to worry about your vitamins accidentally killing you."

The video cut to another anonymous silhouette. "After nearly losing my home, I found out I wasn't alone. Puremetics has one of the highest rates of distributors who declare bankruptcy of any MLM, but they sell the opportunity like it's guaranteed to make you rich."

Vicky felt guilt settle into her bones. She didn't recognize these women's voices, but she might have enrolled any one of them. How many people had Vicky hurt? How many lies had she told to keep her dream alive?

Focus. There would be plenty of time for this kind of self-inflicted punishment. Vicky needed to stick with the task at hand. *Eyes on Christian.*

The CEO was still offstage, yelling at someone hidden behind one of the curtain legs. His arms flailed as spit spewed from his mouth. Vicky leaned in, wishing she could read lips, dying to know what he was saying. Suddenly, Evelyn Davenport stepped out from behind the curtain and ran toward the side of the stage. A disheveled, panicked expression replaced her usually polished decorum. She made her way to the front row and whispered in the ear of a distributor sitting in the end seat.

As the video played on, this nameless distributor began to chant. "Go home, trolls! Go home, trolls!"

Within seconds, everyone around her had joined her rhythmic shouting. They punched their fists in the air, yelling in unison.

"Go home, trolls! Go home, trolls!"

Vicky's heart fell as the words caught like wildfire, the chant growing louder by the second. It didn't take long for their voices to drown out the video. Gloria had anticipated this. Last night, she had been adamant that they needed a confession from Christian. *The video won't be enough,* she had said.

Gloria was right. This wasn't going to work. You would never reach a logical conclusion when emotions were behind the wheel. As brilliant as Anna's distraction had been, everything stood ready to fail without a gut-wrenching punch of truth straight from the monster's mouth.

Vicky felt her stomach tighten as the answer came to her.

She needed to confront Christian.

A shiver ran down her spine as she considered the implications of this impulsive plan. Was Vicky willing to reveal what happened yesterday in Christian's hotel room? Would anyone believe her or just blame her? She had already given up the vision of her empire, recognizing the cracks in what she thought was a flawless life. Now, she was running with a hammer, apparently determined to bring the whole thing down herself.

There was no guarantee Christian would fall for her trap. Vicky could lay it all at his feet and he could stomp it to pieces, deny everything, and twist the story to make Vicky look like the villain. Was it worth the risk? Would she survive such humiliation? And what would happen when word inevitably traveled back to Splendor Springs? What would her neighbors think? Her children? Jack?

So. What.

The realization smacked Vicky in the gut as something deep

within refused to give in to these excuses. She was better than that—or, at least, she wanted to be. What good was an empire if you couldn't look yourself in the mirror and like the person you see?

Vicky ran toward an emergency exit, trying to escape the deafening chants. She was determined to move forward no matter what, so she pulled out her phone and Facetimed Anna.

"What's up?" Anna asked. "Is everything okay?"

"This isn't working," Vicky said, nearly yelling to be heard over the crowd. "They won't listen to reason."

Anna sighed. "What do we do?"

"I have an idea." Vicky was unable to hide the tremor in her voice.

A concerned look washed over Anna's face. "What are you going to do?"

Vicky peaked through the crack in the door, still watching Christian. She took a deep breath and pushed back a tear. "Whatever it takes."

33

Gloria sat on the hard metal chair as her body bowed like a sagging branch. The weight of another disappointment threatened to snap her in half. She had been so sure Christian would buckle under pressure and even more certain his confession would finally see her to the finish line of a journey twenty-nine years in the making. Yet, somehow, Gloria was the one under lock and key while Christian carried on—forever winning a game he didn't deserve to play.

The security officers locked Gloria in the Guest Services room, transforming it into a makeshift holding cell. The climb to the fifth floor and subsequent trek around the stadium's outer ring had been tiring but nothing like the exhaustion of failure. The men barely had time to confiscate Gloria's phone and ask her name before being called away to help with some emergency, leaving her alone to stew in her disappointment without any connection to the outside world.

Gloria sighed. "Looks like I let you down, Fi. Again."

It wasn't just Fiona. Gloria had let herself down—and all the OWLS, Anna, Jane, and everyone else she had dragged into this mess, leaving them all muddied and stained. Her head hung a little lower just thinking about it.

As Gloria wallowed in pity, a small monitor mounted in the corner caught her attention. She walked over and pushed the power button, holding her breath. She was desperate to know what was happening inside the arena. The TV lit up and displayed a live event feed, just as Gloria had hoped. Puremetics purple covered the set's backdrop with *PureExpo 2015* written in bold white letters and a glittery tagline underneath: *Light Your Dreams*. But the stage itself was bare.

Gloria leaned in, turning up the volume, hoping to hear what was happening, but there was no sound. She had no idea if Jane had brought the laptop, whether someone had figured out their plan, or if the video had already played. The only comfort was knowing Emily was stuck at home with a broken leg, along with her disappointing eyes.

The TV screen flickered to black. Gloria rushed to the device, banging its side in a feeble attempt to restore order. Familiar music suddenly burst from its speakers. Gloria frantically turned down the sound, her ears ringing from the volume. A smile crept along her face as she realized what was happening.

"Meet Christian White," the narrator said, "the mastermind behind Puremetics, a company built on deceit and the exploitation of dreams."

"I'll be damned. They did it." Gloria moved her chair closer to soak in this one triumphant moment. She knew each line by heart but didn't mind rewatching every damning fact and brave testimony, knowing ten thousand other people were seeing it for the first time. Gloria hoped her rapt attention would somehow magnify the video's reach.

A few minutes later, the doorknob rattled. Gloria sat tall as her muscles flexed instinctively, ready to fight. She wasn't in the mood to talk to security, especially now. Her mind ran through a list of explanations, hoping to find the right lie that would set her free. When the door opened, she jumped, surprised by who she saw on the other side.

"Jane!"

The teen rushed into the small office and grabbed Gloria's hand. "Hurry!" Jane said. "There's a problem."

"What's wrong? Is it something with Anna? Vicky?" Gloria pointed to the monitor. "The video is working. It's working, Jane!"

"It's playing, but the brainwashed mob isn't listening. The Puremetics huns are chanting like mindless robots: *Go home, trolls. Go home, trolls.*"

This news was disturbingly unsurprising. "How can I help?"

"Mom said Vicky is going to confront Christian. We're worried for her safety."

Gloria didn't need to be told twice. She ran as fast as her sixty-five-year-old knees would allow. They sprinted toward the nearest entrance. With every strike of her foot against the concrete floor, she tried to imagine what she'd do to Christian if he hurt another one of her friends.

"How did you even find me?" Gloria asked, trying to catch her breath.

"Harriet in AV suspected this was where security would put you." Jane slowed down to let Gloria catch up. "Luckily, it wasn't too far."

When they entered the arena, the noise smacked Gloria in the face. The shouting crowd pumped their fists in protest, their eyes and voices growing angrier by the minute. Pockets of people looked more concerned or confused than riotous. They kept their mouths shut and arms down. But the screaming majority made it impossible to hear anything else but their ongoing chant.

"Go home, trolls! Go home, trolls!"

Jane led Gloria down the stairs, maneuvering between staff members and distributors. The people continued to yell, the echo reverberating in Gloria's chest.

Finally, the Jumbotron screens went black. The crowd cheered, believing their protest had worked. Gloria's heart plummeted, wondering who stopped the video and what it meant for their group of rebels. Was this the end? Was it time to give up?

Gloria's chest heaved as she met Jane at the bottom of the stairs. "Where is Vicky?"

Jane shrugged. "Last we knew, she was watching Christian from somewhere in here."

"Where's your mother?"

"She's still in the AV booth with Harriet and Blaze. I wouldn't be surprised if security is already pounding down the door. They would have left with me, but Vicky needed someone to broadcast something." Jane sighed. "I just hope they took my advice and barricaded the door."

The screens suddenly came back to life, drawing everyone's attention. Someone was broadcasting something, but for all Gloria knew, Puremetics was back in the driver's seat. She closed her eyes, hoping Anna and the others were okay.

The image on the Jumbotron bounced. It appeared to be a live feed of a camera someone forgot to turn off. No, not a camera—a phone. It was dangling in someone's hand as they marched down a hallway with clearly marked arrows on the ground. *This way to courtside suites.*

Captivated by the broadcast and the mystery of what was happening, the crowd grew silent. Thousands of phones pointed to the jumbo screens, capturing the moment forever. Whoever was walking down the hall kept their lens pointed to the floor. The clickity-clack of high heels punctuated each second. The image swung with each step as gold stilettos came in and out of the frame.

Gloria immediately recognized the shoes almost as much as the sound of the person's determined gait. She exhaled sharply. "That's Vicky."

"We need to find her," Jane said, picking up speed.

They ran toward the center of the stadium. Gloria scanned the arena's edge for clues as to which door would lead to the correct room. A tall, polished woman with a high bun and pencil skirt stood outside one of the exit doors.

"There," Gloria said, pointing. "That way."

Vicky puffed her chest and wrapped her determined fingers around her phone as she hugged it close to her side. The key to a successful mission was to keep the device hidden without obstructing the lens. One must always keep their prey in sight.

Marching down the long corridor that separated the stadium from the courtside suite where she knew Christian was hiding, Vicky summoned every ounce of courage she possessed. She was used to working for her goals and willing to take risks, and this moment—this hunt—wouldn't be any different.

Victoria Sterling was out for blood.

She barreled through the door into a room resembling a hotel business center. A few leather seats, a long sofa, and a conference table filled the space. Christian stood with his back to Vicky as he yelled into his phone, stuffing a briefcase full of documents. "I don't care if it's already booked. Have the plane ready for me in fifteen minutes."

Target locked.

"Christian White!"

The CEO jumped. His shoulders raised, back arched. He turned, relaxing only a little when he saw Vicky standing before him. As if deciding between fight or flight, he cocked his head and decided the threat wasn't big enough for either.

"I'll call you back in a minute, Brad. I need to take care of a little problem." He ended the call and folded his arms. "What the hell are you doing here?"

"We need to talk." Vicky slammed the door behind her and

stepped further into the room. The sudden quiet made her uneasy after being inundated with all the noise and clatter from the crowds outside. With no one else around, one wrong move could turn the hunter into the prey.

Christian snapped his briefcase shut. "I do not have time for this."

"Then you need to make time." The strength in Vicky's voice felt like a ruse. She tensed her muscles to keep her nerves from turning her into a chattering mess. Only her steadfast determination kept her from falling over. She held the phone close to her side, trying to angle it upward so it would capture Christian's scowl. Of course, even if it didn't perfectly frame him, the lapel pin glistening from his tie would make the audio loud and clear.

"In case you missed it," Christian said, taking a step forward, "We're in the middle of a crisis. Someone is trying to hijack our event."

"Shouldn't you be out there fixing it? Leading your people? Or is running away your thing?" Vicky said, pursing her lips. "Run away, change your name, start over. Sound familiar?"

Christian straightened his spine and clenched his jaw. "What do you want?"

"I want to talk about what happened yesterday—" Vicky paused as the knot in her stomach tightened, "—in your hotel room."

"Oh, please," he scoffed. "Nothing happened. Get the hell out of here!"

"Nothing?" Vicky nearly stumbled at the man's audacity. For the past twenty-four hours, she had tried to squelch the voices in her head rationalizing his behavior. *You're overreacting. You're as much to blame. Nobody likes a tattletale. Just drop it.* She thought back to Blaze, imagining his rage when he heard what happened, reminding herself she did nothing wrong. Vicky deserved justice. "You tried to kiss me, and when I pushed you away, you pinned me down. You assaulted me."

Christian's eyes narrowed with derision. "Assault? Please. Don't flatter yourself. You're the one who kneed me in the gut. As I said, nothing happened."

Vicky's fingernails dug into her palms, her breath seething.

Christian leaned in, his voice low and terrifying. "And if you continue to insist otherwise, I promise you'll regret it. Nobody messes with Christian White and gets away with it."

A voice came from behind. "Just ask his wife."

Vicky spun around, startled to see Gloria standing at the door, out of breath.

"Fucking hell!" Christian slammed his fist against the table. "What do I have to do to get rid of you, Gloria?" He stepped closer and paused, snapping his attention back to Vicky. "Wait, are you two working together?"

Vicky ran to hug Gloria. "I'm so happy to see you." She exhaled, not realizing she had been holding her breath. For all her feigned fearlessness, Vicky didn't want to do this alone. She had spent a lifetime insisting she didn't need help, determined to prove she could climb to the top no matter the circumstance. She now realized it wasn't just a lonely path. It was a dangerous one.

"I've got your back," Gloria whispered. She straightened her blazer and stepped closer to Christian. The silver-haired woman was like a toy poodle facing a bull, but Gloria's fierce expression and unwavering stance made it seem like Gloria had the advantage.

"Now, Christian," Gloria said. "Why don't you tell Vicky what you did to Fiona? Tell her how you ruined your wife's life, kept her captive, and then killed her."

"For the last time, I did not kill my wife!" Chris threw a chair against the wall.

The crash filled the room, but the silence that followed terrified Vicky even more. She reached out and took Gloria's hand as they stepped back.

"It's true, he didn't kill me."

Everyone turned to see who had spoken. The firm, resolute voice did not match the tiny woman standing in the doorway, but it did fit with the determined glare in her eyes and her powerful stance.

Gloria's hands flew to her mouth. "Oh my god, Fiona?" She ran, throwing her arms around the petite woman's shoulders. "I can't believe it," she whispered. "Is it really you?"

The woman smiled, melting into the embrace. "Hey, Glo. It's good to see you."

Vicky had no idea who this Fiona person was, only that she had seen her last night in Anna's car. But the look on Gloria's face—and on Christian's, for that matter—made it clear Fiona was an essential piece of this complicated puzzle. Vicky glanced at her phone, ensuring it was still recording. She hoped this new development would finally get Christian to crack. Despite his temper and a few veiled threats, he hadn't said anything truly damning. But Vicky felt stronger and steadier with each new woman who entered the room.

This battle wasn't over yet.

"Fiona? Where the hell have you been!" Christian yelled. "And why are you here now? Why are *any* of you here?"

The woman ignored Christian's rantings and pulled back from Gloria's enthusiastic embrace. "I noticed you sneaking around the arena with Jane. I was hoping for a chance to talk to you and didn't realize you were heading off to fight a monster."

"Wait, you know Jane?" Gloria's whole body shook, but her eyes sparkled like she was looking at a miracle. "Sorry, that's not important. What I meant to say is: *You're alive?*"

Fiona smiled.

Christian scoffed. "All these years later, and you decide to show up now? After what you did?" He crossed his arms, tipping his head back.

"After what *I* did?" Fiona's nose flared. Her whole body

expanded as every muscle fired. "How about what you did to me?"

"I gave you everything," Christian said. "A big, beautiful home, every luxury and convenience the world had to offer, a name you could be proud of."

"Ha!" Gloria yelled. "Are you serious? Didn't you change your name, Mr. Blackwell?"

"Only because of what *she* did." He turned to his wife. "You didn't just leave. You made me look like a murderer. My business failed because you walked away. Then, after months of searching, I finally found you, and you had the nerve to blackmail me!"

"No, Chris. Before any of that, you broke me." Fiona lengthened her spine. She took a slow inhale and calmly crossed her arms across her chest. "How many black eyes did I endure at your hands? How many bruises did I have to hide? What about the countless degrading remarks, the marital rape, the spiritual manipulation? You ruined my life, and you threatened to kill Gloria if I tried leaving."

The woman took a deliberate step forward, her presence so firm it forced Christian to move back. "I didn't ruin your business. You did that on your own. The scandals, the product recalls, the embezzling? That's all on you. I was just smart enough to take some of the proof with me. It was the only way I knew you'd leave me and Gloria alone for good."

Christian glared Fiona down, but she did not move. "So, the three of you were working together?" he finally said. "Is that what this is?"

"No," Gloria said. "This is bigger than any one of us. Do you know how many people are working to bring about justice? You've made a lot of enemies over the years."

Vicky stepped in. "But you already know that. That's why you were preparing to run again. You know this ship is sinking, but we're here to ensure you go down with it this time."

"Is that a threat?" Christian's face grew red, the anger practically steaming from his ears. He grabbed his stuff and pushed toward the door, grunting as he passed Vicky. He stopped at Fiona's feet, leaned down, and whispered in her ear. "I suggest you disappear again. This time, for good."

Gloria gently pulled Fiona back. "Don't you dare threaten her!"

Christian snarled. "Or you'll do what?"

"Nothing," Vicky said. "I think you've done enough to condemn yourself." She held up her phone. "I've been broadcasting the whole time. Smile for the camera."

He growled and turned to leave. But as he opened the door, he froze. A wall of people blocked the exit. Hundreds of women barricaded the way, filling the corridor and spilling into the stadium. They collectively crossed their arms and glared with righteous indignation. And there, at the front of the group leading the pack, were Anna, Jane, and Blaze.

Christian stumbled backward, pulling on his collar as he struggled for air.

Anna took a bold step forward and smiled. "What's up, Chris?"

34

A massive, righteous mob has the power to reign down chaos. Hand them their sworn enemy, and things can get dangerous. Anna braced herself for what the crowd behind her would do once Christian walked into their path. After all, emotions were running high, and more than one person was eager to see Christian White suffer.

But for once, Anna's active imagination couldn't anticipate what happened next. Instead of confusion, there was clarity. The wall of women barricading Christian White did not bend or break under the winds of outrage, nor did they back down. They didn't flinch when he spat in their faces or push back when he yelled profanities. The group, surging like an ocean wave, moved him along. Hundreds of firm, decisive hands guided him toward his future. There was no escape this time, nowhere to run. With each passing second, Christian slowly succumbed to their quiet strength as they handed him off to the police.

Behind the man marched an unlikely group of misfits—first, his estranged wife. Her quiet, dignified expression resembled the phoenix on Gloria's wall. Born from the ashes, Fiona was flying high. Gloria walked alongside her friend. Her look of relief was an exquisite combination of joy and exhaustion.

Vicky and Blaze were next. Blaze had his arm around his mother as the pair laughed. There was a lightness to their step, one Anna had not seen before. It was as if this journey had permitted them to let go of whatever held them down.

And then there was Jane, who walked next to Anna with her usual snap and curiosity. She was wise beyond her years, unfiltered and unfettered by useless opinions. More than just a daughter, Jane was Anna's most loyal friend, and her heart could barely contain the love she felt.

It was amazing how all these paths had intersected. As the group converged with the officers standing by, Anna felt the victory of crossing a finish line—and the bittersweetness that came with the thought of moving on.

"This is your man," Gloria said as the wall of women purged Christian from their grasp.

The officers guided him out of the building, and the misfits followed behind. They walked outside, squinting in the bright August sun. Anna stretched her arms and wondered what was next. She exchanged glances with Vicky and then Gloria. Neither dared move or speak. This was a holy moment, and nobody wanted it to end.

"I'm going to go with the officers," Fiona finally said, breaking the silence.

Gloria's mouth dropped. "Excuse me?"

Fiona stepped closer and sighed. Her eyes bounced back and forth as if memorizing Gloria's face. "The only way to detangle myself from this man's story is to tell them everything I know and share the evidence I have. An arrest doesn't mean he'll be charged. I need to make sure the police have all the facts."

"Will I see you again?" Gloria reached for Fiona's hand but pulled back at the last moment.

"If I have anything to do with it." Fiona leaned in and kissed

Gloria's cheek. "We've got a lot of catching up to do." She waved goodbye to the rest of the group as she followed an officer to their car. Gloria's eyes stayed with Fiona until she was out of sight.

"You like her," Anna said quietly, piecing together what *close friend* had meant.

Gloria laughed. "What is this? High school?"

Anna nodded, surer than ever. "You *love* her."

"I do—or at least I did." Gloria sighed, still looking in Fiona's direction. "I think she was even interested in me at one point but too afraid to explore that part of herself." She shrugged, her eyes drifting back to Anna. "But that was almost thirty years ago. The truth is, we barely know each other. But I'd like to get reacquainted."

Jane nudged Gloria in the side. "I bet you would."

The group chuckled as Gloria playfully punched Jane in the arm. She wrapped the girl into a hug and pulled Anna in, too. "I couldn't have done this without you," she said, letting go.

Anna looked around. "Are you talking to me?"

"Of course I am!" Gloria grabbed Anna's arm. "You really pulled through, dear. From what I've heard, the plan was dead in the water until you jumped into action. You're full of surprises, Anna Price. I hope you'll consider working with the OWLS on a more permanent basis."

"Really?" Anna was beaming.

Gloria winked. "We'll talk."

Everyone had gathered their things. There was no reason to stick around, but they all felt the pull to stay put—just a little longer. It was a glorious Friday afternoon. Blue skies and a hint of a breeze made the August sun bearable. Vicky moved under the shade of a large oak tree. Her natural magnetism drew the rest of the group to her.

"Some day, huh?" Anna looked at Vicky. "Is convention always this exciting?"

Vicky laughed. "Hardly." She pointed to a group of women in the parking lot. A dozen women in Puremetics t-shirts passed around a lipstick they used as a marker, slashing the logo with a giant, blood-red X. They cheered loudly as they each performed the ritual. "I'm pretty sure this Convention will go down in the history books."

"What does this mean for you?" Anna asked, taking a seat next to Vicky. "What about your business?"

Vicky took a slow, deep inhale as she leaned back against the rough bark of the trunk. The last bit of weight holding her down seemed to disappear as she exhaled. "Well, I'm going to lose a lot of money." She pulled Blaze in close and rested her head on his shoulder. "But I'm going to gain much more in return."

Jane giggled. "Yeah, like your soul."

"Watch it, Jane. You're turning out to be my favorite." Vicky laughed, running her fingers through her long, blond waves. She looked at the sky and sighed. "Maybe I'll go back to school and finally finish college, or perhaps I'll go into business for myself."

"You're Vicky Fucking Sterling," Blaze said, jumping to his feet. He grabbed Vicky's hands and pulled her up. "You could conquer the world if you put your mind to it."

"Language," Vicky said, shaking her head. She pulled Blaze in for a hug. "And thank you."

Jane twirled a piece of grass between her finger and thumb. "What about you, Mom? Now that your Puremetics career has come to an end, what's next?"

Anna looked around at the unusual collection of people that had found a way into her life. On the surface, they had nothing in common. It didn't make sense that they should be friends, but Anna began to see why it worked. Breaking the mold required more than just stepping out of her comfort zone. Anna needed to see all these unique strengths and personalities come together, proving it was okay to be different. After years of trying to fit in, it turns out all Anna had to be was herself.

35

Victoria Sterling was on the hunt.

After weeks of searching, time was running out. But finding the perfect gift wasn't easy. It required an expert eye, patience, and the ability to pounce as soon as a suitable item appeared. Vicky's fingers ran along a shelf of antiques, closely inspecting every potential purchase. She would never attend a house-warming party with some generic, mass-produced candle. The present had to be unique and meaningful—something worthy of Anna Price.

A gorgeous blue and white glass bowl grabbed Vicky's attention. She inspected its hand-blown, fluted edge. It would certainly look nice on the little side table she had helped Anna pick out for the living room. The elevated, almost fragile design was breathtaking but didn't scream Anna. *Next.*

She walked past a cast iron wind chime, a brass candle snuffer, and a beautiful carved wooden recipe box. Vicky's phone buzzed; Jack was calling. She accepted the call and meandered further down the aisle. "Hey, sweetie. What's up?"

"Vicks, Dr. Wilson called. She needs to push back our session an hour tomorrow, and I wanted to confirm that was okay."

Never in a million years did Vicky picture herself going to couples therapy, but now she couldn't imagine how they had gone so long without some outside help. It had been a challenging year full of tough questions, and sometimes even more difficult answers, but Vicky was proud of how much stronger their relationship had become.

"Yeah, that's totally fine," Vicky said, picking up a funky set of bookends. Her phone beeped, reminding her the party started in twenty minutes. "Hey, Jack. I've got to run, but I'm looking forward to tonight! Becki says we must try the lettuce wraps when we go to Jade Dragon's."

"Sounds like an epic date night," he said. "Looking forward to it. Good luck with the shopping and have fun at your party. Love you."

Vicky hung up the phone and walked back to the wooden recipe box. Handcrafted and a little quirky, it wasn't giving her that *wow* factor she wanted, but it was nice. Plus, Anna and Jane loved cooking in their new kitchen. Deciding it was good enough, Vicky beelined to the checkout to get it home and wrapped in time.

As she marched from the far end of the store, her eyes continued to scan, just in case something better jumped out at her. That's when the heavens opened and shined a light on a one-of-a-kind item, begging Vicky to grab the treasure before someone else did.

The perfect gift.

Vicky grabbed the new item, rushed to return the recipe box, and paid before hurrying home to wrap it. She couldn't erase the smile from her face as her car pulled up in front of Anna's house after another successful hunt. Her smile grew wider as she walked toward the front door, admiring the flower beds and quaint porch swing.

The door swung open before Vicky could even knock.

"Vicky!" Jane's eyes lit up, nearly as bright as her hair. No longer just blue, her strands were a spectrum of color. Vicky thought it suited her.

"Hey, you." Vicky went in for a quick hug. It was hard to think both Jane and Blaze would be heading away to college in just a couple of weeks. "Hopefully, I'm not too late."

"Impossible," Jane said with a wink. "The party doesn't start until Victoria Sterling shows up."

Vicky waltzed into the cozy home, still fawning over the paint color she had selected as Anna walked out from the kitchen, carrying a platter of cookies. "I can't get over how great this place looks."

Anna smiled. "What can I say? I had an amazing designer."

"Eh, she was fine," Vicky said with feigned humility. "Nothing compared to the mastermind behind such a bold project." She laughed, shaking her head. "When you told me you had bought Ghostly Manor, I thought you had lost your mind, but the renovation has turned out absolutely adorable."

"I like knowing the place has a history, even a sordid one," Anna said with a smile. "Buying it felt like a revolt—a chance to prove you can't always judge something by its appearance."

"Amen to that!" Vicky hung her bag on a hook, clutched her little gift, and followed Anna and Jane into the living room.

The guests filled the small space, crowding next to one another. It was a hodgepodge of people—typical of any event organized by Anna. Gloria chatted with Blaze in the corner by the built-in bookshelf. Her son waved when Vicky made eye contact. Emily and Fiona laughed on the sofa while Lisa and her new boyfriend rocked in the twin chairs near the fireplace.

Anna put the tray down on the tiny table tucked under the window. "Cookies are warm and gooey. Come and get them!"

Smiles and eyes lit up as the group magnetized toward the

food. Vicky was the first to take a bite, savoring every non-organic morsel.

The room was buzzing with energy, and not just from the guests. Vicky couldn't get over how well the design had pulled together. She had spent hours making the home reflect Anna and Jane's personalities. Recycled hardwood floors and carefully curated furniture from a local antique shop added texture and warmth. A wall of photos, shelves full of books, and plants in ceramic pots gave the space its character. Yet after everything Vicky had done to bring the room to life, the star of the show was the painting over the fireplace Anna had secretly commissioned.

"Oh my gosh! You got the painting! I haven't seen it yet." Vicky ran to inspect it.

"It arrived this morning," Anna said. "Do you like it? The day I signed the papers for the house, I knew I wanted something specifically created for this spot."

Vicky's eyes danced along the canvas. Bold brush strokes and layers of textured paint revealed the outline of Anna's house. Three thick, dividing lines cut the home diagonally, giving the impression of time. The far-left portion of the house was clean and new, while the middle section was tattered and worn down. But Vicky loved the third section the most, and not just because it so beautifully reflected the home's current state. Splashes of color created ghost-like trails of people inside and outside the dwelling, reminding her of what it takes for something to feel alive again.

"It's perfect." Vicky clapped her hands. "Who painted it?"

Anna pointed to Gloria and smiled.

"Gloria!" Vicky said, her voice so loud it bounced off the walls. "You did this?"

Gloria laughed. "I call it *Reclaimed*."

"It's lovely," Emily said, sipping her drink.

"Everything Gloria does is lovely," Fiona added as she squeezed Gloria's hand.

Watching the two women grow into such a loving relationship over the past year had been surprisingly therapeutic for Vicky. Their happiness filled Vicky with hope for Blaze's future.

"Oh! I almost forgot!" Vicky pulled out the gift bag and handed it to Anna. "I have a little housewarming gift for you."

"Haven't you done enough?" Anna asked, taking the bag.

"Just open it," Vicky said, her excitement bubbling over.

Anna pulled out some tissue paper and a small owl figurine. Barely six inches tall, the entire porcelain sculpture was cover with tiny tiles that created a mosaic of color. Hand-painted lines of gold brought the face and feathers to life.

"Oh my god, it's perfect!" Anna admired the details, turning the sculpture in her hands. "I love it. Thank you." She placed it on the mantel and hugged Vicky.

"It seemed appropriate," Vicky said, tossing her hair over her shoulder, "given your official new title."

"Vicky!" Gloria blurted out. "The first rule of OWLS is we don't talk about OWLS."

The room erupted in laughter.

Anna perched herself against the edge of the sofa. "So, Vick. How goes your stuff? I can't get enough of your new blog."

Jane perked up. "*Bold Blunders* is amazing, and that's coming from someone who detests blogs." She stuffed a cookie in her mouth, crumbs spewing as she talked. "Obviously, you can't really call your design work a blunder. You could totally do it professionally. But watching you take on woodworking, archery, and auto shop—that's high-quality entertainment. You're not afraid of failing, that's for sure."

Vicky chuckled. "I got shoved down a path before I knew what I wanted to do, so it's been fun exploring my options."

"When you said you were going to build a rocket, I thought you were joking," Blaze said, shaking his head. "You nearly blew a crater in our backyard. But you stuck with it, and it's been impressive to watch."

"That last model hit nearly two thousand feet!" Vicky put down her plate and smoothed her shirt. "Speaking of which, I just got accepted into UVU's Aerospace Technology Management program!"

Gloria spat out her drink. "Holy shit! Congrats."

"That's amazing!" Anna jumped to her feet, hugging her friend.

"Wow, I never pictured you as the engineering type," Jane said, nudging her.

The engineering type.

For years, Vicky resented being put in a box—forced to wear the labels that came with it. The shiny veneer of a picture-perfect existence had kept her complicit for a long time, but being type-cast as a character that allowed for little variation had become suffocating. After playing the same role for years, Vicky felt trapped, shackled by her own expectations.

It took a long time to realize she had done the same thing to the people in her life. Whenever she met someone, she tried to figure out where they belonged, caging them with the same labels she despised. *The awkward neighbor, the rebellious teenager, the old maid*—only now did Vicky see how limiting it all was.

"You know," Vicky said, more to herself than anyone in particular, "a rocket traveling more than 25,023 mph will eventually escape Earth's gravity."

The chatter in the room died as everyone turned toward her, unsure how to respond.

She folded her arms as she contemplated Newton's Laws of Motion. "It isn't easy breaking gravity's pull. You need a huge reaction—the right fuel to create enough thrust."

Blaze shook his head. "What are you talking about, Mom?"

Vicky inhaled slowly, picturing the person she used to be.

After years of feeling weighed down, stuck by an insatiable drive for perfection, a fire now propelled Vicky toward something new, something better.

"It's just that change requires tremendous energy," Vicky said. She smiled as she scanned the faces of those who had acted upon her with sometimes unbalanced but necessary force, disrupting her path and breaking the chains that kept her caged. Thanks to them all, Victoria Sterling was finally free.

DISCUSSION QUESTIONS

Use the following questions for book club discussions, personal reflection, or writing prompts.

1. Despite exuding confidence, Vicky sometimes has questionable self-awareness. In what ways did she deceive herself, and how did those self-deceptions impact her relationships? What might have been the catalyst for these misbeliefs?

2. Anna is reluctant to attend Vicky's party but is desperate to find her place in Splendor Springs. MLMs often capitalize on people's desire to belong, offering a sense of friendship and community. Have you ever been invited to an event that turned out to be something else? How did you respond?

3. Gloria refuses to change the word *Old* from the *Old Wise Ladies Society*. "Because *old* isn't a bad word," she says. "Twenty-year-old me has nothing on this wiser,

kinder, and tougher version of myself." In what ways would society change if everyone believed this sentiment?

4. Vicky is overly concerned about Jane and Blaze's relationship, mostly because Jane doesn't fit the mold of what she expects from Blaze's friends. Have you or someone you love ever been the subject of unfair judgment? How did you respond, and how does your experience compare?

5. Anna's plastic surgery client, Rachel, is determined to make Puremetics work because she feels she has no other options should her husband leave her. Many women who choose family over career might have similar fears. What does this say about the way society values domestic and emotional labor?

6. Do you think Victoria had a right to look through Blaze's phone? How can parents balance privacy while also ensuring their teens' safety?

7. After learning Blaze's secret, Victoria feels at odds with her religious beliefs. How would you have responded? What are the consequences of choosing faith over people?

8. Gloria was determined to get her revenge on Christian White. Were you satisfied with how the women handed him over to the police? What would you have done?

9. Victoria realizes she has spent a lifetime reducing others to labels. Have you ever felt like you were put in a box? How did that sort of reduction impact you?

ACKNOWLEDGMENTS

There's no way to thank everyone who made this book possible. Every teacher, mentor, editor, reader, and author I've worked with has helped me learn and grow as a writer. Their influence threads throughout the pages even if their eyes or hands didn't directly touch this manuscript. I appreciate all of them.

I'm incredibly grateful for my critique partners, editors, and early readers who saw the gems among the rubble. Their feedback has been instrumental in shaping this story. Thank you to Amelia DeSorrento for your flawless insights and enthusiastic support, which helped me see this book to the end. To Katie Heddleston and Aspen Brown, your eagle eyes and meticulous attention to detail as I finalized the manuscript were invaluable. Thank you to Lauren Miller for giving me insight into the world of Occupational Therapy.

Thank you to my cover design team for your creative vision. To my ARC team, family, friends, and everyone who showed up to give this project love, your support has been a constant source of inspiration.

To Tom, Cami, and Dax, thank you. You are the best crew a woman could ask for. I love you all so much.

As always, thank you, my fantastic reader. Your time invested in this journey is a testament to the power of storytelling. I hope you had as much fun as I did. For anyone who leaves a review or tells others about this book: You are Royal Diamonds in my eyes.

ABOUT THE AUTHOR

ROBIN STRONG is a former university professor, TEDx speaker, and recovering serial entrepreneur. She built and sold three businesses, wrote over 400 articles to an online audience of more than 20 million people, and spoke at national conferences and virtual summits. Now, she enjoys the quiet life in Indiana as a freelance editor with her husband and two kids. Robin is the author of *Gods of the Garden* and *The Scrolls of Prophecy*, a thoughtful and fun YA duet that the Independent Book Review called "enlightening and engaging."

A NOTE FROM THE AUTHOR

If you enjoyed this book, please consider leaving a review online —anywhere you are able. Word-of-mouth is crucial to an author's success. Even a sentence or two can make all the difference. Your time and support is deeply appreciated. Thank you!

- Robin

www.ingramcontent.com/pod-product-compliance
Lightning Source LLC
Chambersburg PA
CBHW032351310726
48973CB00007B/1966